RM JOHNSON

BESTSELLING AUTHOR OF THE MILLION DOLLAR SERIES

The
MILLION
DOLLAR
DESTINY

A NOVEL

THE MILLION DOLLAR DESTINY
A NOVEL

RM JOHNSON

Also by RM Johnson

The Million Dollar Destiny
My Wife's Lover
My Wife's Baby: I am not a murder
Hate the Air
Bishop 3
Bishop 2
Bishop
Keeping the Secret 3
Keeping the Secret 2
Keeping the Secret
Deceit and Devotion
No One in the World with E. Lynn Harris
Why Men Fear Marriage
Stacie and Cole
The Million Dollar Demise
The Million Dollar Deception
The Million Dollar Divorce
Do You Take This Woman
Dating Games
Love Frustration
Father Found
The Harris Family
The Harris Men

THE MILLION DOLLAR DESTINY

A NOVEL

RM JOHNSON

Marcusarts LLC—Atlanta, GA

1

Tangled in the soft white linen of the king-sized bed, Monica savored the warmth of little Nathaniel's four-year old body. He lay sleeping, breathing softly beside her, his head in the bend of her arm, his arm thrown across her belly.

Monica hadn't given birth to the boy, but Nate had recently granted her permission to adopt him. They stood in the law offices of his close friend, and with little Nathaniel holding tight to one of Monica's pant legs, she bent over the desk, grabbed the pen with a trembling hand and signed her name to the adoption document.

Natural born or not, she loved the boy as though she had carried him to term, fed him from her own breasts.

She remembered two weeks ago, coming back to Nate's house for the first time after they last separated, her heart pounding so hard she felt dizzy. When the door opened, Nate was shocked to see her and hurriedly invited her in.

In the living room, the images of the night she was shot over a year ago, flooded back: Monica wearing a bath towel after showering, walking out to see a man pointing a gun at her husband, that man shooting Nate twice then turning the gun on Monica and firing—the excruciating fractioned millisecond of pain she felt of the bullet burrowing into her skull, before she blacked out and fell naked to the floor.

Standing in the living room on the day of her return, Nate's arms around her, Monica told herself she could not be weak; if she wanted her son away from the dangerous man she knew Nate to be, she would have to lie, connive and act as cold and heartless as Nate always had.

Now in bed, she lay in total contentment, the early morning sun peeking through the bedroom's horizontal blinds, casting bright stripes on the comforter. She stared up toward her outstretched arm, the sunlight catching one of the cuts on her 8 karat solitaire wedding ring, making it shine so bright, she had to squint against its glare. It still felt odd and somewhat foreign on her finger, for she hadn't been wearing it twenty-four hours.

"There's something I have to ask you," Nate said, yesterday. He had walked in from work only minutes earlier, and having taken off the gray Armani suit jacket, he hung it over the back of a kitchen chair, and was pacing across the floor while Monica made little Nathaniel a peanut butter and jelly sandwich. "But I'm nervous," he said.

"What are you nervous—" Monica was about to ask, but was quieted by Nate's upheld finger as he bent over and slipped a hand into his suit jacket. He went into the inside pocket, grabbed the item, held it behind his back, then stepped in front of Monica, smiling.

"Nate, what are you doing?"

"Monica," Nate said, no longer smiling, but gazing at her with the most sincere eyes. "I have wished it, dreamt it more times than even I can imagine, but I never thought you'd come back to me. I never thought…we'd be here again with our son, sharing a house, living as a family. Everything is as it should be except…" Nate lowered himself to a knee, pulled his arm out from behind his back to present a light blue ring box. He popped it open, and inside was the most beautiful ring with a stone so bright, Monica was nearly blinded.

Nathaniel rustled beside Monica in bed. She leaned over, gently kissed his forehead. She smiled, thinking about last night's wedding. It was a whirlwind, four-hour affair. Nate said he had a guy standing by a short drive away to marry them.

"A guy?" Monica said, being dragged out of the kitchen by the hand that wore that beautiful new ring. Nate scooped up a giggling Nathaniel under his arm like a surfboard, informing her that the boy was going, too.

On the ride there—it just so happened there was a stretch limo waiting outside the house—Monica couldn't stop staring at the ring and shaking her head.

"What?" Nate asked.

Nathaniel sat dangerously in Nate's lap; Monica figured the child seat was the one thing he had not planned.

"Nothing," she answered, smiling only a little. "I just don't believe you did this."

"Is that it? Because it seems like there's something else on your mind," Nate said with a smile. She was sure he was only guessing, but still she scolded herself for allowing her husband to so easily read her expressions.

"No. It just last time we married there was a pre-nup. You insisted. Is there going to be one wherever you're taking me, a pen lying near it ready for me to sign?"

"No prenuptial agreement this time, if you're cool with that."

Monica nodded. "Yeah, I'm cool with that."

As promised, there was "a guy" in a gray suit, waiting in the small, downtown church courtyard, along with Nate's brother, Tim, Tim's wife and Nate's niece and nephew. It was a beautiful affair.

"Still looking at that thing, huh?" Nate said, jarring Monica out of her early morning daydream. He sat on the edge of their bed, knotting his tie, wearing a light colored, Brooks Brothers suit. It was bought from her store just the other day, Monica deducting her store discount when she rang it up, but Nate refusing, insisting on paying full price.

Monica pulled her hand down, blushed a little. "The ring is beautiful. I still don't believe any of it."

Nate smiled. "I hope you believe me when I say I've been waiting for you. That I know I've made horrible mistakes regarding us in the past, but things have changed; I've changed, and I'm going to be the caring, honest and devoted husband that you've always deserved."

Pulling her son closer, Monica stared somewhat unbelievingly at Nate longer than she should've before answering. "I trust you."

Nate leaned forward, grabbed her chin, kissed her lips and smiled. "No you don't. But I don't expect you to after all we've been through just yet. I'll prove it to you though," he said, kissing the boy on the head before he stood to finish knotting his tie.

"Nate, you have nothing to—"

"No," he said, turning from the mirror. "It'll be fun spoiling you and seeing the crazy look on your face every time I prove what a changed man I am."

Monica smiled, shaking her head. "Well, if you insist, spoil away, Mr. Kenny."

"You taking the day off? We were out pretty late last night."

"I almost forgot," Monica said. "Gotta fly out on business to L.A. later on. I have a face to face with the owner of a similar chain of stores. Hoping she can help me get mine back out of the red."

Appearing disappointed, Nate said, "You're just telling me you're leaving now? When will you be back?"

"Sorry. Slipped my mind," Monica apologized. "But it's a short trip. I'm on a redeye: should be back no later than 2 A.M."

"Well, your son and I will miss you. Be safe, and call me when you land."

Smiling, Monica watched Nate until he left the room. The smile disappeared before he was completely out of sight.

Wearing a nightgown, she hurried across the room on tip-toes and stood by the window, parting the blinds to look out. She listened to noises in the house: Nate descending the staircase, the door to the garage opening and closing, then the big garage door rolling up, as one of Nate's half dozen cars—Monica believed the exhaust note of this one was the new Mercedes SL600—roared to life.

She peered through the blinds again, saw the shiny black sports car pull out, then speed down the driveway and out onto the street.

Combing fingers through her shoulder length hair, she walked back to the nightstand, picked up her cell phone and highlighted the California area number she had saved in her phone. The phone rang five times before a groggy voice said, "Hullo?"

"My flight is on Delta. Will you be there to pick me up like you said?" There was a restless edge in Monica's voice.

"I told you you're wasting your time. I'm not gonna do—"

"Will you be there to pick me up is all I'm asking?" Monica said.

A pause came before a reluctant answer of: "Yeah, why not? I'll be there."

2

"Hurry up, you two. We don't wanna be late for school," Lewis Waters told his daughter Layla and his girlfriend's daughter, Tammi—both of which were five years old. The two had nearly been inseparable since being introduced to each other only months ago. They sat at the kitchen table quickly spooning cereal into their mouths and spilling milk onto the table. "Okay, okay," Lewis said, seeing the mess they were making. "You can slow down just a bit."

The girls giggled, turning their bowls up, sipping the milk from the rims.

The little girl Tammi and her mother Eva moved in at Lewis's suggestion, after he realized the immediate improvement she made in his life. But moving her and her daughter in was about much more than what benefited him: it was what Eva provided Layla. Lewis's daughter had been without her mother since she was an infant: Lewis having walked in one day after work to find his daughter's mother, Selena, had overdosed on heroin. Her head thrown back over the sofa, eyes wide, a rubber tourniquet laying loose under her arm, a needle still hanging from a vein, Layla was screaming on her mother's chest, trying to wake her.

Lewis had grown up without his father, knew the devastating and lasting affects a man's absence had in his life. He had no idea if there would be similar consequences for his little girl growing up without a mother, but he was not trying to find out.

Lewis had other relationships before Eva—briefly dated a woman named Monica he thought could've been the one, but wasn't. Then came Eva. Layla took immediately to her, and they bonded instantly, for which Lewis was grateful, because he still carried a great deal of guilt for the death of Layla's mother, even though he begged the woman incessantly to get off the drugs she had been doing.

Lewis pushed the girl's bag lunches into their backpacks, readying them for school.

"Dad, I think we're ready now," Layla said standing, taking Tammi's bowl and setting the dishes into the sink.

"Okay," Lewis said, ushering the girls down the hallway toward the front door when he was startled by a scream from upstairs. The girls jumped, and terrified himself, Lewis told them to stay where they were.

"But Daddy—" Layla started.

"I said, stay!" Lewis warned. There was no telling what he would find after what had happened to Eva just two weeks ago.

Whipping open the cupboards over the sink, Lewis dug deep into one, bringing out the 9mm. handgun he had hidden there.

"Lewis, why do you have—" Tammi began, but quieted when Lewis shushed her with a finger to his lips.

He hurried up the stairs to the second floor, only to hear Eva scream again. Had someone gotten in on the roof? Climbed through a window?

His back pressed to the wall just beside the bedroom door, Lewis shunned the image of his girlfriend pinned to the bed, her clothes in shreds, some man holding her down at the wrists as he forcefully took her.

"Not again," Lewis breathed. He spun, barreling through the door into the bedroom, holding the gun out in front of him. Looking down the sight, he saw Eva kneeling in the middle of the bed, her hair falling down over her face, crying. She jumped and screamed when she saw Lewis pointing the gun at her.

"Shhh," he said, glancing at the windows to see they were closed. He cautiously checked the room, and after finding no one on the other side of the bed, he stopped in front of the closet door and grabbed the handle. His heart pounding, sweat growing in his palm, he looked over his shoulder, questioned Eva with his eyes as to whether there was anyone hiding inside. She wiped tears from her face and shook her head.

Lewis flung the door open, pointed the gun into the closet, pushed through the hanging garments with his arm, the gun still in his fist. The closet empty, Lewis backed out, closed the door then turned to Eva, his pulse starting to slow. "No one's here, baby," he said, setting the gun on the dresser. He sat down, wrapped an arm around Eva, pulling her close and kissing her wet cheek. "You're safe. There's no one here."

She nestled against him, lay her head against his chest. "How do you know they aren't coming? How do you know the second you leave, they won't come back?"

Lewis didn't know that. He combed a hand through Eva's hair, pulling her closer, kissing her on the part in her scalp. "They won't come again," he breathed.

"But how do you *know*?"

"Because…" he started, careful not to say something to inform her he knew more than he ever let on about her attack. "Because I just do."

Eva shook her head, appearing as though she didn't believe a word he had spoken.

Lewis eased away, dug his cell phone from his pocket, dialed a number then wrapped his arm back around Eva as the call was delivered.

"Who are you callng?"

"I'm going to show you how I know," Lewis said. When his call was answered, a nasally woman's voice said, "Oak Park Psychiatric Institution. How may I help you?"

"Freddy Ford, please?"

Eva attempted to jerk away as though the man Lewis asked to speak to just stepped through the bedroom door. Holding tighter to her, Lewis silently assured her everything was fine.

"Yes," Lewis said into the phone. "I'll hold." He set the phone on his knee.

Eva stared down at it as though it was a dangerous, living thing. When a voice came through the tiny speaker, she gasped and nearly tore from the bed.

"Hello?" the voice called.

Freddy's gruff voice unsettled Lewis nearly as much as it had Eva. Freddy Ford had been responsible for arranging to have two men—the brothers of Freddy's most recent and late girlfriend, Joni—break into Lewis's house and violently rape Eva. Freddy did that because Joni had been shot and killed by police when she and Freddy tried to extort money during a kidnapping. It was information that Lewis offered that helped police find Freddy and take him into custody while Joni lay dead on the pavement, bleeding from a grapefruit sized hole in the back of her skull.

Freddy was sent away to a mental institution, and seeking revenge, orchestrated the rape of Lewis's girlfriend from inside his cell.

On the night of the assault, Lewis found Eva in the ransacked bedroom of his home, lamps broken on the floor, sheets pulled from the bed, long blood smears stretching across the skin of the white mattress. Lewis stood in the open doorway, calling out to his girlfriend, finding her balled into a trembling, bruised and bloodied mess, covering herself with a blood-stained sheet, crying on the other side of the bed. Police had ultimately discovered Freddy Ford was behind the crime, but Lewis never told Eva Freddy had been threatening him and those Lewis loved and that what happened might've been avoided.

Now, Lewis sat beside Eva, envisioning his boyhood friend, Freddy, in sagging jeans, slippers and a bathrobe, standing on the dingy floor tiles of some cold, institution hallway, the phone pressed to his ear, a dying bulb flickering out over his head. "I said hello! Who is this? Who the fuck is this?"

"Hang up the phone!" Eva said.

"I said who…" Freddy said, as Lewis took up the phone, preparing to disconnect the call. Before he did, he heard Freddy say, "This you, Lewis?"

18

Lewis ended the call, stuffed the phone back in his pocket, the intent of the call being to make Eva feel safer when it only appeared to do the opposite.

"He's still locked up," Lewis told Eva, wrapping both his arms around her, kissing her on the forehead. "That's how I know no one's coming. He's still locked up. And he'll never get out."

3

Daphanie stood in her son's room looking down into his crib, while the baby's father, Trevor, dressed for work.

Daphanie dated Trevor briefly on a rebound from being dumped by Nate Kenny. Trevor, who was a banker, was a good man, at least at the time they were involved. He was handsome, bore an uncanny resemblance to Nate, which made it too easy to tell Nate when he called looking to reconcile, that the child Daphanie was impregnated with was his, when it was truly Trevor's.

Eventually, Nate discovered the lie, had himself and the actual father tested and told Trevor the falsehood Daphanie perpetrated. After that, in typical Nate Kenny fashion, he sought revenge.

He proposed to Daphanie, but only under the condition, that once born, she give full custody of her child, along with every right that came with it, to the baby's natural father, Trevor. Nate promised Daphanie that afterward they would get pregnant and start a family of their own. Nate told her it was the only way he could marry her.

Foolishly, Daphanie took the bait, signed away her baby, and on the day of the elaborate wedding she and Nate planned—even that was part of the vengeful plot—he let her stand at the altar looking stupid, bouquet in hand, Vera Wang dress on her back, "DAMN FOOL", stamped across her forehead. But that wasn't the extent of Nate Kenny's wrath: the man had somehow got into Daphanie's accounts, maxed all her credit cards and took all the money she had, leaving her with a single cent, no man and no baby.

She went to Nate, threw herself on his mercy, begged him to get her son back. A smug look on his face, sitting behind his massive oaken desk, he swiveled about in his executive chair and said he had no control over the situation any more. He did tell her that he had spoken to Trevor, and said Trevor would take Daphanie back, allow her to help raise their son if she chose to move in with him.

Daphanie had lost her job, had no money and her credit had been turned to shit. She did the only thing she could and moved in with Trevor.

But it had not been easy. Even though it was Trevor that offered her the opportunity to come back, she believed he did not like her. Maybe it was the pain of being dumped, or the fact that she was willing to give another man his child. Whatever it was, Trevor said few words to Daphanie—got up and walked out of rooms when she entered. On the occasion he did look at her, she could see pain and distrust heavy in his gaze. The few times they "made love" he grunted on top of her, never looking her in the eyes, but at the headboard or the floor, then rolling off the bed, wiping himself with the sheet as he walked wordlessly away into the bathroom. She suffered that for the sake of being in the same space as her only child. Despite Trevor's treatment, she kept telling herself it was worth it.

Two months down…seventeen years and ten months to go, Daphanie thought, staring down at her infant child who had just woken and was smiling, reaching a hand up to her.

"Hey sweetheart. Hey baby," Daphanie smiled at the boy. Ironically, his name was Nate.

"Why did you name him that?" Daphanie asked Trevor the first night she lived under his roof.

"Because if Nate Kenny hadn't alerted me to your lies, didn't convince you to sign your rights over to me, I wouldn't have my son. Our child would've been a bastard. I'm eternally grateful to that man."

Daphanie picked up little Nat. It's what she'd been calling him, because hearing that man's name every time she spoke to her baby was just too painful. Daphanie pressed the baby to her breasts, took him over and sat down with him in the glider.

"Are you hungry, Nat?" Daphanie said, kissing the baby on the head. His last feeding was over four hours ago when she heard him screaming from her room. She climbed out of bed and took Nat down to feed him Similac in the middle of the kitchen, under a low burning overhead stove light. Trevor never fed their baby. It was implicitly stated early on as one of the conditions that allowed her to stay there: she would do all of the off-hour caring.

Now in the little boy's room, Daphanie bounced Nat in her arms, hoping to stop him from recognizing his hunger for she wanted just a little more time with him. The baby's face crumpled, his lips turned downward and he started a long whine, which she knew would turn into a full tantrum if he weren't fed.

"Shhh, shhh, shhh," Daphanie said, bouncing him faster. Nat needed food. But Daphanie didn't feel like feeding her baby food from a can again. It wasn't natural. What he needed, what she knew the baby wanted was what coursed through her mammary glands. She thought of this every time she stood under the hot spray of her shower, dreaming of what was forbidden, massaging her breasts till the milk leaked from her nipples onto the shower floor and washed wastefully down the drain.

Looking toward the door, Daphanie figured Trevor should've been all ready dressed and leaving for work. She knew if she weren't in his path to the front door, he would've never gone out of his way to say goodbye.

Still squirming in her arms, Nat became more restless.

"Okay, baby. Shhh, shhh, shhh," Daphanie said, opening her robe, sliding down her gown strap to expose a heavy breast. She took it in her hand, massaged it gently, squeezing her nipple softly to coax a bead of milk from it. She brought Nat's face forward and immediately he began to suckle.

It had been so long since she fed her child the way God intended. She felt him pulling the life sustaining fluid he needed from her. And finally, after doing all that mothers did: changing diapers, bathing the baby, rocking the baby to sleep, it was only now she truly felt like this child's mother.

She brought Nat closer, lay back her head, rocked slowly in the glider, and closed her eyes trying to suppress the tears that she knew would come. The two months she had been there had been hard, but this made up for it, Daphanie thought. She started to drift off, telling herself if she could have this moment, once every now and again, she could deal with whatever punishment Trevor chose to deliver her.

Suddenly, Daphanie was startled by the opening of the bedroom door, and even more surprised when it wasn't the nanny that Trevor hired to care for Nat much of the time, but Trevor.

"What are you doing?" Shock painted his face. "I said, what the hell are you doing?" he said again, walking toward her, looking as though there was a need to rescue their son.

"I'm feeding our baby." Daphanie pulled Nat closer to her breasts, cradling him tighter.

"I said you were never to do that. All the formula you need is—"

"I don't want to feed him anymore fucking formula. He needs milk. My milk!"

"Give him to me." Trevor said, his hands outstretched.

"No!"

"Give me my fucking son!" Trevor demanded.

Daphanie pushed back in the chair, covering Nat with her arms, but Trevor was on her, his hands wrapped around their tiny baby's body. And he was pulling him like the child was in a wrecked car about to explode: like Daphanie's arms were flames licking his son's skin. She had no choice but release him for fear Trevor would break Nat if they continued to struggle.

"Please!" Daphanie screamed, reaching so far out from the chair that she toppled over, spilling out of it, falling to her knees. She looked up to see Trevor staring down on her, resentment on his face, holding their child as far away as he could from her.

"I told you never to do that. My rules! You don't like them…leave!" He stormed out the room, Daphanie hearing her son scream down the hall as he was being carried off.

4

The downtown bank lobby—floored with granite colored tiles, housed in thick green-tinged glass doors and windows—was busy with early morning traffic. Men and women in business attire stood at the teller stations, others waited to be seen in center lobby chairs by personal bankers.

Nate sat among them, thumbing through a Time magazine, glancing down at the Patek Philippe watch face that peeked from under the sleeve cuff of his suit. Looking up, he stood and smiled when he caught sight of Trevor walking toward him.

The handsome man that even Nate had to admit, resembled him, stood an inch over six feet, was brown skinned, in good shape and had a head of thick, black, neatly trimmed hair. He wore a nicely cut gray suit and held out a hand as he neared Nate.

"Good to see you, Nate," Trevor said.

"Thanks for agreeing to meet with me. I can see your day is already in full swing."

"Never to busy for you," Trevor said. "C'mon back to my office."

Inside, Trevor closed the door on the large space with ground level windows looking right out onto Clarke Street, the avenue bustling with pedestrians and stop-and-go automobile traffic.

Nate watched Trevor take a seat behind his desk, Nate lowering himself into the chair on the other side of it.

"So," Trevor said, scooting his chair forward as though about to get down to some serious paper work. "What brings you by?"

Nate knew what he was about to say would be upsetting. "I was hoping to convince you to tear up the contract," Nate said, deciding there was no polite way to ask for what he wanted, and that it was best to come right out with it.

The smile Trevor wore shrank slowly on his face. "What contract are you referring to?"

"With respect, you know what I'm talking about, Trevor. I think you should give Daphanie her rights back to her child."

Trevor appeared all of sudden uncomfortable in his suit. He loosened the knot in his tie, unbuttoned the collar of his shirt. "That woman tried to pass my baby off as yours," Trevor said, his anger apparent. He pushed back in his chair, stood from his desk.

"And you have the right to be angry. As I do. It was all I wanted, to have a child, and she lied to me, too. It was the reason I did what I did to her: tricked her into giving her baby away. But don't you think she's had enough?"

"No," Trevor said, then leaned over his desk and said it again: "No," before pacing away from Nate. "There can never be enough punishment for what she did to me." He stood, his arms crossed, his back to Nate, staring out onto the congested street outside his window.

"Exactly what do you expect to accomplish by continuing to withhold her rights?" Nate asked.

Trevor spun. "As the paternity test we took confirmed, the baby is not yours, so forgive me, Nate, but what does it matter to you?"

"I was wrong to do what I did."

"She put you up to this? She ask you to come here?"

"No. I've done some horrible things in my life. What I've done to Daphanie, I believe, is one of the worst. I'm just trying to repair some of the damage I've done," Nate said, standing, walking over to Trevor, who was shaking his head as though closed to any reasonableness Nate might've offered.

"She made a mistake, Trevor."

"She tried to keep my son from me."

"So now you're keeping him from her. That will only serve to hurt little Nate."

"I'll be the judge of that," Trevor said, now eyeing Nate as though he were an enemy. "Like I said, he's my son, not yours."

"I know," Nate said. "But if you just consider—"

26

"Thank you for all you've done to get me my boy back, but we'll never speak about this matter again," Trevor said. "If that's not acceptable, then it has been a pleasure knowing you, Nate." Again, Trevor held out his hand.

Nate stared down at it then sadly up at Trevor, appealing to him one last time. "If you'd just—"

"Goodbye, Nate," Trevor said.

Standing on the curb outside the bank, his cell phone to his ear, the warm Chicago lakefront wind finding it's way through the maze of downtown buildings and whipping past Nate, he was heartbroken by the sound of Daphanie's voice. It was breathless and filled with excitement for what she hoped Nate might've accomplished.

"So what did he say?"

"I'm sorry, Daphanie."

She paused on the other end as though there was something more Nate would tell her. When he didn't, she said, "But...he can't just...you have to ask him again."

"I'm sorry, but he won't budge."

"But you have to tell him—"

"I can ask him till I'm blue in the face, but the way he looked at me...I'm so sorry, Daphanie, but it sounds to me he'll never give you your rights back." Nate listened as he heard Daphanie sob. He bit down on his lip almost hard enough to draw blood he was so angry with himself. "Is there anything else I can do? I know you're out of work. I can give you some money. Name a price. It doesn't matter how much. Just tell me."

Nate heard Daphanie sniffling, and he imagined she was drying her face, pulling herself together to tell him what the figure would be.

"Nate," Daphanie said, still half sobbing."

"Yes, Daphanie?"

"I hope you burn in hell," she said, then ended the call.

5

Standing on the porch, looking over the railing to see his Range Rover running, parked at the curbside, Lewis heard the locks on the door of the large brick home being undone.

The door opened and standing behind it was a beautiful, tall and slender brown-skinned woman. She pushed the sun door open and stepped out on the porch, smiling, holding a newborn infant, the baby wearing only a diaper and laughing as he attempted to stick his entire foot in his mouth.

"Brought you these," Lewis said holding out a Dunkin Donuts bag. Inside were two bagels: whole wheat and a multigrain.

"Boy, you shouldn't have," Kia said, leaning her back against the door to hold it open, while still corralling the baby. She wore sweat pants and a faded University of Chicago shirt. "You know I love these things," she said, taking the bag. "C'mon in."

"I can't. Gonna be late for work."

Kia was an ex-girlfriend of Freddy Ford's. The two were together right before Freddy started to lose it, scaring Kia off, she was so afraid of Freddy's violent tendencies. After leaving him, she phoned Freddy to tell him she had aborted their child. He was devastated by the news. The only way Lewis discovered Kia's lie was by coming by her house unannounced one day. It was something that would forever have to remain a secret, for if Freddy were to find out, discover Kia had lied to him about something so important, Lewis was frightened of what the man would do.

"How's the little one?" Lewis said, reaching out, letting the boy take one of his fingers.

"He's good," Kia said. "Getting bigger every day."

Following in her father's footsteps, Kia was a law student who was about to graduate after three long, hard years in school. But looking at her, she appeared more proud of her role as mother than the one she would soon take as an attorney.

"Have you...changed your mind about telling Freddy about him?" Lewis asked.

The smile fell from Kia's face, and she adjusted the baby in her arms, holding him closer. "I'm not. I never will. You haven't—"

"No. That will have to come from you. But I think you got the right idea to keep it to yourself," Lewis said. "I just wanted to know because—"

"You speak to him," Kia said, the faintest resentment in her voice.

"He...he calls me sometimes."

"And sometimes you'll call him, right? I don't blame you. You two were best friends forever. I just can't believe how much he's changed."

"Yeah," Lewis said, dropping his eyes as though he had played some part in that. "I should go. Just stopped by to check on you and little man."

The smile appeared again on Kia's face. She held out a hand, took Lewis in a one-arm embrace and kissed him on the cheek. "I know. My guardian angel: always looking out for me."

From the driver's seat of his truck, Lewis waved back to Kia and watched her close the front door of the house. He reached for the shifter, was about to drive off when his cell phone rang, UNKNOWN CALLER, flashing on the screen.

"This is Lewis," he answered, unsettled. A recorded voice announced: "You have a collect call from..." the voice instructed him to push a button if he wished to accept the charges. Lewis did.

"How you gonna call me then just hang up, muh fuckuh? I thought we were better than that," Freddy said as though their conversation had never been disrupted.

Lewis glanced back up at the house as if to make sure Kia didn't see him, worried she'd guess who he was speaking to. "Needed Eva to know your ass is still locked up."

"Wow," Freddy chuckled. "She stayed with your ass after she was raped, knowing you was the reason I sent them fools for her. She must be the most forgiving female in the Chi."

"She don't know, and never will."

Freddy laughed again. "Still telling lies and keeping secrets. Telling me lies is what got your girl gouged out. Keeping any other secrets from me, dog?"

Lewis bit down, tightening his jaws, wishing he could lay hands on Freddy for what he had done to Eva—one-time best friend or not. "Nah, ain't keeping no secrets," Lewis said, glancing again at Kia's house.

"Good. Cause when I get out—"

"Uh, uh. You ain't never getting out. You rotting in there, right where you belong," Lewis said.

"With these crazy motherfuckers? Fool, I got unfinished business out there—people to end. That bitch Nate Kenny has to die. Maybe you too—haven't decided yet. Nate Kenny, though—definitely. And...probably Kia for running out on me and killing my seed. Yeah, she gonna have to go, too."

"Don't fucking make threats like that!" Lewis shouted, cupping his hand over the phone as if there was a chance Kia might hear from inside her home.

"Lewis getting pissed off, all protective and shit. That's cute," Freddy laughed again. "You a cute, protective motherfucker, but I ain't making threats—they promises. I'm getting out...soon. So never stop looking over them shoulders, playa, cause one day I'm gonna be right behind you."

6

Monica stared at the aging woman who was wearing an old flower-print wool housecoat, slippers and a woolen skullcap pulled over her head. Monica's attorney said Mrs. Ford was in her mid-sixties, but bent over and slowly moving, she appeared well into her seventies. Monica was sure it had to have been from all the stress the woman's psychopathic son gave her throughout the years.

Surprisingly, Monica had gotten further with Mrs. Ford than she thought she would've: inside the door of the modest old home, standing in a living room filled with heavy plastic covered furniture and framed portraits of Jesus, Dr. Martin Luther King and JFK.

Monica's attorney, Joyla Phillips, told her she had reached out to the woman several times, tried to persuade Mrs. Ford to come into the office and give a voice testimony, but the woman was adamantly against it. "I made my last attempt," Joyla said.

"Give me her number and address," Monica said yesterday morning. "Let me see what I can do."

Now, staring at Mrs. Ford, Monica said, "Will you at least consider coming into my lawyer's office to give a statement?"

"I'm not going anywhere."

"I can drive you, or I can have her come here."

"I already told you no, Ms...."

"Mrs. Kenny," Monica told the woman her name.

Mrs. Ford's eyes narrowed with recollection. "You the wife of that man...that man who stole my home from me?"

Monica nodded. "Yes, I am."

"My husband bought that home forty five years ago and your husband stole it from me and Fred and tore it down."

"I know how you must feel, Mrs. Ford. That's why I need for you to—"

31

"No!" Mrs. Ford said, stabbing a finger at Monica. "That man is evil! He made me homeless, forced me to live in a tiny room here with my brother, because my son wouldn't do what he said. He's the reason my son took that boy. He's the reason my son is locked up. Nate Kenny is the devil!"

"Mrs. Ford—" Monica said, but the older woman was already shuffling to the front door. She pulled it open, shaking her head, extending a trembling hand to push open the outer screen door for Monica.

"Get out, Mrs. Kenny."

"But Mrs. Ford, if you could—"

"Just go! Please. Haven't you and your husband caused my family enough pain?"

Monica stared at Mrs. Ford, feeling, because of her association with Nate, guilty. "I'm sorry, Mrs. Ford," Monica said.

Having not driven away, Monica sat behind the wheel of her gunmetal gray Jaguar XJ sport sedan. She pulled her cell phone from her jacket pocket, swiped to her recorder app and pressed the rewind then the play icons.

"…the reason my son took that boy. He's the reason my son is locked up. Nate Kenny is the devil!" Mrs. Ford's angry recorded voice filled the car's cabin.

Satisfied it would help make the case she was building against her husband, Monica pressed the STOP button, slipped the phone back in her pocket and drove off.

7

AERO was the store Monica managed when she had met Nate. When the owner retired and was looking to sell, Monica took money from the millions she won in her divorce settlement and bought the small chain of two fine men's clothing stores, expanded the chain to three, then added spa services to them. For the majority of time she owned the stores, they did extremely well. But lately, sales have hit rock bottom. She wasn't sure if it was the ease and popularity of shopping from online stores: the budget brick and mortars that sold discounted high-end fashions, like Nordstrom Rack, Off-Fifth, or the Neiman's outlet that cut so deeply into her sales, or the idea that she might've expanded too fast. Possibly, it was the combination of all three, but the AERO stores were hemorrhaging money faster than Monica could make it. With the sky-high taxes of her downtown, Gold Coast location, she wondered if she could ever get back on her feet. Her mind stayed occupied with finding solutions and during some very deep, but thankfully short moments of depression, she considered putting the whole enterprise up for sale.

As Monica walked through the glass doors of the store with the high ceilings, oak wood floors and cedar pine rafters overhead, she was again disappointed by how many customers she saw browsing the suit racks or considering AERO's line of very expensive Italian shoes.

She glanced over to the spa side of the store and saw her three female employees, all in black smocks, trying to look busy: polishing the counters and rearranging skin and hair products on the shelves, because there wasn't a single client waiting. Monica hated the idea of having to let one, or quite possibly two of them go, but she would do what she must when the time came.

"Ms. Monica," she heard her name called from the only man she knew in possession of such a melodious voice: her store's second in command, Roland. He was tall, thin, wore a neatly trimmed beard/faux hawk combination, and stayed impeccably dressed in clothes bought from the store with his employee discount. "Such a beautiful smile, girl. Somebody must be in a good mood today," Roland said from the elevated store's cashier station.

She walked the few stairs up and gave him the hug he reached for. After she stepped back, she saw Roland's eyes balloon after glancing at her ring finger. He threw back his head and started fanning himself demonstratively.

"Oh, no! Oh hell no!" Roland said, hurrying down from around the checkout counter, skidding to a halt on the floor in his purple, size 12 heels, then hurrying back up the stairs to grab Monica's left hand and hold it up to his face. "This thing real or did you get lucky at the gumball machine, girl?"

Monica laughed. "It's the real thing, Roland."

"Oh my God! 6 karats?"

"8."

"You go, bitch! Give me five."

Monica playfully slapped the outstretched hand Roland held up.

"All jokes aside," Roland said, embracing Monica again. "Congratulations, girl. You set a date yet?"

"It's done already."

"Well congratulations again," Roland said, sincerely. "Girl don't waste no time."

"Congrats for what?" Tabatha, Monica's store manager and best friend said, walking up behind the two. She was thin, athletically built, with muscular legs and—as she put it—"the tit's of a thirteen year-old." She wore dark slacks, a dark button down blouse, and dark shoes to match her dark moods of late. Tabatha had just separated from the man she thought would finally take her off the market, and she hadn't been the ray of sunshine she had always been in the past.

"Tab, Ms. Monica done gone and got wedded, chile," Roland said, faking a Southern drawl. "Show Tab yo' rang, gurl."

Monica raised her hand, wiggled her fingers. Sunlight caught the diamond, lit the stone up like it was on fire.

"That from Nate?" Tabatha asked.

"Who else?" Monica said.

"And you accepted it?" Tabatha was there the first time Monica set eyes on Nate. It was there in that very store. Actually, it was Tabatha who saw Nate first and thought he and Monica would make a perfect couple. Since, Tabatha had been there through all of Nate's shit: his schemes, his deceptions, Monica's brief affair with Lewis Waters, Monica's divorce to Nate, and even the near-death experience that would've never occurred if Monica hadn't continued to deal with the man. Tabatha continued to tell Monica she would never be able to apologize enough for introducing that man to her.

"Yes," Monica said. "I accepted the ring, his proposal, and we got married last night. Be happy for me, hoe."

Tabatha stared sadly at Monica, shaking her head, her lips pursed sour-lemon tight.

Monica's cell phone rang. She dug it from her purse, glanced at the screen, quickly dismissed the call, and dropped the phone back into her bag. "So, Tab? Anything nice to say?"

Tabatha grabbed Monica's hand, pulled her down the long, brick-walled hallway that led to the manager's office. Closing the door, Tabatha said, "What the fuck is wrong with you? You lost your memory or something? You wanna tell me what you're doing?"

"I'm flying to L.A. today and wanted to make sure you aren't running my store into the ground. That's what I'm doing. You wanna tell me where all our customers are?"

"At Marshall's buying a shirt for $20 instead of buying one here for $120. Can you blame them?"

"That doesn't help me. It doesn't help you."

"Relax. It's early okay. You know these rich folks around here don't start spending money till after lunch. Tell me what you're doing wearing that gaudy ass ring."

"I know what I'm doing. It's none of your business."

"Really? Remember that scar where they shaved your big ass head and cut you open to get the bullet out? Just because your hair is longer, doesn't mean it ain't still there."

Monica's phone rang again. She sunk her hand into the purse once more, saw that the call was coming from the same place and once again, rejected it. She turned her attention back to her friend and said, "Tab, I said I got this."

"Monica—"

"Tabatha! I didn't come here seeking approval. I'm a grown woman, and you ain't my mama, so I can get married without your permission," Monica said. "Besides, there's a reason I'm doing this...why I have to do this."

"Have to? You're not married because you're all hopelessly in love again with that louse?"

"I'm doing what needs to be done."

Tabatha looked to give what Monica said a moment of thought. "If you're going after that man, thinking that you can play his game and—"

"I need to go," Monica said, trying to step away from Tabatha. Her best friend grabbed both of Monica's wrists and held the two of them face-to-face, Tabatha staring into Monica's eyes.

"Whatever you doing, if you think you can beat Nate at his own game, make him pay for the things he's done to you, you're a damn fool. And I'm only saying this because I love you, but leave his ass alone. You'll lose."

"Let me go," Monica said.

"You hear me," Tabatha said, disobeying Monica, holding her a second longer before releasing her. "Don't do it."

Monica stepped away, rubbing her wrists. "Get some customers in here, or we'll both be out of jobs. Hear me?"

"Have a safe trip," Tabatha said, turning her back and stepping out the office.

Monica leaned on the edge of one of the two office desks, set her purse down and shook her head. Her phone rang again. This time she did not look to see who was calling, but took the call. "I don't answer, that means I'm busy. It doesn't mean keep calling."

"You have to help me," the voice on the other end said desperately. "You said you'd help me. It's getting worse. I can't take it here anymore."

"I'm trying, Daphanie. Do you have the contract Nate had you sign, forfeiting rights to your baby?"

"I have it right here."

"Good, I'll get it from you. My attorney will need it to help make my case. Till then, sit tight. I'm flying to L.A."

"L.A.?" Daphanie said. "Why are you going there when you said—"

"To get the woman that's going to help both of us get what we want. I told you all of this. You still have the credit card and the list of instructions I gave you, don't you?"

"Yes, I have everything."

"Good," Monica said. "Like I explained, I'll need for you to take her around, get the things she needs to prepare for her part in all this, okay."

"Yeah, okay."

Daphanie sounded pathetic to Monica. She could only imagine the hell she was going through. The sad reality was Monica knew there was very little she could do; she had already had it determined by several attorneys that the contract was ironclad. If nothing else, she believed, giving Daphanie this busy work would keep her mind off of the gut-wrenching situation she was in, at least for a little while.

"Hang in there, Daphanie," Monica said.

Her voice barely audible, Daphanie replied, "Please, hurry."

8

Wearing a safety construction helmet, eye goggles and holding a pair of protective ear wear, Nate stood a thousand feet from a deteriorating brick building that was erected in 1891. The glass windows had long ago been knocked out the square frames where daylight could be seen making it's way through massive spaces in the building's collapsed ceiling. The structure was initially constructed to house a Singer Sewing machine manufacturing company. It changed ownership several times and had been recently bought for pennies on the dollar by Nate's company. Although the land was far south of Chicago's downtown—almost on the Indiana border—Nate felt the property would be valuable and could sell it for a profit; but the building would have to be demolished first.

Beside him, dressed in similar protective gear, stood Nate's brother, Tim, who was a couple of years younger, a couple of inches shorter, but shared many of Nate's handsome traits. He was not the millionaire Nate was, but a writer, who finally succeeded in writing a series of novels that had elevated him to bestseller status. It was a long haul for Tim: many times Nate needing to subsidize his little brother's pay in order to make sure Nate's sister-in-law, niece and nephew wanted for nothing.

"You sure this was a good idea to bring him out here?" Tim said, raising his voice over the noise of the dump trucks, bulldozers and other heavy construction equipment.

Tim was referring to his nephew, little Nathaniel, who Nate held in his arms. Big goggles covered nearly the boy's entire face. A construction helmet sat askew on his head, and protective earphones covered the boy's ears as he smiled at all the men in work boots, gloves, torso harnesses and helmets working around them.

"You ever see a building implosion before?" Nate asked his brother, lifting his son up over his head, allowing the boy to straddle his neck so that he could get a better look. "You see, we set several charges of dynamite all around the building's base, set them off one after another. It's like taking out the legs of a giraffe one at a time, giving the animal, or in this case, the building, no choice but to fall. The detonation takes out the building's support and it just drops into a cloud of smoke. Coolest thing you'd ever want to see in the world. Right, Nathaniel?" Nate said, bouncing the kid up and down on his neck.

"Right, Daddy!" The boy laughed, swatting the top of Nate's helmet.

"C'mon," Nate said. "Loosen up. Do it for me and be a kid again. This'll be a blast." He elbowed Tim. "Get it."

Tim sighed, appearing more troubled than Nate felt he should've looked.

"Besides, you haven't congratulated me on my marriage to Monica."

"I did, too. Last night."

"You stood there as my best man, trying to hold what you believed looked like a sincere smile on your face. But no, you did not congratulate me."

"You tell me a day before the ceremony you're getting married again when you didn't even tell me that Monica was back," Tim said, yelling over the banging of a jackhammer. "Exactly what are you doing, Nate? You've shit all over this woman so many times and kicked her to the curb, only to call her back again. To what, see if you can ruin her life once and for all?"

Nate turned away from Tim, smiling. He bounced his son again. "Get ready, lil' guy," Nate said, holding up his watch. "Fifteen more seconds, till "BOOM!"

"BOOM!" Nathaniel repeated, clapping. "It's gonna be good, Daddy."

"C'mon," Tim said, his voice still raised. "Tell me what you're doing with her. Tell me what you want from her so I can be clear of who's side I'm on."

"I'm with Monica because I love her, and all I want from her is to love me back and be a mother to our son. Is that enough for you, Tim?" Nate yelled back, scowling. "You approve, or is there something else I need to do?"

Tim took a figurative step back, exhaled. "I'm sorry. It's just—"

"Apology accepted. You care for Monica, don't wanna see her get hurt again, and I appreciate that. But I told you I'm a changed man. So get off my back, already," Nate said as he slid on the big ear protectors, elbowing Tim again, gesturing at the phones he was holding. "You're going to want to put those on. That horn you're hearing: it's a countdown till the building falls. You got six seconds," Nate said, holding up a hand of splayed fingers, then started counting down. "Five!"

"Four!" Little Nathaniel screamed with his father, again, slapping the top of Nate's helmet with his little hands as Tim stared at his brother, seemingly having no idea of what Nate's true intentions were.

"Three!"

"Two!"

"One!"

The last horn blew. A loud, cannon-like bang was heard, then another, and a succession of half a dozen more. Bricks, mortar, steal girders and other debris shot from the lower sides of the building, all shrouded in thick clouds of smoke.

"Daddy! It's exploding!" Nate heard his son happily sing, as the top of the building swayed some, appeared to steady, then suddenly drop out of sight, as though falling into a massive hole that opened in the earth, flattening completely. The ground shook and rumbled around them, and what was once stories of glass, wood, steal and stone was reduced to thousands of pounds of rubble and smoke.

Nate turned to Tim, floating a thumbs-up. "Cool, huh!" Nate yelled.

41

Tim nodded, that mask of concern still on his face, having never taken his eyes off of Nate during the implosion, as though, because of the mistakes made in the past, Nate could never be forgiven or believed or trusted again.

9

6 P.M. and Freddy Ford felt light headed standing down the hall of the main operations desk of the Oak Park Psychiatric Institution. The lights overhead had been dimmed, all the crazies had been medicated and put to bed and change of shift was pretty much complete. So Freddy didn't know why he was left wearing a white staff uniform: waist jacket, orthopedic shoes, badge, and white baseball cap pulled low over his face.

"Ford!"

Freddy spun to see the facility officer walking up quickly behind him. He grabbed Freddy by the arm, tugged him along for three steps, released him, and said, "Follow me!"

"Where have you—"

"Shut the fuck up, and follow me!" Kelly whispered, stopping at a corner of the hallway, glancing back at Freddy before peering around it to make sure the area was clear. He continued on, turning the corner, walking casually, as he probably did every night before going home.

That was the plan he had told Freddy several times during their meetings in the dining and activity room of the facility. On those days, Kelly would stand in front of Freddy, Freddy wearing his bathrobe and slippers in the late afternoon, staring up at the man as though he was being scolded for doing shit Freddy wasn't supposed to have done.

"I'm gonna get you a uniform so you gonna look just like us," Officer Kelly whispered to Freddy just yesterday. "I'll get you a cap, too. Yank it down over your face. Keep your head down. Most of us getting off work after a long day ain't thinking about nothing but getting a drink. And most of us just coming on shift, too pissed off to think about anything but the fact we gonna be here with you crazy fucks for the next eight hours. So you walk next to me, act like you're one of us, and no one should look twice at you."

"What if someone does?" Freddy said, glancing off at one of the psyche patients, an 80 year-old woman, wandering around the break room in nothing but an adult diaper and a t-shirt.

"Then we're both fucked."

Freddy, now in uniform, remembered those words as he walked behind Kelly, deafened by the sound of his own thudding heart, blinded by the vision of them being found out.

"Come on! Hurry up!" Kelly called back.

Freddy picked up his pace, trying not to run, although he so desperately wanted to. He and Officer Kelly were coming up on an exit that would take them out of the psyche portion of the facility. There would be one guard, Kelly told Freddy yesterday. He was told that man would've received some of the money that Freddy paid.

"He'll pass us through. I made sure of that," Kelly said. "Just raise your badge like you been working here for years, like you'll see me do. He'll nod his head and wave us past. The same thing will happen at the next door, the door leading us outside. Do the same thing, and everything will be cool. You understand?"

Yesterday, standing in his bathrobe, Freddy was calm. He envisioned walking the route, performing the actions he was told. There would be nothing to it. But now, nearing the guard at the first door, Freddy shat bricks. Kelly raised his badge, and just as he said, the man waived him by. But the guard's eyes landed on Freddy next, looked at him as though he was not in on whatever deal Kelly struck, and Freddy slowed his stride, looked over his shoulder, and thought of turning, running.

"Ford! What the fuck?" Kelly called, breaking Freddy out of his fearful stammer. He looked at the guard, saw the man nod his head toward the front door. Freddy raised his badge as Kelly had before him, and miraculously, he was passed through.

The heels of their hard soled shoes clicking against the tile floor, echoing throughout the corridor, Freddy moved quickly behind

Kelly as though being chased, his breathing coming so quickly, his head so light, he feared he would pass out.

Thankfully, the next guard post was as easily passed as the first. After a suspicious, but harmless stare from the second guard, Freddy and Kelly walked out of the psychiatric prison facility and into the crisp, night air.

Freddy followed Kelly like a wandering dog, because he was not yet told to stop. Kelly walked into the parking lot, halted at the back of a Chrysler 300 then turned to Freddy. "Get the fuck out of here. You're free."

Surreal wasn't the word to describe the dark, star-filled sky overhead and the vast freedom it represented.

"What?"

"I said, get the fuck out of here. Now!" Kelly said, looking about the parking lot to make sure they weren't being watched.

Freddy turned, was about to run off, but was grabbed by the shoulder of his white waistcoat.

"When they catch you and bring you back here, you breath a word of me helping you get out, know you're a dead man."

Freddy stared at Kelly, the little bit of fear he felt of him while being imprisoned, the little bit of respect he once gave to the man's position was now gone. Freddy chuckled, spit near Kelly's feet and said: "The only way they bringing me back here is dead, so consider this the last time you look at me, motherfucker."

10

The woman that waited curbside at L.A. International airport was not the beautiful woman that used to be Nate's secretary before Monica had met him. This woman wasn't the well-dressed and well-put together woman that, after Nate married Monica the first time, was demoted from being his assistant to his mistress. The woman that Monica saw standing beside the aging, dented and paint-faded early eighties Toyota Corolla wasn't the woman that used to screw Nate behind his closed office door and the woman who ultimately set up the scheme to video tape Nate the last time he and Tori had sex, giving Monica the evidence to prove Nate's infidelity, winning her millions of dollars in her divorce settlement.

The woman that yelled Monica's name from over the roof of the car had sandy brown hair, pulled back into a ponytail, breaking near the ends and starting to kink up near the roots, not flowing, shiny, freshly styled locks like the woman from the past. This woman didn't wear a short designer dress, but a tiny, faded t-shirt, jeans that frayed at the seams, and dirty Converse All-Star sneakers. This woman was the 2016 Tori Thomas.

Dragging her overnight roller bag, Monica said: "Tori?" as though this was possibly an imposter. Monica stopped at the curb, watched Tori come around to the back of the car, and after banging on it with a fist a few times, managed to lift the trunk.

"Flight good?" Tori said, not looking Monica in the eyes, but grabbing her bag, dumping it into a trunk cluttered with old clothes, shoes and papers, then slamming the lid closed.

"Long," Monica said.

"Because California is far from Chicago, Monica." Tori said, sarcastically, walking back around to the driver's side door.

Tell me something I don't know, Tori-2016, Monica wanted to say, but stood watching the disheveled woman about to lower herself into the car.

"Well?" Tori said, staring at Monica from over the roof. "Get in. I got your bag. I ain't opening your door, too."

The apartment Tori drove to was in Compton. Monica's only reference to that part of town was what she saw on old NWA videos and John Singleton movies. Sadly, those depictions were quite accurate, Monica thought as she was driven down the streets lined with liquor stores, weave shops and pay-day loan spots.

Tori stopped the car on a wide street lined with two-story courtyard style apartment buildings then shut the engine off. The car sputtered for a few more moments and fell quiet.

A group of young men wearing do-rags and bandanas hanging under their chins gathered on the street a few doors down. One eyed Monica, looking as though he liked what he saw.

"Are we safe?" Monica asked, fighting a creepy chill.

Tori appeared offended, grabbed her door handle and pushed open the door. "Get out the car, Monica."

The apartment was tiny, had one bedroom, and was filthy. Empty bottles of wine and other assorted cheap liquor lay around the coffee table. Crumpled bags and crushed boxes of fast food littered practically every surface, and an old picture tube TV sat on a plastic milk crate. Monica took in all of that from just inside the door.

Tori went in the small fridge, pulled out a chilled bottle of Jagermeister, set it on the tiny breakfast bar with two glasses she took from the dish rack. She poured a single shot, lifted the drink to her lips then downed it with a backward jerk of her head. Setting the glass down, she filled it again then filled the one next to it, pushing it toward Monica.

"C'mon in. You want a drink?" Tori asked.

"Thanks, but I'm fine," Monica said, stepping in, closing and locking the door.

"Have one. You came all the way to California for nothing. The least you can do is drink with me."

"I came to tell you I need your help, just like I told you from Chicago."

"And like when you were there, I'll tell you the same thing now. I'm not ever going near that man again. He ruined my life." Tori raised the shot glass carefully to her lips, the dark liquor threatening to spill over the rim. She gestured at the room around them with it. "Thanks to him, this is how I live." She downed the drink, wincing after swallowing it.

"I need you, Tori. I can't do it without you," Monica said, catching Tori's eyes narrowing suspiciously on her left hand.

"What is that? I thought you said you divorced him."

"I did. We got remarried again last night."

Tori took a step back from the counter. "You playing games with me?" She said, staring fearfully into Monica's eyes.

"It was the only way to get close enough to him. It was the only way to make this work."

Tori raked fingers through the mess of hair on her head as she picked up the bottle of liquor and slowly topped off her shot glass once more. She looked gravely up at Monica. "He took everything from me. I wanted to kill him."

Nate told Monica that. Last year, upon him flying here to tell Tori face to face that the man she had met only months before, the man that had proposed to her, married her and took all of her money, was a phony: an employee of Nate's hired to take back the million Monica had given Tori of the divorce settlement. Nate told Monica that Tori confronted him with a gun that night, but before pulling the trigger, she was so despondent, so heart broken by what Nate had pulled off, she turned the gun on herself.

"You tried to kill yourself instead," Monica said.

"Yeah. I'd rather die than fuck with that man again," Tori said sadly, finally lifting the glass and drinking her third shot. "You came down here for nothing." Tori started around the counter, scratching her belly under her t-shirt as she headed toward the bedroom. "I don't have any sheets or anything, but you can sleep on the sofa...or whatever."

"I'll give you two hundred and fifty thousand dollars if you help me," Monica offered, desperate.

Tori halted, walked back toward the small kitchen counter, stared in Monica's face and slowly shook her head. Just above a whisper she said, "Not a chance."

"Fine then. Five hundred thousand, Tori. All you have to do is come back with me."

Tori turned around, left Monica again, dragging her feet toward the bedroom.

"Seven hundred and fifty thousand," Monica said, still unable to believe Tori continued away from her. "All right, a million!" Monica said, standing from the stool. "Do this for me, and I'll replace the amount Nate took from you."

Tori pressed a hand against the frame of the bedroom doorway, abruptly stopping. She turned back, appearing far more conflicted than Monica believed she should've been, considering the amount of money she was just offered.

"You wanna live in this shit for the rest of your life, Tori?"

"No. But I don't wanna *lose* my life dealing with your husband. He's an evil, vengeful son of a bitch, in case you still haven't found that out."

"It won't be like that. I promise. C'mon," Monica said, reaching for the bottle of liquor in front of her. "I'll have that drink with you and we can—"

That moment a soft knock came at the door, catching Monica's attention, prompting her to ask Tori who that could've been, but held the question when she saw Tori motioning for Monica to stay quiet, and whispering, "Don't say a thing."

Standing beside her, Monica noticed the deep rise and fall of Tori's chest, and that her eyes were focused on the front door as though whatever was on the other side of it was really, really bad.

The knock came harder. Monica shot Tori another questioning glare.

Holding up splayed fingers, Tori motioned for Monica to stay calm, mouthing the words, "Just chill and he'll leave!"

But Monica knew Tori was wrong, because the knocking came again: angry and imperative pounding, like with the flat of a fist. Like whoever was out there was planning on knocking the door down if it wasn't opened.

"Tori, open this motherfucking door!"

Monica's heart pounded, wondering who was trying to get into the apartment: one of the do-ragged thugs out on the sidewalk? A loan shark or a drug dealer Tori duped? "What do we do?" Monica whispered.

"I said he'll leave," Tori said, her whisper high-pitched and unconvincing.

"I know you the fuck in there, Tori, cause yo' piece of shit car outside! Open this goddamn door or I'll..."

Monica hadn't heard what came next because she was being dragged by the arm by Tori, through the small living room, and into the even smaller bedroom where Tori threw open drawers, stuffing garments and whatever else into a weekend bag she snatched from the floor of a closet.

"What are you doing?" Monica cried over the noise coming from the living room: the sound of a shoulder being rammed countless times into the front door.

"We're getting the fuck out of here!" Tori said. "Come on!" She grabbed Monica's hand, pulling her again, down a short narrow hallway that led to a back door. Tori threw it open to a balcony and a stairway leading to the street below.

A push in the back had Monica stumbling forward, just as she heard the wood-splintering blast of the apartment's front door being thrown open, slamming against the wall behind it, the man calling out: "Tori, where the fuck are you?"

"Go!" Tori said, on Monica's heels as they both nearly fell down the cement stairs that led to the ground floor behind the building. The weekend bag dragging from her shoulder, Tori took off toward a driveway, Monica following her till her attention was pulled away by the big man wearing a wife-beater tee, his arms, shoulders and much of his neck, painted with tattoos.

"Yo! Stop!" he yelled, lumbering and tripping down the stairs.

"Come on!" Tori screamed, and in that cry, Monica heard a fear so pure, suggesting their very lives depended on making it to Tori's car before the man could lay his hands on them.

They turned the corner, Monica panting heavily behind Tori, and the car was in sight. Making it there, Tori sunk her key into the door, yanked it open as Monica ran around the front to the passenger side, jumped in, pulled the door closed, and pounded the lock knob down. But the man, big jeans sagging around his waist, stomping the grass as he raced across the lawn toward the car, was not only coming, but appeared to be pulling what looked like a big, black hand gun from the waist of his jeans.

"Tori!" Monica screamed, grabbing her by the sleeve of her shoulder, shaking her. "Get this fucking car moving!"

The engine revved. Tori shoved the car into gear, stomped on the gas, causing the tires to spin, scream and spit smoke into the air; Monica was pushed back in her seat by the force. She turned up on a knee, looked over her shoulder through the back windshield at the man stopping in the middle of the street, exhausted and breathing heavily, the gun hanging from his fist.

The engine whining, going full speed, Tori hunched over the wheel, gripping it manically, she said, "He gone? Is he?"

"Fading," Monica said, staring out the back windshield at the shrinking figure. "But will he follow you?"

The car rattling as it flew over the street's bumpy pavement, the steering wheel shaking in her hands, Tori turned sadly to Monica, and said, "Not if I go to Chicago."

11

Standing in the small, dark room, streetlamp light cutting through partially opened curtains, Freddy sadly stared down at his aging mother as she slept on the twin sized bed, a skull cap pulled down on her head, wool blankets yanked up to her chest.

He roused her awake with a shake of her shoulder, then pressed a hand firmly over her mouth when her eyes ballooned. Startled, she tried to rise from the bed.

Freddy had shed the mental hospital's white uniform for bagging jeans and a tee shirt he dug out of an unlocked Goodwill donation box, both of which were filthy and smelled slightly of mildew.

"Quiet, Ma," Freddy whispered, looking at the closed bedroom door, making sure his uncle had not been awakened. Freddy's uncle Henry didn't like him, thought Freddy was responsible for his sister losing her house, winding up living here in this tiny room. Freddy knew if the man was to have stumbled upon him, there would've been trouble, and maybe someone would've died.

"It's me, Freddy." He reached up, pushed more of the curtain away from the window, letting more of the outside light in so that his mother could identify him. He felt her calm some, relax her elbows and lower herself back onto the mattress.

"I'm gonna take my hand away now, that okay?"

His mother nodded, her eyes still round and unblinking, her son's hand still covering the lower half of her face.

"Okay? Don't say anything. Uncle Henry can't know I'm here."

His mother nodded again.

Freddy removed his hand, smiled, lowered himself to his knees then wrapped his arms around his mother's shoulders. He had missed her, longed to feel the security of her embrace, knowing she was the only one left alive that gave a damn about him. He felt her heart racing against his.

"Don't be scared, Ma," he said, leaning away from the hug.

She stared at him, the bit of light cast from outside through her window allowed him to see that she appeared only slightly less scared than when she believed a stranger stood over her. She was up on her elbows again. "Can I talk?"

"Yeah, Ma. Just not too loud."

"You're supposed to be in the…how are you here?"

"They let me out. They done some tests, a whole bunch of them and decided I was better. They said it made no sense keeping me in there any longer, so…" Freddy hunched his shoulders, nodding his head. "You glad to see me, Ma?"

His mother looked to search her mind for the right answer. "Yes, Fred."

"I need to say I'm sorry for everything that happened. Your house…me taking that kid and all that other stuff. I needed them to let me out so I can come back here and make everything right."

"Fred," his mother asked, her voice quivering. "Do they know you're out?"

"Ma, I told you, they set me free." Still on his knees, he leaned toward her, took her wrist in his grip. "But they don't want you calling them or looking for me, understand? I told them I would be coming back here, but if you call asking about me, they might think that you don't want me, and they might try and come and get me again. You don't want that, do you, Ma?"

It took tightening his grip on his mother's wrist to get a response, but it was the right one, so Freddy smiled and released her.

"Good," he said getting to his feet, shoving his hands into his jeans pockets and pulling something out. "I'm gonna make everything right again. I'm gonna fix everything. I might even get back with Kia. I know you liked her. What would you think about that?"

"You don't have to do that, Freddy," his mother said a little too quickly. "I think she might've moved or something."

Freddy eyed his mother as he pulled at the crumpled corners and edges of the crinkled and bloodstained bills he pulled from his pocket.

An hour ago, he struggled in the cramped space behind the counter of a small convenience store. From behind, Freddy's forearm was clamped around the owner's neck as the gasping man tried to stomp Freddy's feet, reach blindly behind him to claw Freddy's eyes out with one hand, while the other clutched futilely for the revolver only inches away from his grasp.

In his mother's bedroom, Freddy leaned closer to the window light, counting out $140 of the $160 he had stolen. He held it out to her.

"Go on, take it. It's from working in the cafeteria at the prison. Take it, Ma. You need it, and there'll be more. I told you I'm gonna make everything right again." Freddy lifted his shirt to stuff the twenty dollars in crumpled fives and ones back into his pocket, when his mother gasped.

"Is that a gun?"

"Naw, Ma, you seeing things. You're tired. Go back to sleep and I'll come back—"

Freddy's mother clamped onto her son's hand, sat up in bed and pulled him close to her. "Freddy, it's not too late."

"I don't know what you talking about," he said, using the slightest bit of force to pull away.

"Fred!" His mother whispered harshly like when he was a child and she would scold him for stealing, or fighting, or always saying horrible things about his father because Freddy hated the bruises he'd paint his mother's face with. "You don't have to go through with this."

"Go through with what, Ma? I told you—"

"No one expects you to make things better."

"But I'm going to."

"We can call the hospital, or the police—"

He grabbed her firmly by the arm, pulled their faces close, shook his head and said, "They let me go. I told you that! Now you gotta let me handle things. Will you do that?"

His mother winced and nodded her head.

Still squeezing, Freddy said, "You promise? You ain't gonna call nobody, and you ain't gonna tell nobody?"

She nodded again, this time looking away as though she had lost all hope that she could ever reach her son.

He let her go and stood over her thinking, looking down at the wool cap. After a moment, he slowly pulled his hand from the handle of the revolver.

"I love you, Ma," he said then left to sneak back out the window he had climbed through.

12

When Monica pushed open the front door of Nate's mansion, all the lights were off in the front of the house; it was nearly pitch black in the living room, and she had to smooth a hand across the wall in order to find the switch.

When she clicked it on, the lamps on either of the end tables lit the living room, allowing her to see the half dozen helium balloons tied to the legs, floating above the coffee table and the huge, six foot long banner, colored sloppily in crayon, reading: WELCOME HOME, MOMMY!!!

Wearing a white undershirt, his suit trousers and a bad case of bedhead, Nate sat up on the sofa and sleepily rubbed an eye with his fist. Stretched out across the sofa was little Nathaniel, wearing his Deadpool pajamas, using Nate's lap as a pillow.

"Sur-prise," Nate said, drearily, a sleepy smile on his face.

"What's this?" Monica said, unable to stop herself from smiling.

"He wouldn't let me put him to bed until you came home," Nate said, standing, grabbing the boy from under the arms and hoisting him up, sleeping, into his arms. Walking over with him toward Monica, Nate said, "Trust me. I tried." Holding the child in front of her, Nate puckered his lips, waiting for a kiss.

"Awww," Monica said, kissing Nate, then Nathaniel on his cheek. "That was so sweet of him."

"It was all my idea, ya' know," Nate chuckled.

"So sad. Taking credit from a four-year old," Monica joked, pealing off her jacket, walking toward her bedroom. "What do you expect to get with that?"

"Hopefully, you in bed."

Monica stopped, spun around, staring at Nate with a smile. "Considering how dog-tired I am, I think you might just succeed, Mr. Kenny. But how about you put the little one to bed first?"

Her eyes closed, wearing a sheer nightgown, Monica sat on the bed, facing the dresser mirror, when she heard Nate padding on the carpet behind her. She opened her eyes, spotting his reflection in the mirror as he neared her.

"No fair. I wanted to sneak up on you," he said, placing his hands on her back and rubbing her shoulders.

Monica let her eyes fall closed again and relaxed, for what he was doing felt incredible.

"You're tight, babe. What's bothering you?" Nate asked.

"Stuff didn't go as smoothly as planned in L.A."

"Was it worth going at all?"

"I don't know. Time will tell."

"I'm sure AERO isn't doing nearly as bad as you believe."

"So bad that I could possibly go broke trying to make the stores profitable again. I'm considering options: bankruptcy, selling, I don't know."

"No," Nate said, and Monica felt the intensity at which he massaged her increase. "Those stores, that business, I know means the world to you. Let me look at your numbers, try to devise a strategy to—"

Her eyes still closed, leaning her head to a side, moaning in pleasure—for he was hitting her spot just right—Monica said, "The beauty of numbers is that they don't lie, and these say there is very little hope."

"Then let me give you a small business loan: zero percent interest and you'll never have to pay it back. Do some new marketing, maybe create a stronger on-line store presence, or open another location."

Monica opened her eyes, sat up a little straighter on the bed, and stared at Nate's reflection in the mirror. "You'd do that for me?"

She watched the expression on Nate's face change to something far more perplexed. He pulled his hands away. "Have you talked to Tim?"

"What are you talking about?" Monica said, turning on the bed to face her husband.

"What, you don't think I'm all in on this 'you and me' thing? You think I'm still just playing games?"

Monica smiled uncomfortably. "You wanna know the truth?"

"No point in knowing a lie," Nate said.

"If you think about all the trouble you've gone through to cause me pain, one would wonder why you wanted me back, Nate. Just sayin. What motivated this all-of-sudden change to be remarried again?"

"Fair enough," Nate said, taking a step back. "Three months ago, Nathaniel started waking at all times of night, screaming with night terrors. I'd run in, and he'd be in bed, terrified, shaking, crying that 'Mommy and Daddy got shot. Mommy and Daddy got killed.' I'd pull him close, tell him that Daddy was right here. Yes, I had gotten shot, but that I hadn't gotten killed, and that Mommy was fine, too. He'd keep crying till he fell to sleep, and the next morning, he'd wake forgetting all about what happened, until that moment when he was awakened again by the bad dreams, and we'd do it all over again."

"So you wanted me back so you could have a full night of sleep," Monica said, the words coming out harsher than she intended.

Nate walked around the side of the bed, placed himself in front of his wife. "I was a fool, acting like a vengeful child, wanting to hurt you, believing I had been treated unfairly. I was wrong to have done that—to hurt the woman I loved. And holding Nathaniel those nights, shaking and screaming in my arms, I realized, not only did I hurt you, but him. I asked you back because I love you, because I love him, and because I love us. And part of loving us, is doing whatever is in my power to make sure we're all okay and all our needs are taken care of." He reached out, took Monica's chin in his hand. "That includes giving my wife a loan for her business if she needs it. So, what do you say? Very easy terms and no paperwork required."

59

Monica took a moment, staring up at her husband. She took his hand, gently pulled it from her chin and kissed it.

"Thank you, but no. I'm a big-girl business owner, and I think I'll see first what else I can do before I take any money from my handsome, generous and incredibly caring husband."

13

Tori woke with a start, quickly sitting up in the king sized bed, sunlight cutting into her eyes, the linen twisted around her legs and torso. Heart beating heavily, it took her a moment to realize where she was. Before figuring that out, Monica's terrified voice rang in her head from last night.

"Who the hell was that and why the hell was he after you?" Monica cried, glancing out the back windshield of the speeding Corolla.

They had been racing toward LAX for twenty minutes, Monica asking again, the same question Tori refused to answer.

"I told you, nobody."

"You tell me what I want to know, or forget about the money. Forget about everything!" Monica said, sounding fed up, hammering a fist against the cracked dashboard of Tori's car.

Hands still tight on the wheel, stealing a hateful glance at Monica then looking back at the road, Tori shook her head and said, "His name is Ja'Van. I 'dated' him and he paid the bills and other stuff, cause I had no money. Okay."

"Meaning you were fucking him?"

"Whatever."

"And he was chasing you, trying to kill us, because your pussy was just that damn good." Shaking her head, arms crossed, Monica said, "Lie to me again and I'm jumping on the plane alone and taking my million with me."

The drone of the screaming engine in her ears, Tori glanced over, saw the green dash light in the dark cabin glowing on Monica's face; she looked deathly serious about what she just said.

"His drugs; I stole them."

"What? What did you say?" Monica gasped.

"I stole Ja'Van's drugs and stashed them in the trunk," Tori said, glancing toward the car's hatch.

"Stop the car!" Monica said, reaching over and grabbing a hold of the wheel, trying to steer the car off the street.

On the dark, tree-lined, two-lane road, the car skidded onto the shoulder, kicking up clouds of dirt. Monica pushed open her door, ran around the car and popped the hatch. Tori cut the engine, climbed out and followed, but not before Monica could find and unzip the weekend bag and pull out a sofa pillow-sized plastic bag, filled nearly full with white powder. She snatched it and held it up in front of Tori.

"And you were going to do what with this?" Monica questioned, hysterically.

"You don't know what my life was like there…what I had to do. You don't—"

"You were going to do what with this, Tori?" Monica screamed, her voice disappearing into the dark night sky and into the line of dense trees behind them.

"I needed money. I was gonna try and sell it."

"Where?"

"Was gonna be here, but since we're going to—"

"You were going to try to take this on the plane?" Monica asked frantically, her voice going up an octave. She stared at Tori as though she had lost her mind. "And when TSA found it and charged us with intent to distribute, you were going to do what?"

Tori kicked at the gravel with the toes of her Chuck Taylors. "Don't know."

"And you were planning on doing what with the money?"

"Surviving."

"No. Not this way," Monica said, taking the bag by its upper corners and tearing into the plastic with her teeth, splitting it open.

Tori ran at Monica, but not before the bag was ripped apart, some of the white powder floating about the air, most of it, quickly hitting the black dirt.

Tori dropped to her knees, trying to scoop the mess with her cupped hands, corral it like a child trying to gather sand for a castle. "You know what you just did?" Tori screamed.

"Saved your ass from ten to twenty in prison," Monica said, walking back toward the passenger door of the car. "Get in before we're late for our flight."

Now, wearing the panties and tee shirt she shirt slept in, Tori walked barefoot into the kitchen of the small one bedroom apartment. She pulled open the fridge door, grabbed one of the two cans of Coke Zero—the only items in the fridge—popped it open and sipped from it.

Last night, after landing, Monica drove her here, to this building on State Street in the South Loop.

"Where is this place?" Tori said, walking up the stairs behind Monica, to the second floor unit.

"Where you'll be staying. Belongs to a friend of mine. Nate won't be able to trace this back to me," Monica said, turning the lock then shouldering the door open. Monica flipped a switch on a wall. Lights came on showing them a sofa, love seat, area rug over a worn hardwood floor, and a flat screen on the wall. Personal items sat and stood all over the room: magazines fanned out on the coffee table, crocheted blankets thrown over the back of the sofa and family pictures in frames on the mantel over the fire place.

"It's not much, but compared to where you were, it's a suite in the Trump Towers," Monica said, looking around. "Bathroom's down that hall, kitchen is over there."

Tori walked quickly into the small kitchen and threw open the cupboard doors until she found a bottle of brown liquor. She grabbed it and two glasses.

"You drinking?" Tori asked.

"No. You go," Monica said.

Tori poured herself two seconds worth, took a sip then downed the entire contents of the glass. "Sorry, but I needed that."

"Glad she had something here for you," Monica said, pulling the apartment door key off her ring. She walked it over, set it on a living room end table, along with a folded one hundred dollar bill. "This is for you. It's late. I'll have someone contact you tomorrow morning. I need to get home." Monica spun, and walked toward the apartment door and pulled it open.

Tori stepped out the kitchen, leaned against the frame of the door and crossed her arms. "Hey. So what am I supposed to be doing that's worth so much money to you?"

"Something you've done so well in the past: fuck my husband."

"That can't be all there is. You could've found some trick on 63rd Street and given her forty dollars to do that. Just be honest with me, Monica."

Monica glanced down at the rose gold Omega she wore on her wrist. "Told you. It's late." She started to turn again.

"You dragged my ass all the way from L.A.", Tori said, stepping forward. "I need to know why. Exactly. Now, if you want me to be a part of this."

Staring at Tori, Monica looked to consider what was just told her, and appeared to not want to take the chance in Tori abandoning her. Monica walked to the sofa and set her purse on it: "Tomorrow night, you're going to accidentally bump into my husband at the gym he attends." She went on for the next half hour, very explicitly, as Tori had asked, about her part in Monica's very elaborate plan.

Tori was to get next to Nate, remind him of how much he used to enjoy sleeping with her, then make it happen again. The goal of all that, Monica said, was for her to win sole custody of Nate's son, Nathaniel. Monica had this checklist: requirements that needed to be met.

Pacing across the living room floor, in between the coffee table and the sofa, Monica went on about how her attorney told her Nate needed to be seen as a dishonest and morally corrupt man. His home needs to be seen as somewhere unsafe for little Nathaniel to be raised. And Nate needs to be portrayed as an unfit, and possibly even abusive parent.

"You can't just say those things about him," Tori said from a chair, holding the same small glass of liquor cupped in both her hands. "There has to be proof."

"Nate having an extramarital affair says he's dishonest. There will need to be documentation: pictures, video, of course. But you've done that before. You shouldn't have a problem fucking on film. Will you?" Monica asked.

Tori detected spite and resentment in the way the question was asked, but answered anyway. "No. No problem."

"I'll also have to record you giving testimony of how awful a man he was to you, that he corrupted you, sexually harassed you to sleep with him while you were his employee."

"But that didn't happen."

"But you will say that it did," Monica said, cutting her eyes.

Tori drank from her glass. "And the unsafe home thing? That have anything to do with me?"

"I'll find a way to be out of the house for days on end: a business trip or something. I'll need for you to get Nate comfortable enough to have you over. And then you're going to..." Monica looked disturbed by what she was about to say. "I'm still working this through."

"And then I'm gonna what?"

"You'll...probably have to burn the house down."

"What?" Tori said, shooting up from her seat.

"Not all of it, just enough to get the fire department out. Enough for when this sits before a judge, it will be apparent that Nate having his mistress in the house could've resulted in it burning to the ground, and possibly killing our son inside of it."

Now Tori was pacing, kicking back the last of the liquor in her glass. "Committing arson, Monica. Really?"

"You wanted to know what the million was for."

"And where does the abuse thing come in?" Tori said, back at the coffee table, refilling her glass. "Nate doesn't strike me as the type that'd hit his kid."

"No. He never would."

"Then how..." Tori started, but didn't have to finish the question because the look in Monica's eyes said all Tori needed to know.

"I'm not fucking abusing a little kid!"

"Calm down," Monica said, reaching over and taking the glass from Tori, setting it down. She grabbed her by the shoulders. "I'm not even sure I can make all this happen. These are just plans in my head. He'll have to trust you enough to first bring you into our home, then to take you around our child, and finally to leave you alone with Nathaniel. That may not ever happen."

"But if it does?" Tori said, feeling she might want to reconsider all of this.

"Then you'll have to do what needs to be done. Trust me, it makes me furious, and I want to hit you right now when I imagine you striking my child. But it'll only be enough to cause some bruising, maybe some scarring: enough to where he'll need to be taken to the E.R., so that it can be documented."

Tori brushed Monica's hands from off of her. "And you pretend as though you love that child. You're a horrible person," Tori said, stepping away.

"I do love him," Monica said, raising her voice. "I don't have to tell you about Nate. Everything he comes near dies. I woke from a fucking coma after being shot in the head—all his fault, I might add—to find that my son had been taken hostage. No, I don't want you hitting on my son, but if it takes a few bruises to get him away from that monster: a few scrapes to save my son from being taken again, or God forbid, worse. I'll make it happen. The question is, will you?"

Hugging herself tight, Tori felt all of sudden cold, knowing she didn't have to search for motivation, for Ja'Van was never far from her thoughts. Even now, thousands of miles away, she felt the big man's hand around her throat, the other, forcefully pushing inside of her—not to give her pleasure, but to teach her never to fall asleep on him when he said he wanted oral. Tori lowered her head, and under her voice said, "I won't like it, but yeah, I'll do what needs to be done."

The ringing of her cell phone across the room snatched her out of her thoughts from last night. Tori set down the can of soda and grabbed up the phone, Monica's name flashing on the screen.

"Yeah," Tori said.

"Checking on you, making sure you haven't taken off on me. You still okay over there?"

"I'm fine, Monica," Tori said, resentment in her voice for allowing Monica to put her in this position.

"Just sit tight, and I'll let you know when we'll make our first move."

14

Lying restlessly in bed, Lewis slid a hand under the sheets, reaching for Eva. He was surprised when he didn't feel her beside him. He rolled over and was mildly startled to see her body silhouetted against the light passing through the sheer curtains of the bedroom windows. He sat up, thought to speak, but watched her for a moment, her arms crossed, her body rigid.

"Eva," he finally said. "You okay?" He pushed back the covers and climbed out of bed, stood just behind her, afraid for some reason to touch her. "Baby?" he kissed her lightly on the side of the neck. "Please tell me you aren't still thinking about Freddy. He's locked up and—"

Eva faced Lewis, not appearing worried or fraught with fear like he had imagined.

"I know. I was up all night in bed thinking about it, hating what happened to me. But it wasn't my fault. I didn't cause that to happen," Eva said, sounding suddenly empowered. "You didn't cause it to happen. It just did, and to let it continue to mess up our lives…nah." Eva shook her head, smiling. "I'm not gonna do that." She wrapped her arms around Lewis's neck, and pulled herself into him.

He held her, his head lowered over her shoulder, his eyes closed, happy for her change in thinking, but sad he couldn't tell her that he did have something to do with it, because he knew telling her would be risking her leaving, and she meant too much to him and his daughter.

Breakfast was good. The girls behaved themselves: no hurling Fruit Loops, or splashing milk out of the cereal bowls at each other. During the meal, Lewis stole glances at Eva from over the rim of his coffee cup, making sure she was as carefree as she had said minutes ago.

Noticing his glance after setting down her own mug, she flashed him a reassuring smile, confirming what he had hoped.

At the door, Eva stood in front of Lewis, straightening the collar of his shirt, as playful giggles from the girls came down the hall to them from the kitchen.

"What's wrong? Looks like something's on your mind," Eva said.

"You. You're on my mind, waking up this morning, seeing you just staring—"

"I told you I'm fine, and to prove it, when you talk to him again…"

Lewis shook his head. "I'm not gonna talk—"

"You said he calls you," Eva said, straightening the knot on Lewis's tie. "But I don't even want you to wait till then. Today, call him and tell him I'm not going to let what he did to me control my life anymore. You hear me?"

"Eva," Lewis said, taking her hand.

"Please, Lewis. Do that for me so that I can move on, okay."

15

He wanted it to be a surprise. A block away from Kia's house, Freddy pulled the hood of the coat he was wearing up over his head. It was warm, still smelled new, and late last night he was glad the white boy he encountered walking down the street alone after leaving his mother's place, had sense enough to just take the coat off and not put up a fight.

Freddy slept folded up in it, in a public park, on one of four benches, all occupied by homeless men, overstuffed shopping bags of all their belongings on the ground nearby. This morning, he woke refreshed. He washed his face with water in the park's men's room. Using wadded up paper towel, he scrubbed under his arms and down his pants. In the polished metal funhouse mirror bolted to the wall, he finger-combed his low-cropped hair and beard and straightened the new coat over his old clothes.

Now, walking down Kia's block, Freddy held tightly to the bouquet of wildflowers he stopped into the local Jewel Foods store and bought with the little money he had left from last night's convenience store robbery. Kia would love them, and that could possibly be the thing that would have her take him back. Although the people from the mental hospital, or maybe even the cops, would soon come looking for him, Freddy felt there would be enough time to patch things up with Kia, convince her to follow him somewhere out of state.

Fifty yards from her house, Freddy stopped in the center of the sidewalk, seeing someone standing by an open car door, appearing to have loaded something into the back seat. He stepped up, pulling down on the hood more to hide his face as he neared to within ten feet of the woman. She was bent over, her back turned to him, reaching into the back seat of the car, and although it appeared she had picked up ten pounds or so, Freddy knew, without a doubt, that was his Kia.

He stood silent for a second, hoping she'd turn on her own, hoping for a more spontaneous surprise. She didn't.

"Kia," he whispered, a smile wide on his face.

Kia looked over her shoulder, jumped and released a cry of surprise. She hurried to stand up in front of the door opening, like she was attempting to block something from his sight.

"Freddy?" she cried.

With a sweep of his hand, he brought the hood back from off of his head. "Hey, Kia."

"What are you doing here?"

To Freddy, she sounded concerned and scared.

"I know. I'm looking kind of crazy." He touched his hair, then the whiskers growing long and patchy from his cheeks. "Got to get with my barber and I'll be straight. Till then…" he held out the flowers to her. "These are for you."

"Freddy…I…I don't think you should be here." She was antsy, had raised one of her arms, blocked the part of the open car doorway her body hadn't. Freddy glanced momentarily in the direction of what it appeared she was trying to hide.

"No! Look here!" Kia said, directing Freddy's attention back up to her face. "I'm late for school. Why don't you call me and we can meet later."

"Don't you want your flowers?"

"Yeah." She snatched them from him.

"You aren't happy to see me? I know we were having some fucked up times, but I was thinking that maybe we could work all that stuff out."

"Fine, Freddy. We can do that. But why don't you just leave and—"

Before she could finish, Freddy thought he had heard something that sounded like a baby's cry. Kia stared stupidly at Freddy as if to question whether he had heard the sound. He had, and then he heard it again. Staring her in the eyes, he saw her face fill with horror.

"What was that, Kia?" he asked, trying to look past her into the car again. "That a baby in there?"

"Freddy," Kia said, shaking her head wildly, reaching out and grasping onto the door's opening, as though expecting Freddy to try and rip her off of it. "Just leave, Freddy. We can talk—"

"Kia, I asked you a question," Freddy said, reaching for her.

"Aye, yo!"

There was a crash of a door slamming behind Freddy. He spun around to see a muscular man, roughly Freddy's age and complexion, wearing sweatpants, slippers and no shirt.

"Who are you?" the man called, hurrying down the stairs as though to protect Freddy's ex-girlfriend.

Freddy turned to Kia. "Who the fuck is that?"

She was crying; tears ran down her cheeks. "Nobody. Please! Just leave!"

"Who is he?" Freddy said, grabbing her by the arm and asking again, watching as the man jumped off the last stair, sprinted across the front lawn like fucking Captain America, picking up speed on his way to Freddy.

"Kia!" Freddy said, pushing aside his coat, reaching into the waist of his jeans and pulling the gun. Shoulder high, he pointed it at the charging man. Only then did the man attempt to stop, his heals slipping on the grass beneath him, his arms wind-milling to stop himself from falling. Kia's bloodcurdling scream muted the sound of the gunshot, but the damage was seen in the dime-sized hole that appeared in the center of the man's forehead and the amount of blood and cranial bone that flew out the back of his skull. He fell onto his back, arms and legs splayed like a starfish, onto the grass.

Freddy turned, grabbed Kia by the front of her shirt; she was screaming hysterically, looking over his shoulder at the dead man on the lawn, at the same time, trying to stop Freddy from tearing her away from the car door. Freddy threw her aside, ducked his head into the car to see what he had suspected: a baby. Pulling back out, he grabbed Kia again, yanking them nose to nose, tears spilling from her eyes. She gagged and sobbed and seemed barely able to breath.

"That his?" Freddy pointed out to the dead man.

Kia trembled in his grasp, her eyes shut, tears flooding from under her closed lids. "God, please! Oh, Lord!"

"Answer me!" He slammed her against the car, shoved the tip of the gun's barrel under her chin. "That fucking baby his?"

"No!" Kia shouted, eyes bulging open at him. "He's yours, motherfucker!"

Freddy felt he had been caught in the head with a baseball bat. The world spun around him; he couldn't make sense of what he was just told, but he could feel, and realized what he experienced was complete and total sadness.

"You ain't tell me?"

Kia looked shocked, then angry and through her tears, started shouting. "Tell you? I hate you! You made my life shit," she screamed, her voice so loud, Freddy's ears started to ring. He felt her clawing at his coat, at his face, but he could no longer pay attention to her tantrum. His mind was on the infant in the car: his child, and the thought she would've rather that baby grow up without a father than admit to Freddy that the baby was his. His head quickly flooded with images of Kia's belly round and tight with the growing life he implanted in her: Kia bringing that little life into the world while he lay locked up, medicated out of his mind, staring glassy-eyed at a fucking padded wall. He had thought she loved him. If that had been true, she wouldn't have—couldn't have kept something so important as her giving birth to his child, a secret.

Freddy had felt pain before: standing in a corner, watching as his father used to beat his mother: Nate Kenny stealing his mother's house out from under her: hearing the crackle of a sniper's gunshot, then watching Joni's head explode. Yeah, he had felt loads of fucking pain, and learned the only way to relieve that agony was to make those who caused the pain pay.

But this pain was far worse than the others he'd experienced, this being caused by someone who was supposed to have loved him.

Didn't matter, Freddy thought, coming out from under the blanket of the past, where Kia's screams were muted and muffled and far away. Now he heard them loud and clear, and she was saying something about him rotting in jail, that she never loved him.

He took her by the scruff of her shirt. "Don't say that! Don't say that!" he cried, knowing her love for him and that he'd see her again was the only thing that got him through his incarceration. But she screamed louder, became angrier, as he begged her to stop and to shut up, because he could not take the sound of her setting fire to the last pure thing he could believe in.

She screamed on. "I hope you burn in hell for—"

So Freddy made her stop the only way he could: the sound of the shot echoing over the rooftops of south side Chicago houses; the shriek of his son's cry piercing Freddy's ears as he slowly tucked the gun back into his pants. Holding Kia's lifeless body up by the front of her shirt, Freddy looked back into the car, tilted his head to the side like a perplexed dog, wondering what the boy must've been thinking of the image before him, and wondered now would the baby's life be as fucked as his father's had, after witnessing this.

"Goodbye son," Freddy said, letting go of the infant's mother, Kia's body sliding down the side of the car, dropping to the grass.

Freddy hiked the hood back over his head and strode away.

16

Lewis tossed the bag of bagels to the passenger seat of the Range Rover and set the cup of Dunkin Donuts coffee in the cup holder, deciding he would do what Eva had asked him earlier. He dialed the mental institution. "Freddy Ford, please."

The woman on the line told Lewis to hold. When she returned, she said: "I'm sorry, Freddy Ford is no longer an inpatient at this facility. Is there anything else I can—"

A chill skittered up the length of Lewis's spine. "What do you mean? Where did he go?"

"Sir, are you a family member?"

"No. But—"

"Then I cannot give that information to—"

"Was he transferred? Was he taken somewhere by the police?" Lewis asked, remembering the promise Freddy just made about escaping.

"Sir, I'm not at liberty—"

"Please. Freddy Ford was responsible for my wife being raped. He told me he was going to try to escape. Is that what he did?"

Lewis climbed in the truck, shutting the door and starting the engine. "Please!" Lewis said. "Did he get out of there somehow or not?"

No answer, as if the woman on the other end was deciding if giving out this information was worth losing her job over, then: "Yes, Freddy Ford escaped."

When Lewis pulled up ten minutes later, several police cars were parked at weird angles in the street in front of Kia's house, their lights flashing blue, reflecting off the neighbor's windows. Yellow police tape was stretched across everything, stopping the dozen nosey bystanders from encroaching on what Lewis prayed was not a murder scene investigation.

Lewis threw open his door then hurried out toward the scene. He pressed up behind the thickening wall of on-lookers, attempting to glance at what the police were doing.

"Excuse me," Lewis said, pushing past a young man and an older woman, till the yellow plastic tape hit him in the chest. "Excuse me!" he called out to a couple of the police officers, neither of which responded.

Lewis walked to his left, and from behind one of the police cars, he caught a glimpse of Kia's car.

"What are they doing?" Lewis asked a woman standing behind him.

"Somebody shot 'em'," the woman said.

"Shot who?"

"A dude..."

One of the officers blocking Lewis's view moved to his left, giving Lewis a clear look at what they were doing their best to hide: a body in the grass. Lewis could make out a foot: toes of the shoe pointing upward, then an open palm: fingers splayed, the loop of a key ring encircled the middle one. He shoved someone aside, saw the back of the victim's head: part of which was gone, a wide circle of blood stained grass around it.

"And the dude's girlfriend," the woman finished.

"Do you know the girlfriend's name?"

"Yeah, she lived in that house right there," the woman pointed. "Her name was Kia."

17

After taking Nat for a morning stroll, Daphanie returned home, stopping at the mouth of the driveway, surprised to see Trevor's car parked beside the nanny's when he should've been at work.

Nanny Jennifer was 30 years old, was only mildly attractive in Daphanie's opinion, had a head full of Barbie-Doll quality weave and a voice so high pitched and irritating, dog's howled in agony whenever she uttered a word. Her shapely body being her only attribute, she always walked around in skin-tight leggings and Baby Gap sized tee shirts.

When Trevor had hired Jennifer, he had given her strict hours. She would come in the mornings at 9 A.M., just before Trevor left for work, and would stay until 2 in the afternoon, when Nate's care would be entrusted to Daphanie. Then Jennifer would return at 5 P.M., just before Trevor came in from work. She would ready the baby for bed, then leave at 7 P.M. or a little after, not to return until the next morning.

Daphanie wasn't much of a Jennifer fan, not knowing more about her than she didn't have any children, wasn't married, and had no other job but this one.

In the couple of months that Daphanie had been literally sharing her child with the nanny, Jennifer hadn't much to say. Mornings, Jennifer would walk in the house—she had her own key—set her things down, pour herself a cup of coffee, then reach out for the baby as if expecting Daphanie to hand the infant off like a relay-race baton.

There were times when Daphanie would attempt to update her, telling Jennifer: "He had trouble sleeping through the night", or "I changed him early this morning, so…".

Jennifer would simply take the baby from Daphanie's arms and say, "I know how to take care of him. Thanks."

Every night, lying down next to Trevor, his back turned to her, Daphanie would stare up into the dark room and wonder was it worth enduring the treatment she was receiving just to be with her child? She truly believed she was being punished by a man who hated her and only allowed her to live with him so he could see how she responded to the torture he inflicted.

But every night before falling off to sleep, she told herself it was worth it, and she promised she would do everything possible to make life bearable, possibly even enjoyable.

Some of those nights, Daphanie would slip into the sheets after showering and reach in between Trevor's thighs for him, hoping to repair that connection they had: the connection that had gotten her pregnant.

Before she had left him for Nate Kenny, she did have feelings for Trevor. But the nights of these recent attempts, he would simply roll away, brush her hand back, or say that he was tired. After turning onto her back, frustrated, she would ask herself how he could so easily deny her? Deny himself? In the three months she had been living there, they had sex exactly twice.

Now, walking up the path to the front door, Daphanie knew with certainty that the man hated her. And after hearing the devastating news from Nate Kenny this morning, she figured she would be locked into this situation for the rest of her life, and possibly, could do nothing about it.

But something had to give. What had happened this morning—Trevor tearing their child from her arms, when all she was trying to do was feed him—could never happen again. It was demeaning, demoralizing and agonizing. No, Daphanie couldn't leave, but she would no longer allow herself to be treated like a dog.

Inside the house, she pushed the front door closed with a foot, and called out, "I'm home."

She heard talking upstairs, then laughter.

"What's happening up there, little one?" Daphanie asked Nat in her baby voice.

The infant smiled, and as Daphanie carried him to the stairs, she told him they'd find out.

The door of the spare bedroom—the one next to the baby's room—was cracked just enough for Daphanie to see Trevor and Jennifer facing one another, talking. When she pushed open the door, Trevor took a step back; she saw a faint display of guilt on his face. Jennifer smiled beside him.

"What is this?" Daphanie asked, looking around the room, surprised to see two large suitcases sitting in the middle of the floor and a toiletry bag on the foot of the bed.

Trevor took a step forward between the two women. "After that stunt you pulled," he said, speaking quietly, as if to keep what was being said from the baby right there in Daphanie's arms. "I decided it best Nate have round the clock, in-home care."

Daphanie stared puzzled at Trevor. "What?"

"You heard me."

Daphanie hoisted Nat up into her arms to get a better hold of the baby. She looked over Trevor's shoulder at Jennifer. She glared back at Daphanie, shamelessly.

Urgent questions banged inside of Daphanie's skull, some of which she was afraid to ask. "Are...are you putting me out?"

Trevor took his time answering, as though only then deciding: more games he played. "No."

"Then why is she here?" Daphanie asked, trying to conceal just how angry Jennifer's presence was making her.

"To take care of my child."

"What do you think I'm doing?" Daphanie asserted in a high-pitched shriek. "And he's my child, too!"

"No. You signed him away, remember?" He paused before the next words he spoke. "Until further notice, Jennifer will take over all responsibilities pertaining to the baby. I have to think about whether or not you can be trusted with my son."

"What? No!" Daphanie held tighter to her baby, the child starting to sob, sensing his mother's distress. "Trevor, what does that mean?"

"Jennifer will feed, bathe and clothe Nate."

"No," Daphanie whimpered, glancing at Jennifer with a look, asking her to stop what was happening, for Daphanie believed she could if she wanted, and hoped she might find compassion in her enough to do so.

Jennifer smiled and said nothing.

"If in the middle of the night," Trevor continued, "the baby wakes up crying, you no longer have to trouble yourself with that, either. Jennifer will take—"

"Trouble myself?" Daphanie said. "I'm his mother. It's my responsibility."

"Not anymore," Trevor said, reaching out for Nate. "Now if you don't mind, give me my son. We'd like to spend time with him."

Daphanie's eyes were on Jennifer again; the woman had never once looked away. It appeared she had no fear of Daphanie.

Staring down at Trevor's open palms, Daphanie didn't have to question what would happen if she refused him; he would tell her to pack her things and get out. Considering she still had no job and no place else to go, that plan wouldn't work for her. But what was far worse than being broke and homeless was not being near her son, even if it was to watch someone else play mother to him.

Having no other option, Daphanie handed over the baby to Trevor.

"So what do I do?" She asked.

Trevor glanced at the new live-in nanny, then back at Daphanie. "Whatever Jennifer tells you."

18

Lewis threw open the front door of his house, about to run inside, but stopped abruptly at the threshold; the possibility of Freddy beating him to his home entered his mind. Not taking another step, he called out to Eva. When she didn't answer, he shuddered, glanced around the room and prepared himself for what he'd have to do if he ran upstairs and found Eva with Freddy's gun pressed to her forehead.

"Hey baby, I'm up here," Eva said from upstairs.

Lewis closed the door and hurried to the second floor, down the hall then cautiously pushed open the bedroom door, still not trusting that Freddy wasn't one step in front of him.

Eva stood at the far side of the bed folding towels. "What's up, baby? Everything all right?"

Lewis strode across the room. "You okay?" he asked, looking her up and down.

"Uh, yeah. Why wouldn't I be?"

Lewis stepped away from her, went to the closet, threw open the door and checked it as he had done before. He went to the window, poked his fingers between the blinds and glanced out to the street.

"Lewis..." Eva said, stopping what she was doing. "Why aren't you at work? What's going on? You're worrying me."

She had reason to be worried, Lewis thought. After he was told that the dead woman lying by the car was Kia, his mind wouldn't let him believe that; he had to see for himself. He pushed more forcefully through the crowd, nearly knocking a man down till there was just a single police officer blocking his view. When the officer moved, Lewis gained a clear view of the dead woman's face. It lay on its side, Kia's eyes wide open, staring.

"Everything's fine, Eva," Lewis lied. "But I need for you to pack up enough clothes and whatever else you'll need in some bags to last about a week. I'll go to the girls' room and do the same."

"What are you talking about? Pack?" Eva said, stepping around the bed. "You're telling me you need me and the girls to leave? Why?"

"I'm sorry, but I think Freddy has gotten out."

"But yesterday morning he spoke to you from his cell. I heard his voice."

"I know, Eva."

"And this morning you said there was nothing to worry about. Everything was fine."

"I know."

"And now all of a sudden none of that's true?"

With each word Eva spoke, another second of their getaway time was wasted. For all Lewis knew, Freddy could've been climbing over his backyard fence, looking for a way into his house. "He got out. Shot and killed his ex-girlfriend and the man she was seeing. Now we have to go," Lewis said.

"What? How do you know?"

"Because I spoke to someone at the hospital and they said he escaped."

"No. How do you know it was Freddy that shot her? You see him—"

"I didn't see him," Lewis said, becoming more frustrated. "I just know it was him."

Breathing heavily through her mouth, she shook her head, looking as though she believed none of it. Lewis grabbed her arm, tried to pull her into action; she would not budge. "How do you know all this about him," she said, seemingly deciding: "There's something you're not telling me."

"Eva, we have to go." He tugged at her arm again. She swatted his hand away.

"No!" she yelled. "Tell me the truth."

Lewis whipped his head around the room, feeling there was a chance a bullet would come sailing through a window, or Freddy himself would come running through the door, gun drawn, if they stuck around too much longer. He had no choice but confess. "When Freddy was locked up, he told me he'd make me pay for Joni's death."

"He told you he wanted to hurt me?" Eva's face went blank. Speaking in a whisper, she said, "You knew? He told you that he—"

"That he wanted to hurt *me*," Lewis said, pressing his palms into his chest. "*Me*! I didn't' think—"

"You didn't *think*? You didn't think that making you pay might've meant hurting me? I was raped and you didn't fucking think, Lewis?" Eva screamed, turning away from him. "My daughter was in the next room. The same thing could've happened to her, and your only excuse is that you didn't fucking think?"

"No, I didn't think he'd hurt you. But he did. And now he's out, and it looks like he might be trying to do worse, so I need for you to grab some bags and put your fucking clothes in them and leave, so you don't wind up dead. Can you please do that for me!"

Eva smeared tears from her cheeks, nodding her head. She went to the closet and snatched a weekend bag. "I'll do that. I'll pack our things. We'll leave and you will never have to worry about us coming back."

19

Tabatha took a few moments to go to the office and just sit for a minute, because Monica had left to make a run. Yes, the stores were doing badly, but every now and again, things would kick up, forcing Tabatha to work like a slave. She leaned back in her desk chair, was about to toe off her heals and put her feet up, when she heard a knock at the door.

"Come in," she called, waiting. When the door didn't open, she ordered again: "Come in."

Still nothing. Tabatha got up, cursing under her breath, walked to the door and threw it open. "When I say 'come in'. It means—" she halted when she saw Nate Kenny standing in the doorway. "Nate, what are you doing here?"

"Was passing through and thought I'd stop by. Mind if I step in? Promise it'll only be for a second." He looked over her shoulder into the office. "Unless your busy."

"No," Tabatha said, stepping away from the door.

"Monica's not here?" Nate asked, stepping in.

"She went to pick up food. Not trying to be rude, but what do you want, Nate?"

"How long have you known Monica?" Nate smirked, casually walking through the office, admiring the place as though he had never been there.

"Ten years."

"But you've never really thought much of me, have you?"

"I wouldn't say…"

"You can stop," Nate said, turning, staring at Tabatha. He still wore something of a smile. "Be honest."

"Then no," Tabatha said. "I don't like you at all. I think you're a manipulative bastard, who thinks nothing of Monica and will ultimately hurt her again as you always do."

Nate clapped sarcastically. "True 'ride or die bitch'. Isn't that the term? You'd lay down your life to protect your best friend, wouldn't you?"

"Damn right," Tabatha said, sounding ready to push the office furniture aside and scuffle to prove it.

"I'm glad she has such a good friend in you. Monica told you we remarried, didn't she?" Nate said, holding up his left hand, twisting the wedding band around his finger with his thumb.

"She did."

"So I'd like it if you could respect her decision. Regarding my marriage to Monica, and all matters related, I'm going to need for you to mind your business, or you and I could have some problems."

A look of puzzlement on Tabatha's face, she said, "I don't think I know what you're trying to say."

Nate sidestepped his wife's desk, walked to Tabatha, stopping so close, it appeared he would grab and kiss her. "What I'm saying is, regardless of what you think, this marriage is good for her and for me. I apologized to her for the things I've done, and since I'm here, let me take the opportunity to apologize to you for also putting you through some things. But I want to reassure you, Tabatha, I'm a changed man. I'm truly committed to this. More than anything, I want this to work, so I'd appreciate you not filling my wife's head with all kinds of ideas about leaving or what I might do, or the monster you think I might still be. Knowing that you're on my side would make succeeding with this a whole lot easier. What do you say? We have a deal?" Nate held a hand out to Tabatha.

Tabatha glanced down then backed up, smiling and chuckling. "You've got to be joking. You come into my place of business unannounced, acting like some boy scout. Nate, I see your conniving ass. And sorry to burst your little bubble, but I've already told Monica that remarrying you was a mistake, and I will keep on telling her, hoping that she comes to her senses and seriously considers divorcing you."

Nate stood before Tabatha, the smile no longer on his face. He was frozen, eyes not blinking, just staring her down in a way that made her almost want to scream out for Roland because she felt she might've been in harm's way.

All of sudden, Nate smiled again and turned away from Tabatha.

She exhaled deeply, watching as he turned back to face her.

"Like I said, I'm happy my wife has someone like you in her life. Sorry to interrupt you at work, Tabatha. Have a good day," Nate said, and he was gone.

20

Freddy stood in the bathroom mirror staring at the man he's become: long strands of hair grew in patches from his face. He ran his hand, back and forth, over the buzzed hair atop his head, as though missing the dense mess that used to be there before he was admitted into the psychiatric facility. His eyes were sunken deep into his head, his cheekbones more prominent, as well as his collarbones, protruding from just under the surface of his t-shirt.

He stood, swallowed up in the coat he had taken, the sleeves rolled up as though by a caring mother.

He shut his eyes tight, then opened them again: a trick that seemed to clear the unwanted images that seeped into his head in the past. But an image came. This one he could not shake despite how many times he shut his eyes and counted to ten; it was that goddamned baby screaming its lungs out in the back of that car, his little hands reaching out. All Freddy saw at the time was something alien, something evil, something that he almost pointed his gun at and ended just like he had done to Kia. She deserved it by the way, because she hadn't told him that he had a child, that he had made a life. She kept that from him, so she had to die. But the baby—from that moment to this one—was all Freddy could think about, and only just a moment ago, came to the realization that the baby wasn't something to have been killed, or walked away from. But Freddy had done that.

After he had dropped Kia's body, he remembered the baby shrieking, reaching out his arms…and now Freddy wondered if that was the child wanting Freddy to come back, unstrap him from the prison of that car seat and take him with him. He wondered had the baby known, through some special baby sense, that Freddy was his father, so the child was trying to relate to him that he knew why

Freddy had killed his mother, had forgiven Freddy for that, and wanted Freddy to take him with him so that they could build a relationship, throw a ball when he got older, do shit that his father didn't do with Freddy. But all that was dashed when Freddy walked away and that was eating his ass up inside like a motherfucker.

Eyes open and there he was again in the mirror, the big gun he already killed two people with, sticking out of the jeans that were too big for him, but cinched incredibly tight around his narrow waist—the metal pin speared into the last hole of the belt he wore. He paused, rolled his eyes to the top of his head, searching to make sure he had truly gotten rid of the memory of his baby. He smiled only momentarily thinking it was gone, but spotted it again, heard the echo of the infant and he frowned.

He walked out of the bathroom, pulling the gun from out the jeans, having already decided someone had to pay for what he was made to do, and he knew it was Lewis.

Freddy walked through the bedroom, stopping again at the dresser, noticing the empty drawers that were hanging out: a pair of panties that had been forgotten on the floor. He walked over to the closet: door hanging open, many of the hangers bare.

Freddy had rang the doorbell half an hour ago, holding the gun behind his back, having decided if Eva answered, he was going to dispense with the formalities and just pop her in the head. He would kill Lewis later, because he wanted him to experience what Freddy had already gone through once: losing Joni, and now losing Kia: living after losing the girl he loved.

But the door wasn't open, and Freddy had to go to the back of the house and bust one of the glass squares in the back door window to let himself in. Now, standing in the bedroom, looking at what appeared to be a fast getaway, Freddy figured Lewis must've found out about Kia's death, hurried back here and grabbed the woman before Freddy could find her.

He nodded his head, smiling a little. "Very good, Lewis," he chuckled under his breath. "But this shit ain't over," he said, walking out of the room, but not before reaching down, picking up the panties from the floor and stuffing them in the stolen coat pocket.

21

Lewis anxiously waited at the front door of Eva's aunt's house, one hand around the phone pressed to his ear, the other holding onto his daughter's hand as she asked over and over again: "What's wrong, Daddy? What's wrong?"

Half an hour ago, Lewis was working behind his desk, trying to deal with the information he had just learned about Kia, when his door flew open. In the doorway, stood a huge man in a blue security guard sport jacket and light colored khakis, his neck the size of a tree trunk. In his beefy hand, he held a radio that crackled with noise of people communicating. Lewis believed he heard his name mentioned in all that static.

"Mr. Waters, I need for you to gather your belongs so I can escort you out the building."

"What are you talking about?"

"Mr. Waters..." the man said, sounding not in the mood for games.

Lewis grabbed his office phone, and with the cord trailing behind him, he stepped behind his desk chair, the phone ringing in his ear. "I'm calling Mrs. Roberts," Lewis said to security. "And we're going to straighten whatever the hell you talking about out."

To Lewis's surprise, his boss, who also happened to be Eva's aunt, stepped into the office. Wearing a beige dress, pearls and deep disappointment all over her face, she shook her head at Lewis and said: "Mr. Waters, I need for you to do as this gentleman asks. You are no longer employed here."

After being thrown out of the building, Lewis went to his daughter's school to sign her out.

The pen trembled in Lewis's fist as his daughter's second grade teacher, Mrs. Harrison, watched him sign his name. "Is everything all right, Mr. Waters?"

He looked up startled. "I need my daughter now, please."

Pulling up to his own home fifteen minutes later, Lewis stared at his house through his window, as though wishing he could see through the walls, see if Freddy was moving around in there, maybe hunched behind a piece of tall furniture, or hiding behind a closet door. Lewis pushed open his car door, ran around, unstrapped his daughter from the child seat, grabbed her hand and hurried her to the house.

Inside, he quietly made his way through the living room and up the stairs.

He was there to retrieve something he had foolishly forgotten this morning, so consumed with the shock of hearing Eva was gone for good.

Inside the bedroom, he went into the closet, threw an arm up, elbow deep, onto the top shelf, pulled out an object and shoved it in the back of his slacks. "C'mon, baby. Let's go," he said, halting when he noticed something in Layla's hand. He reached down, snatched what was a cigarette butt from her.

"Where'd you get this?"

"Right there. On the floor," she said.

Only then did Lewis smell the traces of that cigarette he knew had been smoked in this room, and knew beyond a doubt that Freddy had been there. He bent down, snatched Layla close, hoisted her up, pulled the gun and held it out in front of him.

"Daddy! Why do you have—"

"Shhhh!" Lewis said, crouching low, moving quickly against the hallway wall and down the stairs, deciding to leave through the back door, in case Freddy was laying in wait for him. In the kitchen, he saw the glass on the floor, broken from the pane of the door that hung slightly open.

"Arms around Daddy's neck," he told his daughter. She obeyed, freeing both his hands so that he could cock his gun, load a bullet into the chamber before stepping out of the house.

Now long gone from his house, Eva's aunt's front door swung open, Eva appearing behind it. She stood shaking her head, a hand on her hip, her expression saying there was nothing Lewis could say to make her change her mind about anything.

"I need you to keep Layla."

"What? What's wrong?"

"Freddy was in our house. He had broken in, and...I just need for you to keep her until the police catch him or I find out what to do."

"Hi Eva," Layla said.

"Hey sweetheart," Eva said, pained, looking at the girl's little hand being held out before her, but not making a move to take it. "Un uh, I'm sorry, but I can't."

"What do you mean, you can't? I just told you that Freddy was in our house, that my daughter might be in danger and—"

"And what? You want me to jeopardize my family? No! I'm sorry, Lewis."

"C'mon, Eva. If you ever loved me then you'd—"

"I hate what's happening to you. I truly do, but we've have been through enough. I hope the two of you are fine," Eva said sincerely, sadness and worry in her eyes as she stared down at Layla. "But there's nothing more I can do. Goodbye Lewis," Eva said, pushing the door closed.

22

That evening entering Trevor's house, Daphanie felt like an intruder. She walked quietly across the floor, feeling as though if she made too much noise, Trevor might be angered, might not want to put up with all the racket she continued to make and further restrict her from seeing her son, or put her out all together. The man had complete dominance over her, was in control of what was most dear to her. She had zero leverage in the game and it made her angry enough to kill every time he pulled a stunt like earlier, making her aware of how much of a pawn she was.

She thought to call out to him, ask him where their son was, but knew he probably wouldn't have answered even if he had heard her. There were so many ways he disrespected her: ignoring her as though she wasn't even alive was one of his favorites.

On the second floor of Trevor's house, she realized it was past Nat's bedime. She assumed Jennifer would probably be sitting in the baby's room, guarding him like the evil troll under the bridge, and might try to stop Daphanie from even getting a peak at the child. It was a shame that she would have to damn near ask permission from the woman, act meek and non-threatening just to lean over the rail and kiss her son's cheek. But that was the world Daphanie lived in now; those were the rules she had to play by. She had no choice but abide by them.

Coming to the door, she saw that it was ajar. Slowing her pace, Daphanie heard Jennifer speaking, but was unable to make out what she was saying, for her voice was low and the words were garbled. Daphanie figured she was probably reading to her baby. A hot jealously clung to her, seeing that image: Jennifer holding Nat in one arm, the baby's face smiling and aglow as the tramp did her impression of the big bad wolf threatening to blow down the little pig's house. Daphanie needed to make sure that was not happening.

She pressed the tips of her fingers to the door, pushed it open not even another inch to get a better look and froze when she caught sight of Nat's crib in the corner of the room, the baby soundly sleep inside, and Trevor standing in the center of the child's room, his trousers pushed down around his ankles, Jennifer on her knees, one hand cradling Trevor's testicles, the other wrapped around the shaft of his erect penis, giving him long strokes, her head bobbing wildly, as she alternated massaging him with her mouth and hand.

Daphanie's breath caught in her throat. Her lungs stopped working momentarily as she thought of charging in, but could do nothing but watch as Trevor's legs began to tremble as Jennifer started to pull on him faster. Biting his lip, grabbing fistfuls of the woman's hair, Trevor moaned so loudly Daphanie thought the baby would wake. The woman, obviously, a pro at this, stroked and sucked faster until Trevor's body went rigid, Jennifer pulling him from her mouth at the peak of his orgasm, directing him away from her face, still stroking him, shooting his load across the baby blue shag carpet of little Nat's room.

Disgusted at the scene she just witnessed, Daphanie turned away. But when she looked back, Jennifer had spotted her. And there, still on her knees, slowly tugging Trevor's shrinking organ, the woman stared, smiling at Daphanie from around the man's left hip.

Downstairs, outside the back door, Daphanie paced across the backyard deck, her cell phone pressed against the side of her face. "You need to tell me what can be done now, Monica," Daphanie said, trembling she was so incensed and scared of what her future might be.

"You need to calm down, Daphanie."

"I can't fucking calm down!" Daphanie yelled, looking up toward the second floor of the house. She lowered her voice when she said, "If something is going to happen, it needs to happen now."

100

"Tomorrow morning, we'll start. I'll text you the address when we get off the phone. Meet me there at nine then I can tell you what we'll do."

23

"You have reached your destination," Siri informed Daphanie, as she pulled her aging Infiniti sedan in front of a State Street building the next morning. Daphanie closed the GPS application and slid the phone back into her purse.

She paid the meter, took the flight of stairs to the second floor and knocked on the door marked with the number matching Monica's text from last night.

The door opened almost immediately. Monica stood behind it wearing dark tapered jeans, Gucci heels and a silk blouse. Her hair looked as though a stylist just pulled the smock from around her shoulders. Comparatively, Daphanie's hair was pulled back in a fraying bun, wrapped by a little green rubber band, a blue bandana tied over the entire mess. She wore a too-big t-shirt, sweat pants: not the stylish kind, but with the drawstring in front and the elastic around the ankles. She finished the ensemble with an old pair of running shoes and no socks.

"Sorry," Monica said, after getting a look at Daphanie. "Did I interrupt your workout, or your gardening? We could've pushed this back if you were still cleaning the toilets."

"Everyone doesn't have your life," Daphanie said. "So I'd appreciate it if you don't criticize mine."

"Have a seat in there," Monica said, closing the front door.

Daphanie sat down, disappointed to see the place not looking like a military situation room with maps strewn across the coffee table and black and white photos of Nate, taken with telephoto lenses tacked to the wall: tools to aid their strategy in finally bringing him down and taking back her child.

"Coffee?" Monica said. "Looks as though you could definitely use a cup."

"No. I just want to know how I'm going to get my son back."

"I have to be honest, Daphanie, I haven't figured that out yet. But understand, this is about you helping me first then I will help you. That was our arrangement. You remember that?"

"Fine," Daphanie said, shifting to the edge of the sofa. "Can we get on with it?"

Monica raised a finger, turned toward the kitchen. "Tori."

Daphanie figured this would be the precious cargo Monica flew all the way to L.A. to transport back. She moved around on the sofa and looked toward the kitchen doorway to see a woman step into the living room. She was 5'3", thin, with full lips and flawless light brown skin. Her sandy colored hair was a mess—maybe as bad as Daphanie's, but she did not seem to care. The strands fell in her face and down her shoulders as if it was an intentional style. Under the woman's little, faded t-shirt, Daphanie saw she had rather large, perky breast for a woman her size. She wore dirty, faded jeans, bunched up at the bottoms and stuck into Doc Martin's boots. All in all, the woman was beautiful in a dusty-desperate-thumb out-hitching a ride on the side of the road-damsel in distress kind of way.

"Daphanie," Monica said, "That's Tori. Tori, that's Daphanie."

Daphanie slowly rose from the sofa, and not knowing why, wiped her palms on the front of her pants; she was just a little nervous.

"Go ahead...you two shake or something," Monica said.

Daphanie stepped from around the couch and walked over to Tori as though the woman were a wild dog that may bite. She held out her hand. Tori, popping gum, one hand on her hip, reluctantly held out the other: tragically chipped orange polish colored her fingernails.

"Hey, I'm Daphanie."

"Tori," Tori nodded, dapping Daphanie up instead of shaking hands.

"Okay," Monica said. "This is our team. Now that the two of you have been introduced, this is what will happen next."

As instructed from the list Monica had written and included in the envelope she had already given Daphanie, she took Tori to a hair salon, where it had taken nearly three hours for the big woman wearing a freeze-curl hairdo to complete Tori's cut, color and style. But when she finished, Nate's ex-mistress emerged from the chair looking stunning and Daphanie could understand what Nate found in her. Of course Daphanie did not tell Tori that, just looked down at the list Monica had scribbled out and said, "C'mon. We still have a lot to do today."

On the drive to Water Tower Mall, Tori tried to start conversation; Daphanie ignored her. Tori clicked on the radio to an R & B station. Daphanie reached over and immediately shut the radio off. "If it's not yours, don't touch it," Daphanie scolded.

Walking through the mall, Tori followed Daphanie, slowing down occasionally to look into store windows. Daphanie would call for her as though Tori was a disobedient child.

"Hey, hey," Tori said, stopping for the last time.

Daphanie turned to see that Tori had stopped at the entrance of the mall's food court.

"We need to stop for something to eat. I'm hungry as hell."

"We don't eat until after the clothing stores. C'mon."

At Neiman Marcus, two beautiful women walked to the front of the store when Daphanie mentioned who she and Tori were and that Monica Kenny had sent them. Both women were tall. Thin and model-like in their demeanor, they carried garments back and forth to the changing room on their very high heels, continuing on about how beautiful Tori was and how well every size 2 garment fit her. They practically dressed and undressed her in the changing room's three way mirror: unzipping her trousers, unbuttoning her blouse, reaching around her waist, fastening her belt, while Tori stood there, holding up her arms, seemingly wishing to be anywhere else but there.

"What do you think?" One of the girls asked Daphanie after they had finished dressing Tori in an ensemble of pink and white. All of the outfits were banging, all of them costing hundreds of dollars.

"Is that what Ms. Kenny told you to dress her in?" Daphanie asked.

Both women nodded.

"Then it doesn't matter what I think. Wrap it up and we'll take it all."

After carrying the bags to the car and locking them in the trunk, they left Daphanie's Infiniti in the parking structure and walked down Michigan Avenue to Saks Fifth, for it was only a few blocks away. It was a warm spring day, the sun was out, and the sidewalks were thick with people wearing everything from business suits to tennis shorts, flip-flops and tank tops.

Daphanie weaved in and out of pedestrian traffic, her mind set on finishing the task at hand, no matter how little she believed it would actually help in improving her home situation, which she was anxious to get back to, for she had no clue as to what was happening there now. She had tried three times already to call Trevor, but the man would not answer.

Standing behind a rack of dresses in Saks, making sure Tori could not see her, Daphanie had left a message last time Trevor's voicemail picked up.

"If you won't answer, the least you could do is allow me to have that woman's phone number so that I can call and see how my son is." Realizing how demanding her tone might've sounded when and if Trevor finally did listen to it, and that it might prove to worsen her situation, she said beseechingly, "Please," before she hung up.

More outfits were bought at Saks and were carried back to the car. Slamming the trunk closed, Daphanie climbed into the driver's seat, pulled shut the door and was about to slip the key in the ignition.

"You got a problem with me. Why?" Tori said from the passenger seat. She wore a big dark pair of brand new Prada sunshades on her face.

Daphanie paused, thought to answer her, but didn't. She slid the key into the ignition, was about to start the car when Tori covered her hand, stopping her.

Daphanie closed her eyes, took a breath and said calmly: "Take your hand away, or I swear you will regret this day for the rest of your life."

Continuing to test her, Tori waited a beat before doing as she was told. A second after that, Tori said: "I don't get it. I mean, Monica hasn't really told me nothing about you, but I don't want to be here just as much as it seems you don't. I'm making the best of it, because I have no choice, just like you."

"You don't nothing about me, okay," Daphanie said, angrily turning in her seat to face Tori. "I don't know who the hell you are, other than some slit Nate was bending over his desk until he got tired of you. Despite what Monica says, we don't have shit in common other than her making me drag your little prissy ass around, buying you shit, when I have real problems to solve. So do me a favor: never talk to me again, unless it's one hundred percent necessary."

24

"You can tell me the truth, please," Lewis said, sitting on the old, plastic covered sofa. He had just gotten up from his seat across the living room of Freddy's Uncle Henry's house, where Freddy's mother now lived.

He had walked over and sat down next to her, after already having asked her twice if she had seen or heard from her son. Both times she pretended as though she had no idea of what Lewis was talking about. But he could see the worry in her eyes, could feel the tension in her body, and he watched as she nervously twisted and tore pieces from the sheet of paper towel she rung in her hands.

"Has he come here?" Lewis tried again, knowing Freddy had nowhere else to go.

Mrs. Ford shook her head, her eyes turned down toward the paper towel, her hair long, wiry, mostly gray and parted down the middle.

"Has he called?"

"I said no," Mrs. Ford said under her breath, then looked up, seemingly to check if Lewis believed her.

He stood again, took the old woman's hand, shook it gently then said goodbye, believing she would hold firm to telling him nothing. But at the door, he couldn't force himself to open it, remembering Kia's body lying spread out on the grass. He saw her head: the huge hole blown out of the back of it, and finally her eyes: staring wide and accusingly at him, as if to suggest that if he had gotten there earlier, she wouldn't have been dead.

"Did you know Kia, Mrs. Ford?"

Mrs. Ford turned, looked over her shoulder at Lewis, showing on her face, the closest Lewis saw her come to a smile that afternoon.

"Yes, that was Freddy's little girlfriend for the longest time. She was gonna be a lawyer, right?"

"That's right. She was a semester away from finishing. Told me she had a job lined up downtown at a big law firm and everything."

Prideful, Mrs. Ford smiled wider. "I always knew that girl would make it."

"She had a little boy, too," Lewis said walking over and sitting back down beside Mrs. Ford.

"Oh," Freddy's mother said, the information seeming to come as a mild shock.

"Your son is the father. Did you know that?"

Mrs. Ford turned away, twisting the paper into a tighter rope, as she rocked back and forth on the sofa.

"Kia was a wonderful mother. She would've been so good to that child."

"Would've?" Mrs. Ford asked. "Why you say—"

"Kia's dead, Mrs. Ford. Freddy killed her. Shot her in the head."

"No, no, no!" Mrs. Ford said, standing from the sofa, spinning in a circle, as if looking for somewhere to hide from the news. "My boy wouldn't—"

"Mrs. Ford," Lewis said, standing.

"No!"

He grabbed the older woman, turned her to face him. "Freddy killed her. He wants to kill another man, and he might even be after me. Please, you have to tell me if he's come here and exactly what he said to you."

25

That night, after dressing in the newly purchased cross trainers, the body hugging tank top and the black athletic stretch leggings, Tori stepped out of the woman's locker room in the highly exclusive Gold Coast Fitness Center.

"That is where he'll be," Monica said this morning, walking over to a small chest of drawers in the dining room. She pulled one open, sifted around and brought back a card, handing it to Tori. "That's the card to the gym. Use it to get in. You look enough like my girlfriend; they won't ask any questions."

"And what am I supposed to do at a fitness center?"

"Work out. Walk around, talk to men who talk to you until Nate sees you. When he does, ignore him. Trust me, after while, he'll come to you."

"And when he does, I tell him..."

"Exactly what we agreed on. Times were hard in L.A. You're house sitting a friend's place. You don't have any money. You're lonely, and no, you wouldn't mind if he comes over. I'm sure he'll ask," Monica said, snidely.

At 4:45, a knock came at Tori's door. When she answered it, Daphanie stood there, not saying a word, just stared past her into the house.

"What?" Tori said.

"I'm here to pick you up. Don't act like we hadn't gone over this with Monica this morning."

"Okay," Tori said, sensing serious attitude from the woman. "So you just gonna stand there, or are you gonna come in?"

"I'm fine right here," Daphanie said.

Tori shook her head and threw her hands up. "Fine. Give me five minutes and we can leave."

Now, walking out onto the fitness center floor among the scores of men and women in workout clothing—shorts and tees, weight gloves and sneakers—Tori looked around, feeling the weight of men's eyes on her.

She walked to the lat pull down machine, took a seat, grabbed the bar over her head and did a couple of repetitions. On the third, a man wearing a too-small t-shirt, exposing the lowermost part of his huge belly, asked if he could show her the proper way to do the exercise. Tori smiled and said she was fine doing them the way she always had. When he asked if she was sure, Tori smiled and very politely said: "I'm here to get a work out, not to be picked up by men. Now if you would excuse me," she said, stood and walked away.

She worked out for another forty-five minutes, dividing her time between the Stairmaster, the treadmill and a rowing machine. Exhausted and covered in sweat, Tori stood from the rower, blotted her face and neck with her hand towel and checked the time: 5:47 PM.

She had seen no sign of Nate. Daphanie would be in the parking garage at 6, so Tori started toward the locker rooms, perfectly content with not having run into the man.

"Leaving so soon," Tori heard someone ask behind her.

Turning slowly, Tori forced a smile to her face, and doing her best to control her nerves said: "Is that you, Nate?"

He was as handsome as he every was: beautiful smile, straight white teeth, curly, well trimmed black hair, and that smooth, golden brown skin, pulled tight over the muscles he wore so well under his workout clothes. It was hard to believe she was right there in front of him: the man she had loved, the man she was supposed to have married, the man that once wanted her to have his baby.

Nate extended a workout-gloved hand. "Look at you? How long has it been? What are you doing in Chicago? I thought you were a Cali-girl now?" He spoke to Tori like they were old college classmates, like the last time they saw each other, they were on good terms, not wanting each other dead.

"I..." Tori had to force herself not to stammer, not to freeze, to remember that succeeding at this assignment, this job, this whatever-it was, would be the difference between her living the life she had been accustomed to when she was a human being, or going back to living like an animal. "I..." Tori cautiously placed one of her gloved hands into his. "...can't believe it's you. It has been a long time."

They spoke where they were for five minutes, Nate telling her that he had finished his work out, but if she would wait for him, he'd be happy to walk her out.

Inside the locker room, Tori paced quickly back and forth across the carpeted floor, her cell phone to her ear, ringing.

"What is it?" Monica answered.

"He found me!" Tori said. "He's waiting outside the locker room because he wants to talk some more. What do I do?"

There was a longer pause than Tori felt comfortable with, and she wondered if Monica was having second thoughts about putting the woman that her husband used to fuck, back in front of his face.

"Monica! I said what do I do?"

"Right," she said. "Go out there and talk to him. You know what the endgame is. Get us there!"

Nate walked Tori to the elevator. Once the doors closed them alone inside, Tori recited the reason she was back in Chicago, leaving out the bit about Ja'Van and how badly she had been treated.

In the parking structure, Nate gave the valet the keys to his car then asked for Tori's. She told him she wasn't driving.

"So you're letting me take you home, then."

"You don't have to. I'll Uber it."

"Not a bother?" Nate insisted, as the vested valet ran off to get his car.

"Really," Tori said, scanning the parking structure, hoping Daphanie wasn't circling. "I'm good, really," she said, realizing just how much she wanted to be away from him, how frightened she was feeling of him that moment. He looked at her oddly then smiling, he

113

said, "Okay. Okay, but give me your number. We should get together. There's something I really want to talk to you about."

Tori glanced down at the wedding band on his left hand, realized things never changed, and questioned was she really to go back into that life. She smiled.

"Okay, here's my number. You got your phone?"

26

Monica let the drapes fall back as she saw Nate pulling his car into the driveway. She stepped away from the window, carried her wine glass back to the kitchen trying to suppress the mild twinges of jealousy, knowing it was her that placed the temptation before her husband. She didn't like thinking about what might've taken place at the gym—didn't like imagining her husband fawning all over his ex-lover. Monica had to continue telling herself it was for a reason, and if nothing else, her cell phone in her hand proved it.

After Nate shouldered his gym bag, kissed Monica on the cheek and took off, she went into the family room where Nathaniel was was watching TV and sat on the sofa behind him.

"What we watching, baby?" Monica asked.

"Bubbles and Martian Frog," Nathaniel said, not turning away from the cartoon that played loudly on the flat screen.

"You mind if I talk to you for a moment?" Monica asked, reaching for the remote.

He didn't answer, but appeared not to like the fact his show was turned off when he spun around on his bottom to face his mother. Monica slid off the sofa and sat down on the floor with her son, crossing her legs "Indian style".

"I had a conversation with Daddy the other day that I wanna ask you about." While she spoke, she activated her phone recorder. "Daddy said, not long ago, you were having really bad dreams."

Standing in the kitchen now, Monica held the phone, listening again to some of the recording.

"…and…and then," Nathaniel's little voice came frightened and small from the cell phone speaker. "I tried to wake Daddy up. But he wouldn't wake up." Then Monica heard her own voice ask, "And why wouldn't he wake up?"

"Because…because the bad man shot him."

"And did that make you feel scared? Did that make you feel unsafe? Did you think the bad man was going to shoot you next?" Monica had said.

She stopped the recording, feeling terrible about using the boy, about steering his recollection of that event in a way that would serve her best. But if she were to succeed in what she was attempting, she would have to put her feelings aside.

She stood, her hands resting on the edge of the sink, her eyes closed as she tried to redirect her thinking, force herself into the mold of a woman who loved her husband and was ecstatic about being newly married again.

"Babe, I'm home," she heard her husband call from the front room. "Where are you?"

Eyes still closed, she exhaled then called back. "In the kitchen."

Seconds later, Nate walked into the room with her, set his bag on one of the chairs, and from behind, gave her a hug and a kiss.

"How was the gym?" Monica asked, her voice monotone, not yet succeeding in her attempt to fake the happy newlywed. "Anything exciting happen?"

"Nope. Good workout though," he said, going to the fridge, pulling out some juice, Monica watching as he took swigs straight from the bottle. "Where's the little boy?" Nate said.

"Family room, watching TV."

Nate started off, but stopped short of the door. "You okay? I can sense something's a little off."

"I'm fine," Monica said, forcing a smile and pressing fingers to her temple. "Just a little headache. Took some aspirin. I'll be fine."

Nate nodded, gave her an A-OK smile then disappeared out the room.

Monica turned back to the window, telling herself she needed to get her shit together, but this: Nate stepping out felt all too familiar. It hurt like hell years ago when she found out he was cheating, and even though she cared nothing for him and she was the orchestrator for this new infidelity, she believed it would feel no less painful now.

Later that night, Nate rolled from on top of Monica, pulling her naked body around the waist, urging her to straddle him. That was how Nate always liked to finish off their sessions: her taking control, making him come when she decided. But making love to him had been hard. Lying under him, closing her eyes, making enough noise so he felt she was enjoying his efforts—she could manage. But giving him pleasure when she convinced herself she was very close to hating the sight of him would require her most skillful lying.

Monica straddled him and lifted up enough to feel him slide slow and hard into her wetness. She bit her lip, cursing the pleasure she felt, and begin to gyrate and roll her hips with intent of getting this over with. There was work that had to be done: climb out of bed once he had fallen to sleep, research the internet from the home office, find whatever else possible she could to strengthen her chances of removing little Nathaniel from Nate's care.

One hand on her ass, with the other, Nate urged Monica toward him, took her breast in his mouth, began to suck and push deeper into her. She felt herself getting wetter, felt her body responding to his, betraying what she wanted. She cried out, bore down on him, rode him harder, feeling the characteristic numbness in her lips and tips of toes that came just before an orgasm. She tried to fight it, tried to pull herself from him, but he roped his arm around the back of her neck, locking her down in such a way that she could not move, could only feel him slide quickly in and out of her. She felt her juices spilling out of her, coating his stomach, his thighs, allowing her to slide about only enough to give her even more pleasure. Hating herself, Monica shrieked, pulled her breast from Nate's mouth, lunged forward and pressed her lips to his, riding him faster until she felt the gush of his warm fluid explode up and inside of her.

Panting heavily, her eyes wide, the side of her face pressed against his chest, she asked herself exactly what the hell she was doing.

"Wow," Nate panted, gently combing his fingers through Monica's hair.

"Yeah," she breathed, closing her eyes, feeling embarrassed and ashamed from the pleasure she took.

"You enjoy that?" Nate asked, and Monica could feel him shifting under her so that he could look in her face.

Staring at him, sweat dripping from her brow, Nate carefully moved the strands that fell over her eyes out the way. "Yes," Monica said.

"Glad to hear that, cause it felt...I don't know," Nate said, quickly looking off, then back again. "Kinda like you didn't."

Monica attempted to climb off of him.

"No. Don't go," Nate pleaded.

Monica rose up, her palms on his belly, her breasts hanging over his face. He caressed one of her nipples when we he said, "Never mind what I said. Guilt, I guess."

"For what?" Monica asked and for the briefest of moments, she thought he might confess to meeting Tori this evening.

"For mistreating you so badly to think that you'd never be able to enjoy making love to me again."

"Oh," Monica said.

She was thankful that the room was just dark enough so that he could not fully see the disappointment on her face.

"But you're bigger than that," Nate said. "Obviously you are, or you couldn't have married me, you wouldn't have agreed to be a family again, and you wouldn't be in this bed with me right now."

"You think?" Monica said, chuckling a little at Nate's arrogance, his ignorance or both.

"How could you be?" There was a lighthearted tone in his voice.

"Hmmm," Monica said, as though joking. "What if I told you I didn't come back for any of that, but to set you up, get you comfortable, then think up some brilliant and diabolical scheme to take your son from you so I could raise him all by myself?"

Nate laughed, but Monica felt her husband's dick quickly deflate inside of her as he slowly wrapped his hand around her neck, squeezing her, not enough to strangle, but enough to cause her alarm.

"If you did that—knowing how much our son means to me—" Nate said, his voice lowering to barely above a whisper. "I'd take everything you held dear, destroy it, then set your entire world on fire. I wouldn't even care if I went up myself in the blaze, as long as I knew that you and all you loved had been incinerated." He squeezed her just a bit tighter then released her. "But I know you'd never do that," Nate said, reverting back to the loving, caring, devoted husband he was pretending to be. "Because we're a family again, and that's all that matters. Right?"

"That's right," Monica said, feeling Nate gently pull her down so that he could give her a kiss and hold her body close to his.

27

The next morning, Monica stood, washing her face in the bathroom basin, wondering had she said too much last night, alerting Nate in some way to what she was planning? After the frightening threat he delivered to her, he said nothing else on the matter, just held her close to him. A moment later she heard him lightly snoring. Now, ringing the wash cloth, folding it and draping it over the rim of the sink, she told herself she could never be that careless again.

Monica threw on her bathrobe and walked out into the kitchen, surprised to see that Nate wasn't alone.

"Lewis?" Monica gasped.

"Hey, Monica," Lewis said, not sounding terribly happy to see her.

Monica knew Lewis Waters better than she would've liked. She knew him intimately, having slept with him back when she was first married to Nate. It was a scheme Nate devised, hoping to get Monica to cheat: break the terms of their prenuptial agreement and forfeit money coming to her in a potential divorce settlement. Sadly for Nate, the plan backfired and half the fortune he was trying to protect went to Monica anyway.

"What are you doing here?" Monica said, looking across the room, glancing at the five year-old, sitting at the kitchen table, scribbling colorful lines on a single sheet of notebook paper, big headphones covering her ears, obliviously bobbing her head to whatever was playing on her MP3 player.

"Freddy Ford," Lewis said, gravely. "He got out."

Monica flinched. "What? How you do know?" Last time Monica saw the man, she had visited him in the mental institution: her form of therapy, proving he had no power over her: telling him to his face he'd no longer haunt her dreams and her every waking moment. It had worked, but she was scared as hell now.

Lewis glanced at Nate as if for permission to tell the truth about all that was happening.

"Just tell me!" Monica demanded.

"I go by his ex-girlfriend's house some mornings to check on her. When I went yesterday, she had been shot, was lying dead on her front lawn, surrounded by police cars."

"And Freddy Ford did it?" Monica asked. "You sure?"

"Not sure, but he kept telling me he was going to break out. Kept talking about this list of people he was going to kill when he got out."

"A list?" Monica asked, praying she wasn't on it.

"He doesn't want you," Lewis said. "He never did. Shooting you that day in the head was a mistake. He always tells me that."

"I'm the one he wants," Nate said bravely, as though he had nothing to worry about. And despite how much Monica convinced herself she loathed him, Nate was once her husband—was her husband again—and she felt concern for him now.

"I spoke to the police," Lewis said. "But there's no proof it was him."

"But you said he broke out of the hospital," Monica said. "And he said he was going to kill her. Shouldn't that be enough for them?"

"Sweetheart," Nate said, hugging his wife with an arm. "The girl dying was unfortunate, but odds are, Ford had nothing to do with it. At this very moment, he's off his meds somewhere harmlessly wandering about in his bathrobe, relieving himself in the grass and playing with it."

"You don't know that! We have to do something," Monica said, feeling less safe with each passing second.

"Lewis coming here, informing us was him doing something. Besides, I have a gun here now," Nate said. "Let Ford come. Things won't happen the same way they did before. I can protect myself."

"And what about me? You couldn't protect me last time. What's changed?" Monica said, sounding more spiteful than she intended.

"And our son? Did you forget about Nathaniel? He was right here in this house when we were gunned down. He's had nightmares about it. We can't let that happen again? We have to move him until Ford is caught."

"Nathaniel's staying right here in this house with me—with us."

"No, Nate!" Monica said.

"There's nowhere safer for him."

"Nate, you can't seriously—"

"That's the last word said on the subject." Nate said.

He was being the arrogant fool Nate often morphed into during situations like these. She knew the stupidity came from his need to makeup for Nathaniel being stolen from him. He needed to prove that not only was he a loving father, but also a competent protector. But Monica knew thinking like that might only serve to get him, or quite possibly, all of them killed.

She looked again across the room at the little girl sitting at the table. For the short time Lewis and Monica were in a relationship, she played Mom to Layla. Monica cared a great deal for her then; she still had feelings for her now. "And what about her?" Monica said.

"She's the other reason I'm here," Lewis said. "I don't know if Freddy wants me as much as Nate, but I can't take that chance. Layla needs to be somewhere safe."

"You can't think that place is here," Monica said, staring spitefully at her husband.

"I had just gotten off the phone with Tim," Nate said. "He said he has no problem keeping Layla till this blows over."

"I'm sure Tim wouldn't have a problem keeping our son, either. Why don't you just ask him?"

"Because as I told you before, our son is staying with his father."

28

Tori lay on the living room sofa, scrolling through past selfies on her cell after just finishing a bowl of Cap'n Crunch cereal. She paused on a picture of her smiling and squinting against the California afternoon sun. Her hair was all over her head, the front pulled down, her attempt to cover a pretty bad black eye. It was a week old, and pretty much gone, but laying on the sofa that moment, she enlarged the screenshot with her thumb and forefinger, paying close attention to the bruising, and the healed cut that came with the clubbing right hand Ja'Van had thrown at her one night while sitting in the car. The hit that night came as no surprise; it was a common occurrence: a slap here if she came out her mouth the wrong way, a punch there if she wasn't as "in the mood" to fuck as he felt she should've been. She endured that for the year they "dated."

Those twelve months were torture, so she took to liquor to help her cope. First a couple of drinks at night, soon after, indulging in the afternoons as well, then getting to where by the end of the day, she found herself finishing off bottles and standing outside the liquor store waiting for it to open early the next morning.

Tori darkened her phone, set it on the coffee table beside the bowl of sugary milk and told herself not to think about that man. She lay her head down, closed her eyes, only to open them again at the sound of her cell ringing. "Hello," she said, answering.

"I know a place that has the best coffee and bagels in the city. Where can I pick you up?"

It was Nate, and Tori all of sudden felt uncomfortable, like she was being watched. She glanced at the windows in the living room and at the door, making sure it wasn't slowly opening.

"It's early." She walked over, twisted the knob and made sure the bolts on the front door were locked. "Just after ten."

"That's not early, Tori."

"It's eight in California. So it's early to me," Tori said.

"Sorry, but just got some disturbing news a while ago, and I decided to go in late today. Besides, believe it or not, I was meaning to reach out to you."

"Why?" Tori said, worried.

"Just tell me where I can pick you up?" The request sounded more like a command than anything else, like Nate was up to something: plotting, like he was so good at doing.

"Probably not a good idea," Tori said. Monica would be pissed if she found out that Tori rejected Nate's invitation, but she still wasn't certain she could have any dealings with Nate without them ending in tragedy. "Maybe another time."

"Really Tori, this has been on my mind—"

"I said no, Nate," Tori said, startling herself at how abrupt she was. "I'm sorry. Just tired, okay."

After a pause, Nate said, "Okay. I...I didn't meant to upset you. Maybe another time."

"Goodbye, Nate." Tori hung up and immediately it started ringing again, Ja'Van's name flashing across the screen, along with the picture he insisted she use as his contact photo: freshly braided ponytails falling all over his head, him grinning into the camera wearing a fresh set of gold plated grills over his teeth.

She hesitated a moment, then picked up. "Hello."

"Bitch! Where the fuck you at?"

"Ja'Van, I need for you to calm—"

"You hear me, silly bitch? I said—"

"And did you hear me, you punk-ass, shrimp tandoori dick, motherfucker?"

The phone got quiet, Tori knowing he was on the other end blowing up like a puffer fish, ready to explode; she could hear him breathing. She continued. "You right, I was a silly bitch for letting you beat me. But bet your black ass, that won't ever happen again."

"Oh no?"

"No."

"No?" Ja'Van yelled.

"Hell no!" Tori countered.

"Say that when I come for your ass."

Again Tori glanced up at the windows and the door. "Fool, you don't even know where I am," she shouted into the phone. "If you do, tell me. Come on, punk, trick-ass bitch!" Tori said, intentionally enraging him. "Tell me where I am so you can come get me."

There was a momentary pause.

"That's right!" Tori said. "Weak ass, limp dick, pink-pantie wearing hoe!"

"It's all right," Ja'Van said, his voice now calm. "You gotta come home, bitch. And I'll be in your crib, like I am right now, on the sofa, watching motherfucking Xfinity. And when you walk in that door I'm gonna tie you face down to the bed and whoop your ass till you bleed."

Ja'Van ended the call, leaving Tori staring down at the phone, her mouth hanging open, her body covered in a cold sweat.

She punched another number into her phone, held it to her ear.

"Hello, Nate. Yes..." she said, trying to smile, while at the same time, wiping a frightened tear from her cheek. "I changed my mind about that bagel."

29

When her doorbell rang, Tori answered it wearing jeans that clung to her curves perfectly, a form-fitting pink sweater and plain white tennis shoes.

"You look beautiful," Nate said, standing in front of her, wearing a crisp spring-weight gray suit. He held out his hand as if wanting to shake.

Tori hesitated a moment, reminded herself of her reason for standing there, then opened her arms and said, "We go back too far for handshakes, man." She wrapped her arms around Nate's neck, not hating the feeling of his body against hers as much as she thought she might've.

Nate took Tori to a tiny café on Rush street: chairs and bistro tables sat out front, shaded by old oak trees. He ordered: café au lait and a chocolate croissant for her, and a regular brewed dark roast and a multi grain bagel for him. He took their order to go, and they walked sipping their drinks and pulling pieces of their pastries from their small white, wax paper bags.

Nate had asked her what really brought her back to Chicago.

Tori told Nate she needed a new start. "Things aren't going well right now. Haven't been for a while. You know, money and stuff. Can't find work." She glanced at Nate, then away.

"But the gym last night is not cheap. How do you—"

"The friend I'm apartment sitting for—It's her membership."

"Got it," Nate said.

They walked for quite a while longer under the sunny sky, an occasional breeze coming off Lake Michigan just blocks away, neither one of them saying a word, Nate's attention seemingly held hostage by something else.

"Everything all right?" Tori asked, looking at Nate concerned.

He turned to her as though just realizing she was there and smiled. "Sorry. Head is spinning with stuff."

"What stuff?"

"Not sure if it's a threat or not, but you ever have a crazy person after you?"

Tori's eyes lit up a bit. "Boy, if you only knew," she said, laughing in spite of herself.

"I think I might have something like that going on now, but...it's only because I deserve it," Nate said, popping another piece of bagel into his mouth.

"You deserve a psycho stalker after you? I don't get it."

"All the bad stuff I've done in the past—this guy is part of that. It's one of the reasons I'm trying to fix those things. If I change, maybe the crazy stuff won't happen anymore." Nate stopped walking, as did Tori. "It's the reason I asked you out. I want to apologize."

"For what?" There were so many horrible things he had done to her she wasn't sure to which he referred.

"For everything. Just everything. And especially the thing in California: you know what I'm talking about."

"Yeah," Tori said, under her breath. "I know."

"The situation you're in now: you having to come back to Chicago—that have to do with what I did?"

She nodded her head, wondering how he could be so foolish as to think it didn't. "Yeah, Nate. It does."

He started walking again, Tori following his lead. Nate looked away, shook and frowned, as if scolding himself. "Like I said, I'm trying to be a better man now. Not be so...I don't know... vengeful. Is that the right word?"

"Yeah, that's definitely the right word."

Nate laughed, his smile genuine one, like he was really happy to see Tori. "I want to help you get back on your feet. Is that okay?"

"Of course it's okay, Nate. Let's make it easy. You took a million dollars from me, so you can start by giving that back, then stack another mill on top for pain and suffering," Tori said, smiling, but dead-ass serious.

Nate smiled with her, even laughed a little as if Tori was kidding. "I'm trying to be a better man, but I'm not trying that hard." He reached into his pocket, pulled out a neat square of crisp, new hundred dollar bills, held together by a platinum money clip. He looked over his shoulder, quickly counted out the seven bills that were there and folded them. "I'm going to check on some things. I think I might be able to give you some good news next time I see you."

"There's going to be a next time?" Tori smiled, knowing Monica would approve of that news.

"Like I said, I wanna make sure you're good. So yes, there will be a next time." Till then, will this keep you?" Nate handed Tori the roll of seven hundred dollars.

"Sure, this'll work. And I appreciate the bagel, but next time how about we do dinner?"

30

Lewis hadn't given up on Eva even though she had dismissed him so easily. He rang her phone like crazy until she finally picked up. After she said hello, Lewis said: "Just meet me. I can explain everything, and I really want to see Tammi. I miss both of you," Lewis begged, his cell phone clutched tight in his hand.

Eva rejected his request, told him there was nothing more to talk about. When Lewis told her that he felt their time together as a family and the commitment they had shared was worth at least fifteen minutes of her time, she went silent on the phone.

"Eva...you there?"

"Okay," she said. "I'll meet you."

She had chosen a public place—Chipotle in Hyde Park— because she said she didn't want to be alone with him, and she said she wouldn't cry if people were around.

She had been wrong about that; five minutes into Lewis's argument, the tears started to run down Eva's face. She grabbed stray napkins that had been sitting on the table before they had gotten there and dabbed them against her cheeks.

People had already started looking, throwing glances at Eva and Lewis in between bites of their burritos. He saw people whispering, but cared absolutely nothing about that, considering he was about to lose the woman he loved.

"We were living together," Lewis said. "We were making a home—a good home for our family, and now you wanna just leave?"

Eva shook her head, strands of her black hair falling in her face, as she dabbed more of the wet napkins to her cheeks. "When I thought it was just some random event, something neither of us had anything to do with it, those men doing that to me was the hardest thing in my life I've ever dealt with, but I believe I was handling it. But finding out you're the reason it happened, *and* that you could've saved me from it if you just would've been honest. "No Lewis," Eva said. "No matter how much I love you, I can't ever come back. I'm sorry." She grabbed her purse, slid out the booth and was about to hurry away when Lewis stood and caught her by the wrist.

"You can't go. My little girl...you're her mother now. She loves you. I love you." He felt more stares on him: people listening to everything he said. "I'm so sorry, but nothing like that will ever happen again."

"You don't understand, Lewis. It's not the assault that hurts so much, it's the lie," she said, gently taking her hand from him and walking away.

31

After work, Nate stood at the bedroom window, still wearing his work slacks, a bathrobe thrown over his white undershirt. He stared outside, felt reassured, hoping his wife would feel the same and would stop worrying.

This morning after Lewis gave them the news of Ford's escape, Monica wouldn't stop pacing in and out of the living room, wouldn't stop insinuating that Nate cared nothing for their son.

"All right!" Nate said, springing from the sofa, clicking off the curved 70" Sony, mounted over the fireplace. He grabbed his cell off the coffee table and dialed a number.

"Who are you calling?" Monica said, standing halfway between the living and dining rooms.

"Someone who should help you feel safer."

Whenever Nate needed sensitive information gathered, whenever there were matters he felt were dangerous or needed a certain forceful delicacy he was incapable of, Nate called in his private investigator, Abbey Kurt.

The woman served several years in the military, both in the states and abroad. She served five years on the police force, and a couple with the Illinois Bureau of Investigation, before leaving to start her own service. Nate valued her commitment to him so much and in turn, paid her so handsomely that for the past eight years, he's been her only client, making herself available at all hours of the day for his potential emergencies.

Now, peering back through the blinds down to the front walkway of the house, he saw the 5'4", lean, very compact and muscular woman, wearing a tailored pants suit, speaking into a walkie-talkie, as tiny droplets of rain started to fall from the sky. An automatic rifle was slung over her shoulder, as well as what Nate believed, were a pair of night vision goggles.

He turned away from the window when he heard the bathroom door open. Monica walked out in a nightgown, toweling her hair dry. She still appeared more worried than Nate ever wanted to see her.

He held out his hand. "Come here."

"Nate there's nothing you can say that'll make me think staying here with that man on the loose is the right thing to do."

"Just come here, please."

Monica dropped the bath towel on the bed and walked barefoot over to her husband.

"They arrived and set up while you were showering. Look out there and tell me what you see," Nate said, gently urging her forward with a hand on the small of her back. "Go on."

Monica peered out between the blinds. "Looks like a high school student, dressed as a high school principal."

"Very funny. That's my private investigator. You see what she's toting?"

"A big gun."

"Exactly. A big, automatic, military issued gun. Her, and the three other men and one other woman she brought to guard our home," Nate said, letting the blinds fall closed. "If Ford is out there, and if he's thinking about trying to come here again, I promise, he will get cut in half before he steps foot on our property." Nate stared oddly at Monica. "But it's still not enough. You still don't feel safe, do you?"

"Yes, Nate. I feel safe now," Monica said, easing away from him.

"No you don't. I can feel it and I can see it all over your face."

"Okay, you're right, and I'm wondering why aren't you worried about the same?"

"I told you, I'm not fleeing my home because—"

"Because someone's trying to kill us in it?"

Nate spun around after having paced away from Monica. "Then leave!" he said throwing up his hands, frustrated. "I'm sorry. I didn't mean it like that."

"I know you didn't."

"I meant, if you don't feel safe here, you can stay elsewhere till Ford is caught."

"You should come too."

"How many times must—"

"Then I'm taking my son."

"No, you're not."

Monica stood, staring at Nate from across the bedroom, wondering how a man could be so arrogant that he was blind to putting both his and his son's lives at risk.

"Are you sure?"

"If you don't feel safe in your own home, then you shouldn't remain here."

"Fine. I'll start considering places tomorrow."

32

The rain was irritating, almost maddening. It saturated Freddy's coat, making it hang heavy on his narrow shoulders. The hood drooped down over his forehead, forcing him to lift it every few moments so that he could continue to watch the police car that sat curbside in front of Kia's house.

He didn't know what time it was. He didn't have a watch, and the cell phone he had taken off the girl he robbed earlier, he tossed, because the battery had long ago gone dead.

Freddy stared out from behind the bushes lining the house next door to Kia's. Since he had left her and that man dead on the grass, he had been hearing her voice whispering in his head, seeing her face, staring at him lovingly, begging him to come back and see about her.

Whether walking down the street, hood pulled over his head, or ducking into an alleyway when he spotted a police car rolling down the street, he'd shut his eyes and then open them, but the image of her face never blanked away. It was always there, one thin red line of blood crawling down the center of her face. But Kia wanted to talk to him, make sure he was okay, and she wanted to apologize for keeping their child a secret.

Freddy took a step out from behind the bushes, still shrouded in the shadow of the house, so that the cop dozing behind the wheel of the cruiser could not see him. He scanned the area where Kia's car had been, thinking there might've been a chance his son was still there, that he might've fallen out of the car during the investigation and had just been overlooked, like a key or a coin slipping unnoticed out of someone's pocket. But Freddy didn't see the boy.

He took another step toward the street. He wondered what the baby's name had been, wondered what he looked like when he smiled, wondered what he smelled like, and what it would've been like to pull him close, snuggle him in the crook of his neck, feel him squirm and hear him laugh.

"No!" Freddy said, trying to shake the thoughts from his head. "They're gone!" But only Kia was dead. The boy was still alive. His son was still breathing, and all of a sudden, Freddy was overcome with dread and guilt, knowing the baby was most likely surrounded by strangers, wondering where his mother and father were. Then again, he could've been in the back seat of that police car Freddy was staring at that moment. They could've set him there, given him a bottle, planted him as a trap for Freddy, because they knew no good and caring father would just leave his son on the side of the street to die. A good father would eventually come back for him when he realized it was probably bad to have killed the mother.

Rain running down his face, Freddy smeared it away with a hand so that he could see. He cut across the grass away from the police car then stepping onto the sidewalk, he turned back. His hands pushed down into the big pockets of the coat, the hood shielding his face, he walked with purpose and caution toward the car.

As he neared its backside, he could hear that the car was not running and he could see the haze of dash lights from inside. Five feet away, he hesitated a moment seeing no movement inside, just the back of an officer's head lying against the headrest.

Across the slippery wet grass, Freddy stepped up alongside the passenger side, looked inside the back seat, expecting to see his son. When he did not see him there, he felt himself getting anxious, but calmed some, knowing the officer would probably know where his boy was. The cop would have to tell him, so Freddy could tell his son he wasn't alone and unloved. Freddy knew what being abandoned and scared felt like and he had to make sure his son never experienced those feelings.

Freddy leaned forward, peaked into the car. Both front windows were rolled partially down—the driver's side more than the passenger's. Inside he noticed the officer was sleeping. He walked around the back of the car, staying low, his right hand finding the gun on the bottom of his coat's big pocket. He pulled it, but told himself he would not use it. He had killed a state trooper last year when he was on his way to Atlanta then buried another cop while in Georgia, but that was only because he had to. Still, at times, he saw in his head, both dead men's bodies: one on the road, the other crumpled at the bottom of the ditch Joni helped him dig. This officer he wouldn't kill, Freddy promised himself, as he pulled the gun from his pocket. He just wanted to know where his son was. When the officer told him, Freddy would make the cop take him to his baby so Freddy could apologize and reunite with his child.

Looking inside the car, he noticed the officer was female, her face laying to a side, her shiny black hair pulled back into a bun, a walky-talky clipped to her vest—crackly radio chatter spilling low out of it; she was breathing and sleeping peacefully. Freddy lifted the gun and stuck the barrel into the opening of the window, not because he meant to hurt her, only because this, he knew, would be the incentive she needed to tell him what he wanted to know.

Holding the gun pointed at the officer, rain falling even harder around him, pelting the metal roof of the police car like millions of little bullets, Freddy tapped on the glass with a knuckle. When the cop stirred, Freddy whispered loudly over the rattle of rain: "Hey!"

The cop opened her eyes, blinked and froze as though she knew exactly what was happening. Freddy could feel the energy surrounding them become a thousand times more tense.

"Look," Freddy said, pushing the gun deep into the window's opening, where his knuckles bumped against the glass. "I just wanna ask you some—"

But the officer whirled, and before Freddy could react, he saw her hand reach down then come up. There was an explosion of light, a cannon-like pop, the sound of metal tearing and a pain so intense, he believed he would lose consciousness. Almost at the same time, he reacted, squeezing the trigger of his gun: another explosion of white light and sound, then the interior windows of the car went red with the blood of the officer, pieces of skull and brain clinging to the dash and windows.

Freddy stumbled away from the car, limping fast as he could go, his hand pressed to his thigh then fell in the middle of the street. His head whirling, he saw lighted squares appear in the façade of two houses. He pulled himself to his feet, and quickly leapt away.

33

She showered, toweled off and stood naked in the bathroom mirror staring contemptuously at herself. All of her questions had been answered, seeing that woman pleasure the father of Daphanie's son. Why had Trevor been treating Daphanie so awfully? Why had they made love so infrequently? And why did it seem he could've just as easily tossed her out on the street, not caring how he was going to raise their infant son alone? He was not alone; the woman who was supposedly there only to help care for Nat was taking care of Trevor too.

Daphanie wondered just how much more of this she could take: how many more lashes of the whip was Trevor going to inflict upon her before forgiving what she had done.

She rolled out several sheets of tissue and dried her eyes, staring at the bathroom door, not wanting to step out into the bedroom with Trevor.

They had seen each other several times after the event: Trevor walking past Daphanie in the hallway, saying nothing to her half an hour ago when she walked out of Nat's room, after kissing him goodnight. She wasn't even sure if Jennifer informed him that the two of them had been seen by her engaging in their disgusting act.

Daphanie pulled her night gown off the hook on the back of the door, slipped into it, and after a deep breath, opened the door and stepped out into the adjoining bedroom to see Trevor, having already showered and wearing pajama bottoms, inside the blankets, reading a paperback.

She stood at the foot of the bed, staring at him, saying nothing.

He appeared to ignore her for as long as he could then set the book face down in his lap. "What is it?"

Daphanie swallowed the lump lodged in her throat, knowing each word out of her mouth was another straw on the weak-legged camel's back, another crack in the dam, that additional pound on the doomed plane that was already carrying too much cargo to stay in the air. "I'm sleeping on the sofa tonight." She walked around the bed and reached for her pillow to take with her.

"Leave it," he said, already taking up his book and reading again, as if nothing she said mattered. "You're sleeping right here as you're supposed to."

Angered, Daphanie said, "You've been having sex with that woman…that prostitute," she said loud enough for Jennifer to hear through the walls "And then you let the slut—"

"Lower your voice," Trevor said calmly into the pages of the book, still not looking up. "And come to bed."

"You let that skank care for our son!"

"I said, lower your voice and come to bed!" Trevor yelled, slamming the book down beside him.

"Why? We aren't fucking! The two of you are. Why can't she sleep here and I take her room?"

"Because I say you can't!"

"I'm your son's mother, yet you treat me worse than some trick you pulled off the street. You're allowing her to do everything I'm supposed to be doing for my child," Daphanie said, feeling that she was breaking down and hating herself for showing Trevor how weak she was. "Are you testing her to see if you can all together replace me as Nat's mother? What if something happens to you?"

Trevor looked away, as if for the first time realizing just how terribly he was treating her.

"Answer me!" Daphanie screamed.

"You're his mother. You always will be," Trevor said, looking her in the eyes. "And God forbid, something happens to me, I've taken steps to make sure he'll be taken care of properly."

"What does that mean, Trevor?"

"It means what I said it means. Now get in bed. I'm tired and I have to work tomorrow."

Daphanie said, "You're doing this for no other reason than to punish me."

"You're right." He reached over, clicked off the bedside lamp, casting the room in darkness. Rolling onto his side, pulling the blanket over his shoulder, he said, "And if you don't like it, you're more than welcome to leave."

34

The next day, Monica sat in the back office of her clothing store, checking her watch again, waiting for her manager, Tabatha, to walk in.

Earlier at home, she had served Nate coffee after pouring milk into little Nathaniel's bowl of cereal.

"Thank you, Mommy," the child said, spooning a heaping serving into his mouth.

"You're welcome baby." Monica looked up at Nate across the table. Bringing his coffee cup down, he smiled and picked up his tablet to read the morning news. "Eat up," he told his son. "We want you to be big and strong when you grow up."

"Didn't know what I was thinking last night," Nate said to Monica. "I'm sure one of my downtown properties is vacant. I'll have it checked out. You can stay in one of them till this thing with Ford is over."

"Thanks," Monica said, setting her coffee cup into the dishwasher. "But what if he's able to look up properties in your name. What if he can find me that way? I'll just get a place. I don't want to take any chances."

"Don't be ridiculous. The man doesn't even have a high school diploma. He's half crazy. What makes you think—"

"What man, Daddy?" Nathaniel said, milk dripping down over his chin.

"Nothing you need to worry about, lil' guy."

Monica leaned over Nate, kissed his lips. "If safe equals ridiculous, then I wish you'd be more ridiculous. I wish you'd go insane. I have to go to work."

In her office, she thought about her husband's nonchalant attitude and prayed that his instincts were true. It was a frightening

147

thing that was happening, but Nate's carless response to it would only strengthen her position regarding her custody suit. She could hear Joyla's voice asking the judge what kind of man would demand his son remain in a house he knew was unsafe? What kind of father would put his son in harm's way when he was warned that a killer was on the loose and gunning for him?

Monica's office door opened. Tabatha stepped in surprised by Monica's presence.

"Just got remarried and so sick of Nate already you're leaving the house early. I told you this thing you're doing is a mistake."

"I need to stay with you for a while."

"How long and why?" Tabatha said, setting her purse down on her desk.

"It's complicated. A day or two," Monica said, knowing it might've taken as long as two weeks for her plan to even start to develop. "It shouldn't take much longer than that."

"What shouldn't?" Tabatha asked, closing in on Monica and staring in her face. "Is he hitting you?" She reached to brush the bang that was falling over Monica's left eye, out of the way.

Monica swatted Tabatha's hand. "No, he's not hitting me! You know I don't play that. You think I'm crazy?"

"You remarried Nate Kenny, that's all I have to say. Now I'll ask you again? Why do you need to stay with me?"

"We had an argument last night," Monica lied. "Came out his mouth in a way I didn't like, and I need for him to see that I'm not there because I have to be, but because I chose to."

Tabatha stared at Monica, her lips pursed into an expression that said she didn't believe a word her friend said. "Whatever. Move in whenever you want."

35

Daphanie sat down on a park bench with her son, hoisting him into her arm, kissing his cheek, believing the hell she was going through was worth it just to hear him laugh.

This morning, she made Trevor's breakfast, served him and sat across the table from him, watching him eat, as though they were happily married. It was what he demanded.

Daphanie didn't mind so much. At least the nanny wasn't there. Jennifer's ass slept in, and Daphanie wouldn't care if she never came out of her room.

Wearing a shirt and tie, Trevor crunched on a piece of toast and looked over at Daphanie. "What do you have planned today?" he asked.

Daphanie was shocked by the question. He hadn't inquired about her day in months; he never cared what she was up to. As long as she dropped whatever she was doing the moment he called and ran to do his bidding, he was fine.

"I…" she stammered. She was on-call for Monica, but of course she could not say that. "I…I don't know. Was just hoping to spend some time with Nat."

"Don't call him that," Trevor said, frowning. "His name is Nate. *Nate!*" Trevor said, pronouncing the name as though Daphanie was an imbecile. "If you can't—"

"I'm sorry. I was hoping to spend time with Nate."

Trevor sipped from his mug of steaming coffee and set it down. "It's going to be a nice day today. I think it might be a good idea if you took him to the park."

An intense excitement bubbled up in Daphanie, so much that she was near jumping from her chair and clapping her hands. She calmed herself and asked: "Alone? That woman doesn't have to come, does she?"

Trevor went about eating the last of his eggs, sopping up the running yolk with the corner of his toast and popping it into his mouth. He chewed, sipped more of his coffee, making Daphanie wait, then said, "No. I think you and our son could use some time alone."

Daphanie stood smiling, leaned across the table and kissed Trevor. She had no intention of kissing him anywhere else, but he turned his face so that her lips could land on his cheek.

"Thank you so much!" Daphanie said, elated.

He nodded, wiped his mouth again, stood from the table and said, "You're welcome," once he was halfway out the door.

The day was a beautiful one as Trevor predicted, and Daphanie sat on the park bench bouncing Nat on her hip, thinking of earlier this morning when Jennifer walked into the boy's room and asked Daphanie what she was doing.

"Dressing Nate. I'm taking him to the park."

Standing in the doorway, a hand on the frame as if to stop Daphanie, Jennifer said, "No you're not."

Daphanie finished pulling Nat's pants up, lay him in the crib then turned to deal with Jennifer. Walking toward the younger woman, Jennifer first looked shocked then narrowed her eyes as though she wouldn't have been afraid of a fight if it came to that.

"I get it," Daphanie said. "You got your claws in a man that makes some money and now you're able to put to use those exquisite dick sucking skills you've been practicing since twelve years old."

Jennifer's eyes blossomed wide and her mouth dropped open.

"Understand this, I am and always will be the only mother of that child," Daphanie said, pointing to Nat. "And although Trevor's letting you blow him in the baby's room, fuck him on the kitchen floor or eat his ass in the bathroom, I'm still the one he chooses to share his bed with. Now if you'd excuse me, I'm going to finish dressing my son."

"Say whatever you want about me, old hag, but you still ain't taking that baby out of this house," Jennifer found the courage to say.

Hoisting Nat up onto her chest, Daphanie turned to Jennifer. "Why don't you call Trevor and let him tell you why you don't know what the fuck you're talking about?"

Now, smiling in the warm sun, Daphanie's cell phone rang. She set Nat back in his stroller, saw Trevor's name on the screen and answered it. "Hey, I'm at the park with Nat...Nate. How's your day?"

"It's good," Trevor said, Daphanie unable to determine what his emotional state was by his even tone. "Come by the bank. Pick me up. It's lunchtime."

Daphanie was a little shook by the strange request. He's never asked that before. "Everything okay? Your car working?"

"Yeah. Just pick me up in fifteen minutes. I'll be out front."

The phone went dead, and even though it was another demand from Trevor—not caring that she was enjoying herself with the time she barely ever got with her son—Daphanie had a smile on her face, imagining the three of them having lunch together.

Fifteen minutes later, Daphanie pulled to the curb in front of the downtown bank Trevor managed. He opened the back door of the Infiniti, kissed his son, had a short baby-talk conversation with him then climbed up front, not looking at or speaking to Daphanie.

Daphanie turned to him: "So where to?"

"Just drive for the moment."

In the time she's known Trevor, she's learned not to question a request of his.

"Don't you want to put your seatbelt on?" Daphanie asked, thinking it odd that whenever he drove he would buckle up, but as a passenger, he always chose to ride without the restraint.

"Just drive, please," Trevor said.

She pulled the car slowly into the flow of afternoon traffic.

Daphanie hadn't driven for two blocks down Wabash, when Trevor told her to head back to the bank. She was at a red light and turned to him.

"Why? I thought you said we were going to lunch."

Trevor was not looking at her, but out the front windshield. "I said it was lunchtime. Not that I wanted lunch. Just take me back."

Outside the bank, Daphanie shifted the car in park and turned in her seat to face Trevor. "What's going on?"

"I considered what you asked for last night, and I've decided to give it to you."

"What are you talking about, Trevor?"

"From now on Jennifer will sleep with me and you can stay in the guest bedroom."

Daphanie sunk in her seat, feeling what little ground she had on the intruder had just been snatched out from under her. "Trevor, no. I didn't mean to say—"

"But you did say." He stared right in her eyes. "You did say that was what you wanted. Correct?"

Daphanie sadly nodded. "Yes."

Trevor leaned over his seat, said goodbye to his son, tapping the little boy on the tip of his nose. He pushed open his door, but before stepping out, said: "Have all your clothes out the drawers and closet and into the other room by the time I get home, please."

Daphanie gasped, wanting to say something to stop what she knew might be the change that would ultimately have her losing her baby. The door slammed shut and her cell phone rang. She answered it.

"Daphanie…Monica. Be at the townhouse to pick Tori up in half an hour."

36

From the passenger side of Nate's Bentley, Monica dropped her cell phone back into her purse, before he could see that she had just hung up from a call. Nate climbed in the car after filling it with gas, and smiled at her when he reached to start the car. "Still excited?" Nate asked.

"How can I be when I have no idea of where we're going?" she said as he pulled off onto the street.

Nate had come by Monica's store unannounced again, was standing in the center of the floor holding a bouquet of flowers, little Nathaniel standing beside him, when she came out of her office with Tabatha. Walking behind her, Tabatha spotted him from down the hallway—before Nate laid eyes on either of them—and out the corner of her mouth said, "Tired of this fool dropping by here whenever he wants."

"My husband is not a fool, but I know, Tab," Monica said back, seeing that Nate had finally spotted them.

"You need to tell him something," Tabatha whispered, the two of them closing to within twenty feet of Nate.

"I said I know, Tab," Monica said, smiling, holding out her arms to hug Nate as she approached.

"These are for you," Nate said, holding up the beautiful gathering of flowers.

"Yeah Mommy, those are for you," Nathaniel said.

The child being there was the only reason Monica hadn't gone off about him just popping in. She bent down, hugged the boy, nuzzled his neck, lifted him up and spun him around. "And I love them. Almost as much as you."

Now from the passenger seat of his car, Monica watched as Nate drove through doors of a wrought iron security fence, and onto a huge property with neatly trimmed grass that rolled over tiny hills, leading to a large white stone home, four columns standing tall in front of it.

"Where are we?" Monica said.

"Patience, baby," Nate said, grabbing Monica's left hand, bringing it to his mouth and kissing it. He parked the car in the circular driveway in front of the mansion's door and shut off the engine. "C'mon, get out and I'll show you."

They walked up the path to the wide stairway of the home: Nate and Monica on either side of the boy, holding the child's hands.

The front door was huge: a beautiful dark wood framing a thick, gold trimmed window. Nate turned the knob on the door and pushed it open.

"What are you doing?" Monica said. "You can't just walk into someone's house."

"After you, my dear."

Monica walked into a foyer larger than most people's entire living room. The floor was marble, black, shiny and so clear, she could see her reflection underfoot, staring back up at her. Further in was as spiral staircase and hanging over it was a gigantic crystal chandelier. The empty house stretched out far and wide in front of her, doors leading to who knew where on all sides of the front and dinning rooms. The ceilings were incredibly high, adorned with the most ornate molding, the walls covered with a tan, parchment-like wallpaper that Monica could not resist but reach out and touch.

"You have to tell me now," Monica said, turning to Nate. "What are we doing here? Whose house is this?"

Nate looked down at Nathaniel. "Why don't you tell her?"

"Yours, Mommy. Daddy bought it for you."

Monica stared oddly at Nate. "Why would you—"

"You just moved back in, and you're leaving me again so that we're living apart. I can't have that."

"So you bought us a new house?" Monica said, trying to sound mad. But turning and taking another look at the beautiful space, trying not to imagine herself living there.

"Yes," Nate said. "Tell me you don't love it."

"I...I don't not like it," she said, doing everything to hold back the smile coming to her face.

"You were right. There were some bad things that happened in our home. We need a fresh one to go along with our fresh start."

If this were only true, Monica thought. If only Nate was the sincere man he was trying to portray, she could relax, enjoy this—love this. But...she turned to him, the smile mostly gone from her face. "I'm assuming we can't move in now."

"I pushed as much as I can. I have a contract on it, but with closing and all of that...no sooner than two weeks from now."

"Then I still have to leave. I'll be staying with Tabatha."

"Or we can just leave. Like I said, go somewhere until this house is ready. "C'mon," Nate said, taking Monica by the shoulders. "We can go away, let the police do what they do, catch Ford, and when that's over, we come back, move in, and everything will be perfect."

"You know I can't just leave with what's happening with my stores."

"And I told you, I'll help you take care of that. You trust me when I tell you that, right?"

Nate had been working very hard to gain that trust, and if she didn't know that he was about to sleep with his ex-mistress, Monica would've foolishly and eagerly bought all the shit Nate was selling. But having that information was what made it hard to continue to lie, at least convincingly. Nate read the answer on Monica's face before she could speak it.

He nodded sadly, squeezed her shoulders, let her go and took a step back. "Not a problem, but I'm not giving up on us: on this," Nate said, glancing over at Nathaniel, who was running wildly up and down the length of the living room. "You hear me?"

"Yeah," Monica said, watching the boy she knew she would be soon taking from him. "I hear you."

37

From the moment she shut the door on the car, Tori sensed the Daphanie chick had another attitude, or hadn't shaken the one it appeared she had from last time she chauffeured Tori around. All that did was piss Tori off, considering she was the one doing the heavy lifting in Monica's little scheme.

"Where are we going?" Tori asked.

Daphanie shifted the car in gear and drove off without answering.

"It's a simple question. Why can't you answer it? Where are we going?"

Daphanie slammed on the brakes, nearly jerking Tori out of her seat.

"You knowing or not; does it make any fucking difference? You're going to have to do whatever Monica says anyway, or do you think you have a choice?"

"I—" Tori began.

"What?" Daphanie said, cutting her off. "She has total control over you; you damn near have to ask her for permission to take a piss."

"Why the hell you going off on me? I just asked a question and you bitchin me out."

"Because I'm tired of you acting like you got a say in this. You are nobody, you mean nothing, and you're only here because your ass is desperate," Daphanie said. "Whatever she tells you to do, your going to do it, because the only other choice you have is to tell Monica to go to hell and leave whatever you're trying so desperately to get from her on the table, and we both know you're not going to do that. Now are you gonna say 'fuck Monica' and get out my car, which is what you should do, or are you going to shut up and let me take you where Monica wants you to go?"

Tori shook her head, crossed her arms, and said, "Drive."

Daphanie stuck the key in the ignition, but didn't start it, just sat there, her head lowered.

Tori glanced over at her. "What? You haven't gone off on me enough? Trying to think of more shit to say before we leave. I said you can drive."

"I'm sorry," Daphanie said, facing Tori. "What I said…I wasn't even talking about you. I was talking about myself. You haven't done anything to me. So the only person I have to blame for my situation is myself."

Tori sat up a little in the car seat. "Don't be so hard. We've all been a little stupid, that's why all three of us are here."

"Yeah, but not as stupid as I've been."

"I got taken for a million dollars. Who does that?"

Shaking her head, Daphanie said, "Nothing compared to what I lost."

"Really? What is that?"

Daphanie filled Tori in on the brilliant plan Nate ran on her to get her to give up her son, as well as telling Tori about the lunchtime announcement Trevor just sprung on her.

Before Tori had heard all of that, she really couldn't stand Daphanie, but after hearing the mess the poor girl had gotten herself into, Tori's heart was starting to break for her.

"So that's why you're playing errand girl for Monica?"

Daphanie nodded "She's going to help me get back my son."

"Really?" Tori said, sounding unconvinced. "Monica's gonna do all the things you haven't tried yet?"

"I tried everything. I've gone to every lawyer, investigated every loophole, tried to negotiate with Trevor: would've given both my eyes if that would've gotten my son back."

"And Wonder Woman Monica is gonna do more?" Tori said, still sounding skeptical.

"She has money and—"

"So Trevor will allow Monica to buy you custody of your son? All I know of him is what you just told me, but he doesn't sound like he'd go for that."

Daphanie shook her head, and under her breath said: "No, that really doesn't sound like him."

"So Monica will pay lawyers to tell you what you've already heard? Cause you said you been to all of them, right. And they told you..."

"Contract is airtight," Daphanie said, her voice even lower than before.

"You can't really think that woman is going to go harder to rescue your baby than you already have, especially considering you were one of the two bitches Monica found out used to fuck her husband? I mean, I hate to say it, Daphanie, but I think you're being played."

Daphanie pressed back in her seat, looking helpless, shaking her head.

Tori stared, watched a tear roll down the side of Daphanie's face. Tori spied a travel pack of Kleenex in the dash cubby, yanked one and held it in front of Daphanie, which she took and blotted her cheek.

"What did I do?" Daphanie moaned.

"Told a man the baby you were carrying wasn't his and got caught. You fucked up."

More tears fell, and Daphanie softly banged her skull against the car's padded headrest.

"So what am I supposed to do?" Daphanie said, pulling herself up to face Tori. "Just give up?"

"Absolutely not. First, you need to tell Monica you're not gonna be her bitch anymore, and if she doesn't have a real plan to get your kid back, then you won't be able to wait. You might have to just take what's yours."

"Okay," Daphanie said, dabbing a ball of the wadded up Kleenex under her jaw, drying the tears. "What do you mean by 'take'? How am I supposed to—?"

"I don't know."

"I don't have any money, so how—"

"I don't know," Tori said, shaking her head.

"If Trevor has the custody papers I signed—"

Throwing up her hands, Tori yelled, "I don't know!" She stared at Daphanie who stared right back, not angry or startled, but desperate and needing to know whatever possible path she could take to winning her son back.

"My bad for yelling. All I know is, if I had a child and someone took him from *me*—my fault or not—I wouldn't be able to live. If some man was holding my baby hostage, I'd do everything short of…" Tori paused, staring unblinking into her imagination. "No…there's nothing, absolutely nothing I wouldn't do."

"I don't know what that means," Daphanie sniffled. "But this is killing me right now."

"Then maybe it's time you do what it takes to live."

38

Tori following just behind her, Daphanie yanked both the glass doors of Monica's store open, as though her body, or the anger surrounding it was too big to fit through just one of them. She had known Monica owned this store—which was beautiful, Daphanie thought and hated to admit—but she had never actually walked into it.

"Can I help you?" a tall, thin black man with a sexier walk than Daphanie's, asked. He wore pink leggings and a matching tiny pink hat balanced on his head just so.

"Where's Monica?" Daphanie said, her tone very direct.

The man leaned back, pursed his lips and pressed the tips of his forefinger and thumb together. "May I ask why you'd like to see her?" Roland said.

Daphanie glanced around the store. There were only three customers there, but they were all looking her way as if expecting her to make a scene. "Because I fucking said! You taking me to her, or do I have to find her myself?"

Roland nodded, snapping a finger at her. "Got it," he said, pursing his lips even more. "Follow me, girlfriend."

Daphanie looked back at Tori. Tori gave her a look that said she was following Daphanie's lead. Daphanie walked down the long corridor, stopped behind the man, and waited as he knocked on the door.

Waiting beside her, Tori leaned over and whispered in Daphanie's ear. "Don't lose your nerve. Give it to her good."

"I got this," Daphanie said, nudging Tori off of her.

"What, Roland?" Monica's voice came muffled from behind the office door. "I told you I was busy."

"You have...guests that want to see you. And one of them is pretty insistent."

When the doorknob turned, Roland stepped aside. The door opened. Monica gasped and her eyes bulged.

"I'm sorry, Monica," Roland said. "I tried—"

Paying no mind to the man, Monica grabbed Tori by the shoulder and yanked her in before Roland could finish apologizing.

Slamming the door, she said: "What are you doing here? Have you lost your mind?"

"Whoa! Why you yelling at me?" Tori said, holding up her hands, brushing Monica away. "Daphanie's here to see you. She's the one that's driving, remember?"

"Daphanie?" Monica said, staring surprised at her. "What are you thinking coming here and bringing her? Do you know—"

"Monica—" Daphanie started.

"No! You don't talk! Do you know what would happen if Nate saw either of you walking in or out of this store? You have any idea how often he just fucking pops up without calling? You have any idea, if he got wind of this, what he'd do?"

"Monica—" Daphanie attempted again to speak.

"No!" Monica barked, stopping her with a pointed finger. "He finds out what we're doing, he wouldn't tell us. He'd plot and plan on a way to end all three of us. Is that what you want?"

"No," Daphanie said. "You know it's not. But you're not doing anything for me, Monica."

"What?" Monica said. "Doing for you? I told you that would come after you take care of my business first."

"Exactly what is the 'that' you're talking about? I need to know, Monica. What more are you going to do to get my son back that I haven't done already?"

"Daphanie, I don't have time for this. I have too many other—"

"Then make time. I'm doing everything you ask of me. Why don't you do what I fucking ask of you for once."

"Mmmph! Heard that!" Tori said, then looked away when Monica shot an angry stare at her.

162

"Don't look at her. Look at me, Monica. Tell me," Daphanie said.

"Well, this minute, I can't tell you specifically what I'm doing, but—"

"Then tell me what you have planned."

Monica hesitated, looked as though she was trying to devise a plan of action that very moment.

"I think the only plans she's made is for me to try to fuck her husband," Tori said.

"Shut up, Tori!" Monica snapped.

"So nothing?" Daphanie said. "You've just been playing me?"

"No, Daphanie," Monica said, sounding sincerely apologetic. "But my situation is just more important than yours right now."

"Which means if I want my son back I'll have to wait for whenever you're ready to do something, or..." as Tori said, "...get him back myself."

Monica nodded sadly. "I'm sorry, but I'm afraid so."

More disappointed than angry, Daphanie nodded. "I don't have to say I never want your sorry ass to call me ever again, do I?"

"I guess not," Monica said, softly.

"Good." Daphanie turned, headed toward the exit and said, "Let's go, Tori."

When Daphanie pulled open the office door she was surprised by a handsome, brown-skinned, well-built man with a head full of long, unkempt curls. He was holding a fist up about to knock. Daphanie excused herself, walked past the man, but a few steps down the hallway, she noticed Tori wasn't behind her. She turned, looked back down the hall to see that the man had grabbed Tori's hand and was saying something to her.

"Tori," Daphanie called. "You coming or what?"

Tori hurried down the hall, then walked beside Daphanie.

"I thought the plan was for you to fuck Monica's husband," Daphanie said. "Not any guy that walks into her office."

"I'm sorry men think I'm fly. Don't hate," Tori smiled.

"Tori!"

Tori stopped, hearing her name called from down the hall. She turned to see Monica, her arms crossed, not looking particularly cheery. "I need to talk to you a moment."

39

This morning, Lewis had gotten up, put on a pair of nice slacks and shoes, a crisp white shirt, expensive Swiss watch and climbed into his Range Rover. All those items were either bought for him, or he had purchased with the money Nate Kenny had given him when they had first met: money that was given Lewis when he was paid to seduce Monica so that Nate might divorce her without paying the penalty of giving her half his millions. Since then, Lewis hadn't really bought any clothes or spent his money on expensive things. That wasn't who he was. All he wanted was a decent woman and a decent job to enable him to care properly for his daughter. He had neither of those things now, which was why he had been dropping by businesses: Home Depot, Dick's Sporting Goods, even a couple of Jewel's grocery stores: anyone he thought might hire him. All of them told him he could apply online, and each time he was told that, he walked away, his head hung, understanding the very reason why that was the new form of applying for gigs; none of the employers wanted to stare in the faces of the poor, desperate fools they chose to reject.

That afternoon, he dropped by Nate's brother, Tim's house. When he walked through the door, Layla ran over and jumped in his arms, nearly knocking him over, she was so excited to see him.

"When can I come home, Daddy?"

Lifting her up and hugging her, he looked thankfully over her shoulder at Tim for doing him such a favor. "I don't know, sweetheart. Soon, okay."

After his visit with his daughter, Tim walked Lewis out to his truck, Lewis telling him just how appreciative he was for what he was doing for him.

"It's no problem at all. She's wonderful and my kids love her," Tim said. "Is everything okay? Any word on this Ford character?"

"Things are as good as they can be," Lewis said. "But I'm tense: looking over my shoulder everywhere I go, thinking I'm seeing him, hoping if I ever do, it won't be after he's already pulled the trigger on me."

"Don't talk like that, Lewis," Tim said, putting a friendly hand on his shoulder. "Everything's going to be okay and Nate said..."

"Not really caring about anything your brother has to say right now."

"I know. He's had his days of being a complete asshole—most of his days, but you can go to him for anything. He feels responsible for all this."

"That's because he is."

"Yeah, I think he's starting to realize that, and trying to make up for it." Tim extended a hand, which Lewis took. He held it a little longer than a normal handshake, hating himself for the beggar he knew he'd sound like, but he also knew he could not afford the burden of pride.

"Would you happen to know anyone who's hiring to do *anything*? I just lost my gig and...you know."

The look on Tim's face said it all. "I'm sorry, but if I hear anything, you know I'll give you a call," Tim said.

He sat in his truck, watched as Tim walked back up and into his house. Lewis slid the key in the ignition, started it up, and watched as the gas needle lifted just a hair above "E", the gauge an almost direct reflection of his bank account.

He cut the engine off, slumped in his seat, realizing there was nowhere for him to go.

"You're nothing but a fucking loser!" Lewis breathed, feeling he was in no better place than he was years ago, when he was living in the projects, doing cuts at the barber shop for ten bucks a head. His hand gripping the steering wheel, he saw marks from the tattoos on his forearm peek out from under the cuff of the white collared shirt he wore, reminding him, no matter how he tried, he could never hide or forget who he really was: a thug from the streets, plucked from them due to a sequence of events and given access to a world where he didn't belong: a world where people had educations and money, where the women didn't abuse drugs while pregnant, and die of drug overdoses while attempting to raise their children—his world. His little time pretending to be the man Nate paid him to become must've still had Lewis thinking her deserved what only those smart, moneyed people had: loving partners, families and good jobs. He didn't deserve any of that shit, because he wasn't one of them.

Lewis released the steering wheel, banging his fist angrily on the dash, looking back at Tim's house, fearful of how he'd be able to afford all his little girl needed if he couldn't even find a fucking job. He dropped his face in his hand, squeezed his temples enough to cause him pain, breathed deeply and told himself to calm down, that something would come along if he just didn't lose faith.

Lewis's cell phone rang.

He glanced at it from under the visor of his hand, grabbed it from the center console, saw that it was Monica and quickly answered it, hoping that she was fine and this was not some cop calling him after finding her phone near her dead body. "Hello."

It was Monica asking if Lewis had heard any more about Freddy: if he had been caught, or if had reached out to Lewis again.

"I haven't spoken to him. It was always the hospital phone I called him on, and there's no telling where he could be now."

"That's what worries me," Monica said.

He sat on the phone, listening to her a second then said: "I'm leaving Tim's. I'm near your store. I can come by if you want," he said, believing she'd feel safer with him there, even if for a little bit.

After reaching the store, Lewis was told Monica was in her office. He walked down the corridor, was about to knock on her office door, when it flew open. Two women stood behind it: both attractive, but the shorter one definitely caught his attention, and he noticed she was staring up at him, too.

The older, taller woman stepped around him, leaving Lewis there, holding his hand out, hearing himself asking the young woman what her name was. Before she could answer, the woman down the hall yelled it and asked if she was going with her.

167

"Maybe I'll see you later, Tori," Lewis said, after she pulled her hand from his.

Tori didn't respond, just smiled, and hurried to catch her friend.

Monica walked up to Lewis, told him to have a seat in the office then she walked out into the hallway, calling the girl, saying she wanted a word with her.

Monica walked back in from the conversation and closed the door, shaking her head as though she had many more troubles to worry about than Freddy sniping for her.

"What's wrong?" Lewis said, sitting on the office sofa.

"Nothing."

"You sure."

"Those women that just left my office kinda work for me, and one of them just quit. And of course, this is the worst possible time. And because of the very sensitive nature of what she was doing for me, I have no idea of who I can call to replace her."

Knowing an opportunity when was sitting right in front of him, Lewis stood from the sofa and asked, "Am I able to do it?"

Monica stared, narrowing her eyes at him, as though only that moment, did she realize he was a possibility, she nodded her head, and said: "Two questions. Are you able to keep a secret, and can you start today?"

40

When the door of the townhouse opened, the girl Lewis had just met at Aero stood behind it.

"Hey," Tori said wagging a finger at him, a smile of recognition on her face. "You're the guy from..."

"Yeah, I am. Monica sent me over to see if you needed anything," Lewis smiled. "I'm your new driver."

Tori said she needed food, so they ended up walking down the chips and soda aisle at the Michigan Avenue Jewel food store. She pushed a shopping cart as Lewis hung back a couple of steps, trying not to, but admiring the way the faded denim of the woman's jeans clung to her hips and ass: the way she walked in her sneakers as though barefoot across a wet bathroom floor, just coming out of the shower. He knew he was fresh out of a relationship and knew he wasn't supposed to have been thinking like that, but not by his choosing, he was single again and that was just how single men's minds worked.

"I said do you know what aisle the cherries are on?" Lewis heard Tori raising her voice. He blinked, looked up to see her facing him, a hand on one of those curvy hips.

"I'm sorry, what did you say? I didn't hear you."

"If you weren't staring at my ass, maybe you would've."

After finding the cherries, Tori set a large bottle of them into the basket beside the Jay's Hot Stuff potato chips, the two liter bottle of Coke Zero, the box of microwavable cheese sticks and the big bottle of Kraken spiced rum. With Lewis following, she pushed the basket to the self-checkout station.

"That's all you're getting?" Lewis said. "Since we're here, maybe you should get some real food."

"And maybe you should mind your business. Whatcha think?"

"Okay," Lewis laughed, raising his hands. "Here's me minding my own business."

Lewis pulled the Range Rover to a red light and turned to Tori. She was a beautiful woman, but she appeared damaged, like she had been through a lot of shit: jacked up stuff that she hasn't been able to shake. Monica hadn't told Lewis anything more about this Tori Thomas than that she'd be working for Monica over the next few weeks. "Where do you wanna go?"

Tori sunk down in the passenger seat, scanning what lay outside the windshield for ideas. "I don't know. I got something Monica wants me to do tonight, but I don't wanna go back to the house yet. I feel like a prisoner there." She looked to give the question a bit more thought, then said, "The movies. I think there's one down the street."

"The movies?"

"I'm just killing time, dude. Just drive, okay."

After a ten second deliberation in the parking structure as to whether or not Lewis would accompany Tori or wait in the truck like a real chauffer, they agreed he would go.

They sat in a relatively empty theater, a seat between them, not speaking at all, but watching the latest X-Men flick: Apocalypse.

Pulling up in front of Tori's apartment building, Lewis climbed out, grabbed her groceries from out of the back and walked them around to her.

"Big bottle of liquor," Lewis said, holding the bags. "I hope you have some real food in there to eat; those cheese sticks alone won't soak up all that alcohol."

"Guess I'll find out," Tori said, grabbing hold to the bag that Lewis hadn't fully let go of. Their eyes met: Lewis—noticing how sad Tori's appeared—could not help but say, "You want some help?"

"I don't think so." She took the bag and started up the walkway.

Not having anywhere else to go, and not wanting to be alone, Lewis asked, "You sure?"

Tori stopped, her back still to him. After a second, she turned and said, "Fuck. Why not? Come on."

Lewis had thought the woman sitting across from him on the small apartment deck, drinking her third Kraken and Coke, looked slightly familiar, but after finally coming out and telling him the truth about being Nate's mistress, he realized he had seen Tori once before.

She went on to tell him why she was there now: everything that happened in L.A., and that the apartment wasn't really hers, and that Monica was paying her to seduce her husband.

Laying back on the folding chaise lounger, Lewis almost choked on his mixed drink. He sat up quickly, nearly falling out of the chair. "You're me!" he said, pointing at her with the hand he held the drink with.

"What do you mean?" Tori said, taking a sip from her glass.

"It's how I know Monica and Nate. He had hired me, bought me clothes, gave me money, fake name and shit, and stuck me in a house so I could sleep with his wife." His head buzzing a little, Lewis said, "She has you doing exactly what Nate had me do to her."

"Wow, then they truly deserve one another. By the way, how'd that work out for you?"

Lewis stood, stepped over and sat down next to Tori. "Doesn't matter how you got caught up in all this, you seem like a nice enough chick who just needs some money. Like I said, I know, cause I been there. But be careful, Tori. There's a lot more going on with those two than you know." He stood, taking one of her hands in his and shaking it. "Just sayin…from the little time we spent together, I think I like you. I'd hate to see you get hurt again." He brought her hand to his lips and kissed her knuckle. "I'm gonna let you go. You got my number. Call me when you ready to do some real grocery shopping," Lewis smiled. "Cause sooner or later, you gonna need some food up in here."

41

Later that evening, Tori stood in the bathroom mirror wearing nothing but a bra and panties as she applied purple eye shadow, mascara, just a touch of blush on her cheeks and a very special shade of plum lipstick—something that used to be Nate's favorite.

Earlier at the store, after Daphanie told the woman off, Monica had Tori follow her to the changing rooms, where she slid a key into one of the doors, pushed it open and motioned for Tori to step inside.

"In there?" Tori said. "For what?"

"Because I don't need Nate dropping in and seeing the two of us talking. Did you think I was joking about that?"

Tori stepped in. Monica followed, closing them inside.

"So are you quitting on me too, or is that just Daphanie?"

"I'm not quitting, Monica."

Monica closed the distance between the two of them, getting up in Tori's face. "So that means you have to act like you have some sense."

"Monica, I'm doing what you're telling me to do. I've already met with Nate twice and we're supposed to plan something tonight."

"Good," Monica said. "You call him, have him come by the apartment and get him drunk, get him high, whatever it takes, but you move things along."

"This shouldn't be rushed or he's going to suspect something."

"Then you make sure he doesn't, because it has to done. After what happened a moment ago, things have to be expedited, because I no longer trust you not to eventually expose everything I've planned. The sooner he sleeps with you, the sooner he trusts you, and the sooner we can get on with the rest of this," Monica said.

"It's like that then?"

"If you expect to still get your money, you goddamn right, it's like that."

After she drove Tori home, Daphanie shut the car off and turned to Tori. "Still not gonna tell me what the dragon lady wanted to talk to you about?"

"Nothing worth repeating," Tori said, digging her cell phone from her jeans pocket. "But can you stick around another second while I make this call? Just feel a little better with you here."

"Of course," Daphanie said.

Tori dialed a number, then stared at Daphanie when her call was picked up. "Hey Nate," she said. "We still getting together tonight? Okay, great!" Tori said, faking enthusiasm and showing Daphanie a phony smile. She told Nate he can pick her up at the apartment, gave him the time, then said she looked forward to seeing him.

When she ended the call, Tori said, "That's what Monica talked to me about, speeding things along with Nate."

"He's not a fool, you know."

"Yeah," Tori said. "I know, but this is my part of the deal."

"Whatever you say."

"You going home to get your son?"

"Yeah, just don't know how yet. I'll figure it out."

"I know you will," Tori said, staring at Daphanie for a long, somewhat uncomfortable few seconds. "Should we...uh, hug or something?"

"Have you stopped hating me?"

"Yeah."

"Then yeah," Daphanie said, extending her arms, hugging Tori. "Be careful, okay."

Hugging Daphanie back, Tori said: "Always, girl."

Now after pulling on a pair of comfortable, hip-clinging, faded jeans and an equally worn t-shirt, a deep V in the neck to expose her

174

perky cleavage, Tori walked out of her room to answer the doorbell that rang for the second time.

She shot a glance in the bedroom's full-length mirror, then hurried out of the room in her bare feet. At the door, Nate looked incredibly handsome, wearing dark slacks and a black shirt. He was cleanly shaven and his hair was freshly cut. He took Tori in with his eyes from head to toe, smiled then said, "You look great, but..."

"Thank you. I know we were supposed to go out, but you'd never believe the day I've had. Can we order in instead? I have all the wine we can drink." She smiled sheepishly. "What do you think?"

Two hours later, strategically placed candles burned around the room, soft music played in the background and the glow of the flat screen TV lit a coffee table covered with packages of half eaten Chinese delivery and two bottles of wine: one of which was empty, the other three fourths gone.

Tori and Nate sat on the couch, laughing, his arm stretched across the spine of the sofa. Her buzzing head leaned against his armpit, but the only articles of clothing that had been shed were the shoes Nate kicked over an hour ago. As Monica so desperately wanted, Tori hadn't been able to take advantage of the fact Nate had been drinking. She hadn't made a move for the man's zipper to rub the throbbing erection in his pants, because there wasn't one. Neither did he attempt to slip a hand up her t-shirt, or move in slowly, eyelids drunkenly low, for an open-mouthed kiss.

For the last two hours, Nate and Tori, half watched Mad Max Fury Road, ate, and got wasted, laughing like old friends, which Tori realized, they kind of were. But the echo of Monica's voice, letting her know there was still work to be done, was unrelenting.

Tori leaned up off Nate, reached for the second bottle of wine and emptied equal parts of what was remaining into the glasses that sat on the table. She handed Nate his, then took up her own.

"To..." Tori said, pausing for Nate's suggestion of something suitable to toast.

"To bumping into each other at the gym."

"Sounds good," Tori said, then brought the glass to her lips, took a drink, and while looking over the rim, watched Nate do the same.

He lowered his glass, smiling.

"So..." Tori said, "How about a kiss?"

Nate smiled wider, actually looked a bit embarrassed, and chuckled. "I'm honored, but like I said, I'm a married man now."

"So," Tori said, her voice low and throaty. She leaned toward him, running a tongue over her lips. "It can't be our little secret?"

Nate leaned back. "I don't think so. I'm really trying to do the right thing now."

"But you're here."

"Because I said I would have some good news for you, but I haven't found out yet," Nate said, his words slurring only a little. "But you wanted to get together tonight, so here I am."

"Does your wife know you're here trying to give your old lover some good news?"

"No. She probably wouldn't understand."

"Understand what?"

"That I'm trying to make up for past behavior. I've told her...keep telling her," Nate said, his eyes momentarily glassing over as though reliving every example of Monica's distrust, every time she stared at him with disbelieving eyes. "Maybe it's too late. I mean, I was a really bad man: the way I set you up like that, took all your money." Nate sat up on the edge of the sofa, set his glass back on the table. "You seem like you're okay now, but I can only imagine what life had to have been like for you after what I did."

"Wasn't that bad." Tori tried to smile, laugh away that period in her memory when she was dirt poor and dependent, but when she thought about the hard times she suffered, living in that shit hole Monica dragged her from, all she could think about was Ja'Van. Yeah, there were the roaches that would scurry across her counters when the lights were turned on, and the rats she'd hear scrapping around in the walls when they were off, but still, Ja'Van, and his methods to keep Tori in check was the worst of it.

"You want to tell me about it?" Nate said.

"Nice try, but don't think that's such a good idea." She walked across the room with her glass, stopped at the window and fingered one of the drapes aside to look out. From behind, she heard Nate ask again to speak to him, saying that she could trust him. Based on past experiences, no she didn't think she could. But he had done just about all the harm he could do to her, so maybe unloading the shit she was carrying in her head at the feet of the man who caused it, might actually do her some good.

She faced Nate. "You really wanna hear this?"

"Only if you want to tell me."

Tori swallowed what was left in the glass and went on the frightful, almost twenty minute journey, back to her past, recounting every painful moment for Nate, who winced and frowned and uttered compassion-filled noises at all the right parts. When she was just about finished, Tori grabbed the bottom of her t-shirt and elbowed it over her head, pulling it off.

"Hold it," Nate said. "What are you doing?"

"You wanted to know what I went through," Tori said, her words slightly slurred as she reached behind her back and undid her bra.

"Tori, wait," Nate said as the bra dropped to the floor, exposing breasts dotted with dozens of dime-sized, darkened, craters of healed wounds around each of her nipples.

Nate's mouth dropped open.

"Cigarette burn scars," Tori said, standing shamelessly in front of Nate, her arms at her sides. "He'd hold me down when I 'did wrong' and put them out on me."

Nate gasped. "I'm so sorry," he said, his voice barely a whisper.

"Not a big deal," Tori joked sadly. "Nothing compared to this," she said, turning around to show Nate a back covered with thick lines of raised scar tissue. The lines crisscrossed her skin, looking like grill marks on barbequed meat; they stretched from the small of her back, all the way up onto her neck, and into the fine hairs on her nape.

Nate slowly stood from the sofa, walked over, picked Tori's bra and shirt from the floor, held them out to her. She took them from his hand, feeling no shame, and put herself back together while he stood with his back turned to her.

"You can turn around now," Tori said.

He turned, looked at Tori, guilt in his eyes. "This man you were with, why'd you stay with him?"

"I couldn't afford to leave," Tori said sadly.

"Because I took all of your money?"

Tori smiled, pointed a finger at Nate. "Bingo. Tell him what he's won, Chuck."

Nate said nothing.

Tori watched him look away then watched his eyes darken and narrow a moment as though suppressing evil intentions. He walked to his suit jacket on the back of one of the dinette set chairs, pulled out a pad of some kind and a pen and leaned over the table.

"Tell me his name, address, cell number and whatever other information you have on him," Nate asked.

"Why?"

"After the things he did, do you care to know?" Nate said, the pen still to the pad. "Does it really matter?"

"No. It doesn't."

Tori gave him the information he requested, to include the make, model and year of Ja'Van's car.

"Thank you," Nate said. He closed the pad he had written on and slipped it back in his pocket.

42

One leg of his jeans pulled off, his foot propped against the sink of the filthy gas station rest room, Freddy took the wad of paper towel he had cranked out of the wall machine, wrapped around his hand, then poured cheap liquor from the bottle he purchased at the store across the street. He pressed the pad of paper towel against the open wound. It burned like a motherfucker, and Freddy shut his eyes, clenched his teeth and suffered through the searing pain, behind the locked door and under the flickering overhead bulb.

When he pulled the folded towel away, it was pink from the quantity of blood it had absorbed. He looked down at the wound and almost puked the only thing he had eaten in twelve hours: a McDonald's McDouble cheeseburger.

The pain was horrific, but Freddy was lucky that cop hadn't blown his head off.

He limped away from there as fast as he could, his leg feeling as though it had been amputated at the thigh. He found his way into an apartment building doorway, across the street from a CVS. The rain was coming down harder, flowing over the street gutters, the water being kicked up like tiny tidal waves as cars sped through it along the street. Despite his hood, Freddy's face was dripping wet; the coat had been soaked through down to his t-shirt, down to his jeans; even his underwear clung cold and sopping wet to his hips.

Across the street from the convenience store, Freddy pulled off the coat, wincing as every little movement caused him extreme pain. He wrapped the sleeves around his narrow waist, letting the garment drape over his torn, bloodstained jeans.

Onto the store's counter, Freddy dropped a 99-cent pair of scissors, a cheep Bic razor and a tube of crazy glue. An elderly lady with dyed, jet-black hair, rang the items up and asked if he had a CVS discount card.

"No," Freddy said, looking behind her at the counter wall. "Where ya'll cigarettes? You don't have no Newports back there?"

"We stopped selling cigarettes, sir. That'll be $3.68."

In the gas station rest room, Freddy took the two torn sides of his wound (thankfully the injury stopped bleeding) pressed them together and squeezed several bead-sized droplets of the glue into the line of ripped flesh. The bullet was still in there, but he had heard of people who lived after being shot: like Fitty Cent, who Freddy thought he heard still had a bullet somewhere lodged in his face, and he was doing movies and shit. Freddy set the tube of glue down then clamped both hands over the injury, holding the injury together for twenty seconds until he felt the glue would hold. When he slowly pulled away his hands, the skin did not separate.

He stood in front of the sink, cranked out another dozen perforated squares of paper towel from the machine and wrapped it around his thigh. He pulled up his jeans and took his gun from off the corner of the sink and shoved it into the small of his back.

Freddy looked in the mirror, seeing a gaunt man with hollowed out cheeks, sunken eyes and hair that had grown wild over his face for what looked like years. But Freddy had killed another cop, so the man in the mirror would be the man the police would be looking for.

From the little CVS plastic bag, Freddy pulled out the scissors, tore away the packaging then started hacking at his beard. When he finished, he went on to the hair on his head, pushing soap from the dispenser into his palm, getting a lather going with a little tap water and slathered the suds over his face and skull; he shaved himself completely clean with the razor.

When Freddy toweled off, he looked even more malnourished, more like those starving big-headed Cambodian refugee children with flies all over their faces. But what was most important was that Freddy no longer looked like the man who smoked the chick cop the other night. Hopefully, this would buy him the time he needed to find his baby.

43

With an exhalation of relief, Monica set her two large suitcases down just inside the front door of Tabatha's condo.

"You staying for a couple of days or a couple of years?" Tabatha said, sipping from a purple wine cooler.

"You could've helped," Monica said, going into Tabatha's fridge and pulling out the last bottle of what her friend was drinking. Monica cracked the seal, twisted off the cap then turned up the bottle and did not stop drinking till more than half of the contents was gone.

Tabatha stood, leaning against a kitchen wall, staring at Monica. "You wanna talk about it?"

"Talk about what?" Monica said, turning up the bottle again, leaving just a corner of the beverage in the bottle. Shaking what was left, she said, "You got anything else in here to drink? Maybe something less for teenagers?"

Shaking her head, Tabatha grabbed a bottle of bourbon from one of the lower cupboards and set it on the counter in front of Monica, along with a short glass. "We're going through a slump, but we're gonna be fine. The stores will be profitable again."

"I'm not worried about the stores right now," Monica said, pouring her glass a quarter of the way full with the dark liquor. She took a sip.

"Then what are you worried about? I know it couldn't be your marriage to Mr. Wonderful."

Monica had lowered herself onto one of the stools alongside the breakfast counter. She had no intention of telling Tabatha what she had planned, knowing she'd be scolded and condemned, but it had become hard holding it all in; she needed someone to hash things over with—someone besides Tori or Daphanie—someone who wasn't directly involved. "No," Monica said, taking another drink. "It's not the marriage. It's the fucking top secret, covert operation to win sole custody of Nate's son, that's starting to drive me a little bat-shit," Monica said, reaching across the counter for the bottle. Tabatha had grabbed it before Monica could, and slid it out of Monica's reach.

"You wanna explain to me exactly what the hell you're talking about."

"Well…" Monica started.

"Hold on," Tabatha said, reaching behind her, into the cabinet. "Let me get a glass. Think I'm gonna need something stronger when I hear this."

Monica told Tabatha the plan she had devised, at what stage she was at, and her assessment of how things were going.

Shaking her head, pacing in front of Monica, holding the half glass of liquor, Tabatha said: "All to get custody of Nathaniel?"

"That's right."

"But…you fucking have custody of the kid," Tabatha said, incredulously. "Nate let you adopt him, right?"

"But I don't have sole custody."

"Ooh, I get it," Tabatha said, sarcastically. "It's not that you really want the little boy yourself, you just don't want Nate to have him."

"That's not true. I'm doing this to protect Nathaniel."

"You're doing this to spite Nate," Tabatha said, walking toward Monica, a tinge of anger in her voice.

"That's not true!" Monica said again, standing from the stool.

"You married the man you supposedly hate. Dug one bitch from out of a hole, flew one in from out of state to seduce your husband," Tabatha said, standing directly in front of Monica, staring her in the face. "Then you're planning on burning down half your house, for what—to give your son a better life? You're full of shit, Monica!" Tabatha turned and paced away, leaving Monica there, her mouth open, seemingly not knowing how to answer. "What if this plan doesn't work out the way you're hoping?"

"It'll work out."

"Really? Those tricks all up in the store today, acting a fool, when you know Nate's been dropping by lately for no reason at all: is that an example of your plan working out?"

"It won't happen again."

"Ever wonder why, all of sudden, he's been there every fifteen minutes? Think he might suspect you're on some shit?"

"He doesn't suspect anything. I'd know."

"Yeah," Tabatha scoffed, guzzling the last of what was in her glass. "Because Nate's so transparent, right. Because he's not one to plot and scheme without you knowing."

"Look, I have everything under control, all right."

Shaking her head sympathetically, Tabatha said from across the room, "No you don't. And I'm only saying this because I love you, and I care, but since you've been with that man, you've never been in control. Never."

Monica tried not to think about all the examples Tabatha could've sited that second to support her statement; she didn't want to think about anything except how nice things would be when all of this was over. "So what? You saying I should just shut down everything because I hit a couple of bumps."

"Monica, the bumps are a warning ahead of the cliff that you're just too blind to see coming." Tabatha walked back over to Monica, set down her glass, took Monica's away, and grabbed both her friend's hands. "If you hate the man as much as you say you do, then once and for all, leave him the fuck alone and live your life. But if you actually have feelings for him, which you must to have put up with him for all these years, then admit it, tell everyone who disapproves—even me—to fuck off, and continue living a happy little life with him and your son."

The thought of that reality popped into Monica's head for a brief moment. It would sure as hell be easier than what she was attempting now. But how could she do that after all he has done to her? How could she do that when Nate was probably just one more date away from hooking back up with his mistress?

"No," Monica said, pulling her hands out of Tabatha's grasp. "I know what I set out to do, and it's what's going to happen. Whether you like it or not."

Tabatha nodded sadly. "Okay, Monica. You know what's best. I'm going to bed," Tabatha said, then turned and left the room.

44

Ja'van Richardson sat at the bar of a dark, corner dive, lit by neon Budweiser, Pabst Blue Ribbon and Colt 45 signs. Even though California state law banned smoking in any public place, there were gray ribbons from orange lit cigarette tips spiraling into the dank air all throughout the bar.

A J-Cole song played over the speakers. J-Cole was the truth in Ja'Van's opinion, but the music was too fucking loud and the fat ass bartender wouldn't turn the shit down, even though Ja'van told him he'd give him five dollars if he did.

The half dozen dudes—to include Ja'van's boy, Todd—slightly bobbed their heads while drinking from beers and short glasses of liquor. The rest of the bar was filled with wobbly circular tables and miss-matched chairs, at which older men and younger unattractive women with chunky backsides sat. At a table in one far end of the bar, sat a woman in a tailor-made business, pant suit and nerd glasses. In the opposite corner of the bar was a ten by ten foot area of floor tiles, a wall in front of it, covered with square stick-on wall mirrors; it was the designated dance floor.

Three thick, twenty-something women, wearing skin-tight, thigh-high dresses, gyrated rhythmically on high-heels while watching their reflections: their cellulite dimpled thighs and heavy breasts testing the fabric of their outfits.

Ja'van turned back to the bar and took another sip of his double Jack and Coke. "Next time the bitch in the red dress walk up here, I'm gonna holla at her ass."

Todd glanced over his shoulder at the girl Ja'Van was referring to; she flipped her shiny black weave back and fourth over her face as she danced. Todd nodded, chuckled and said, "That hoe ain't thinking about you."

The song ended. An old Ludacris cut blared through the speakers. The woman Ja'van had been eyeing sidled up between him and Todd and ordered a Long Island Iced tea. While the girl waited, she twisted her hips sensually between the two men, Ja'van never taking his eyes from the girl's ass.

"Nine dollars," the bearded bartender said.

"I got that," Ja'van said, sliding a ten-dollar bill over the bar.

"Thank you," the girl said then took hold of the drink, wrapped her lips sensually around the straw and sucked it like she was trying to give it pleasure.

"What's yo' name, girl?"

"Creesha."

Ja'van pulled a hand out of his pocket, set it flat on the bar, then angled his palm up to show the corner of a tiny, clear plastic bag: a corner of it filled with white powder. "You wanna party wit' me, Creesha?"

Inside the men's room, the four drinks Ja'van drank earlier were fucking with his head, and the way Creesha's ass cheeks spilled out that dress creeping up her hips as she bent over to snort another line, had his dick hard like an aluminum baseball bat.

Creesha stood up quickly from the sink, inhaling hard, blinking her eyes and rubbing her nose. "Goddamn, that's some fire shit!" she said, glancing quickly in the mirror, finger combing her hair. She leaned in to Ja'van, and air-kissed him on the cheek. "Thank you, baby. I gotta get back out to my friends."

"Ho...ho...hold it," Ja'Van said, hurrying around in front of Creesha, blocking the door with his wide body. "Ain't no need to rush, girl. We just gettin' started."

Creesha smiled. Not as wide as before, but still showing teeth, said: "Really, I need to be getting out of here."

"C'mon, give me five minutes of some of that," Ja'Van said, his eyes dropping to the curves of her hips.

Creesha all of a sudden went straight faced, pointed a finger at him, bangles clanging together on her wrist, and said, "Look nigga, I said I ain't fuckin' wit' yo' bitch ass. Now move yo'—"

But before Creesha could utter another word, Ja'Van said, "Fuck you talking to? I was trying to be nice, but fuck it now." Ja'Van reached out, grabbed the girl by the arm and started to drag her toward one of the stalls.

Wobbling on her heals, Creesha swiped at Ja'van's arm, knocking it away. Ja'van whirled around, slapped Creesha across the cheek. She twirled, spun around and landed on her ass. Ja'van reached down, grabbed a fist-full of her weave, hoisted her up and dragged her into the stall, threw her to the floor and started unbuckling his pants.

"Bitch think you gonna get something for nothing," he mumbled as though talking to himself. "Bout to teach dis fat ass bitch a lesson."

"Excuse me."

Ja'van heard someone say behind him. He spun around to see a small-framed, but chiseled woman standing just outside of the open stall doorway; he realized it was the nerd that had been sitting, her knees all clamped together, in the corner of the bar.

"It appears that woman does not like what you are doing to her. Maybe you should stop."

Ja'van thought the liquor, the drugs or his boy, Todd was playing a trick on him. Whichever, he ain't have time for it. "Bitch, get the fuck out of here before I have you choke on my dick first."

"I'm not going anywhere," Abbey Kurt said.

Ja'van turned fully, stepped out of the stall, leaving Creesha on her knees, staring wide-eyed, unbelieving, yet thankful at the woman.

Ja'van rushed Abbey Kurt, a hand outstretched to grab her by her shoulder.

With little effort, Abbey sidestepped him, swept his ankle with her foot and shoved him in the back. Ja'van fell forward, his chin colliding into the porcelain sink, breaking his jaw with a loud snap. Immeasurable pain coursed through his skull at the same rate warm blood spilled over his lips. He staggered to his feet, feeling as though his lower jaw had been unhinged—might drop out of his mouth, but the woman was still there: blurry, but in front of him. He raced at her again, lunging with both outstretched arms. Abbey reached behind her, came out with something small in her hand, then with the flick of her wrist, it extending into something longer: a three segmented, iron police baton. She swung the small bat-like weapon, striking Ja'van across the forehead as he barreled toward her. He saw stars against the blackness of his closed eyes then felt a wall collide against his skull.

He hadn't known if he had lost consciousness for a split second, but he was on his back when the bathroom light slowly came into view. He could hardly see; everything was hazy. He could still hear the bass-heavy music in the bar outside the restroom door, the dripping of one of the faucets and the suited woman saying to Creesha: "Get up. Go. You don't want to be here to witness this."

Ja'van heard the hurried "clops" of the big-booty bitch's shoes rush out of the restroom. He heard the small metal bolt slide into its catches on the door lock then heard the slower steps of the suited woman nearing him.

"Wook...yuh...yuh...don't have ta'..." Ja'van tried begging, but his broken jaw hurt too much and the blood pooling in his mouth made it hard to talk.

"Shhh," the suited woman said, standing over him. All Ja'van could see was the gray smear that was her suit. He felt her rolling up the legs of his jeans.

"Why...why...yuh..." he said, wanting to know why she was doing that, who the fuck she was and why she was even here.

"Ja'van, I'm here on behalf of Tori Thomas," the woman said, having read his mind. "You've done some not-so-nice things to her," Abbey Kurt said, as she continued rolling his jeans up. She pushed his socks down to expose the very center of his shin. "She has a friend who has been greatly angered by that, and he has sent me here to ensure that you'll never touch Ms. Thomas again."

"I...I...won't!" Ja'van stammered, spilling more blood onto his shirt.

"I know that," he heard Abbey Kurt say. "But first, a lesson must be taught. I'll do that by breaking your legs, your arms and several of your ribs. I would recommend bracing yourself," he heard the suited lady say, as he saw the blurry vision of her raise the baton over her head, then quickly, as though chopping wood, bring it down on his leg. He heard a jarring 'pop', similar to someone smashing an air-filled paper bag, then felt a pain so great, so blindingly excruciating an enormous white light exploded in his brain, then the world went suddenly black.

45

The next day, Nate pulled open the restaurant door for Tori and allowed her into a beautifully decorated dining room. They were greeted by a smiling hostess and asked if they'd prefer to dine inside or outside on the street front patio. "It's a beautiful day. Let's sit outside," Tori said. It was a decision she had no say in, but was made by Monica over twelve hours ago.

Last night after Nate left her, Tori sat on the arm of the sofa, a half smile on her face, a sneaking uncertain suspicion in her head that—at one time she never would've believed it possible—Nate was truly changing: that if he wasn't yet the better man he hoped to be, she believed he was definitely moving in that direction.

Tori glanced down at her cell phone on the sofa cushion and frowned. She was to call Monica when the "date" was over, before Nate made it home, and give her an update of what happened.

She grabbed the phone, dialed Monica's number and slid off the arm and down onto the sofa cushions, where she lay on her back. As the phone rang, she felt guilty for what she was doing: trying to help bring down a man who was trying to do better: a man who had already given Tori a fist full of cash, promised her good news, and taken the info of her crazed abuser, with what she figured were plans to convince Ja'Van to leave her alone. No, what she was doing didn't feel right at all, Tori thought as Monica answered the phone.

"He just left," Tori said.

"And…" Monica sounded anxious and uncertain. "How did it go? Did you have sex?"

"No. That didn't happen."

"Why not?"

"Because he didn't want to."

"It's not his job to determine that," Monica said. "It's yours. What didn't you do? Did you come on to him? Did you make him know sex was what you wanted—that it was okay for him to—"

"I know how to seduce a man, Monica. Especially your man," Tori said, hoping to piss Monica off. "I was standing nearly butt-ass naked right in front of him," Tori said, "ready to go, but he didn't want it. Okay."

Silence for a second, then, "What do you mean, 'He didn't want it?'"

"He said he's a married man now. That he loves his wife, and he wasn't here for that."

"I…I don't believe you," Monica said, sounding as though she didn't know what to believe. "Did you push him?"

"He's not going to do it. He said he's a changed man."

"Then you fucking change him back!"

"Look," Tori said, sitting up on the sofa. "I'll take your money if you wanna give it to me, but why go through with this if he's finally acting right?"

"What did you say to me?"

"I was just sayin…"

"I'm not paying you to just say anything. You still want this money?"

"I wouldn't have come all the way to Chicago—"

"Answer the question. Do you want it?"

"Yes."

"Then you better start acting like it, or I swear, you won't see a dime."

Sitting with a view of the street, Tori watched cars as they passed, trying to catch glimpses of the drivers, as well as an occasional look at the faces of pedestrians passing in front of her.

"You okay?" Nate asked, after swallowing another bit of the baked salmon sandwich he had ordered. "You seem preoccupied. Something bothering you?"

192

Tori was bothered by the fact that she knew she was being watched. She wasn't sure when exactly it would be, but Monica said explicitly for her to come to this restaurant, to sit outside, and she would arrange for someone to snap pictures of her and Nate.

"And even though nothing happened tonight, I, my lawyer, and the judge—whoever that will be—will need to be able to look at the pictures and assume you're fucking. So act accordingly."

"I'm fine," Tori said, trying hard to appear carefree, when she was near going crazy not knowing who'd be taking the pictures of her, where that person would be or when. "Awww, but it's so sweet that you're concerned." Tori leaned over and kissed Nate on the cheek, her lips lingering near his ear long enough for a photo opportunity. "I know you said you weren't interested, but I couldn't help myself."

She started to pull away, watching Nate appear to blush, but before leaning back into her seat, she intentionally knocked his fork off of his plate, into his lap.

"Hold it, hold it," Tori said, reaching down between his legs to retrieve the fallen utensil. She looked around, as if guilty of an obscene gesture, then smiled to Nate who appeared embarrassed. "Don't look like that. People'll think I'm trying to give you a hand job or something."

"Boy, you haven't changed a bit," Nate laughed.

But you sure have, Tori thought, glancing out onto the street, and telling herself she hoped whoever Monica tasked to take shots, was at the right place at the exact right time.

"So I brought you here to give you the good news I was trying to deliver."

"And seeing as though I'm never mad at anyone with good news, I give you permission to give it to me," Tori said.

"Well," Nate said, as though nervous. He dabbed the corner of his mouth with a napkin. "I moved my secretary off my desk and gave her to my VP. I needed to wait a few days to see if it was a good fit. Everyone's happy, which allows me the opportunity to say: I want you to come back."

Tori had a hard time comprehending at first what Nate had said, because she just knew she had not heard him right. She squinted as though her vision and hearing were connected and said: "Come again."

Nate laughed. "I knew you'd react this way, but I want you to come back, work for me. With a huge raise of course. I know how much you loved that job. You were great at what you did. I was the one that messed everything up by...you know."

Tori let her mind run with the possibility of what was just presented her and thought of how wonderful it would be. She would have independence: could buy a nice condo downtown, a nice car, some clothes that she picked out by herself and bought with her own money. And there was the bonus that she truly did love that job, loved walking among the business people downtown, taking the elevator to the fiftieth-something floor and staring out the big windows at Lake Michigan. But sadly, Tori "worked" for Monica now, so she couldn't just accept Nate's offer...unless Tori was foolish enough to tell Nate everything.

"And what makes you think you wouldn't mess it up again, me walking in and out of your office every other hour looking as sexy as I do? You know how I don't like to wear panties under my skirts." She winked at him.

"Yes, you are as gorgeous as you've ever been," Nate admitted. "But like I said..."

"I know, I know. You're a changed man."

"That's right," Nate nodded. "So," he held out a hand. "We have a deal?"

Tori leaned forward, wanting nothing more than to take Nate's hand and accept the job, but having run over every possible scenario in which she was freed to do that, she couldn't see one that was actually plausible, without telling Nate everything Monica was up to, then hoping he'd forgive her, which she knew he'd never do. "So you told your wife I'll be working for you again?"

"I'll tell her before it happens, that way—"

"That way she'll trust you to rehire the woman you used to cheat on her with?" Tori said, shaking her head sadly. "Nate, you're claiming this 'changed man' stuff, but you take me back, in your wife's eyes, you'd be doing exactly what the old Nate used to do. There's no way she'd believe I'd be there to be anything more than an in-office piece of ass," Tori said, feeling like a damn fool for turning down the great opportunity.

"Don't say that! I never saw you that way," Nate said.

"Fine. But you know all that would do is make your life at home a living hell, and even though I should want you to be miserable for what you did to me, I think I have to reject your offer and spare you the torment."

Disappointed, Nate said: "You sure? I would eventually convince her to believe me."

"No. You just have to think of another way to pay me back for ruining my life."

Nate laughed. "I'll start working on that today. Till then, there is one more bit of good news I have for you. I had an associate of mine fly to L.A. and have a face-to-face with your friend Ja'Van Richardson. I think I can say with complete certainty, you will never have to worry about that clown harassing you again."

Tori jumped out of her seat, leaned over the table and wrapped her arms around Nate, kissing him all about his face, not because she hoped Monica or Monica's photographer would get great incriminating snapshots, but because she was so happy with what Nate did for her.

46

Monica had circled around the block the restaurant was on
several times until she saw Tori and her husband take seats outside.
She drove into a small parking lot across the street, pulled the car
into a snug spot between a large car and a huge SUV, obscuring her
just enough to where she could not be seen, but had a view of her
husband and his ex-mistress.

Sitting and waiting, Monica thought back to her argument with
Tabatha last night. She flipped and turned in her best friend's
guestroom, unable to sleep for thinking about Tabatha's suggestion:
drop the plan to steal Nate's son, for Monica already had partial
custody, and just be the child's mother and the man's wife—if she still
loved Nate like that. But that was the million-dollar question: did she
still love him? Did she even like him?

In the parking lot, behind the wheel of her car, the digital
camera on the dash, waiting to be grabbed the moment she saw Nate
and Tori take their seats, Monica found herself hoping they'd never
show. She tried to convince herself she felt that way because she
was tired and didn't feel like doing the work of aiming the lens,
pressing the button and capturing proof of her husband's misdeeds.
She realized that was only half true. The work wasn't the issue, but if
Monica never saw what Tori said Nate was doing, it would've
remained the word of a money-desperate, scorned ex-mistress,
versus her husband's. But Monica saw that they did sit down, and
they did everything Monica had ordered Tori to ensure they do.

Now sitting behind the wheel of the car, Monica thought about
the ring Nate had bought her, about the wedding, about the offer of
the loan, and helping her fix her business and the house he was
attempting to purchase. All those promises it took to make her believe
again—to trust that her husband had truly changed. And she possibly

could've forced herself to believe him, if it weren't for the snapshots she was cycling through on the digital camera she just used to catch Nate and Tori doing what Nate promised he'd never do again.

Up until this point, Monica had held out a sliver of hope that maybe Nate was telling the truth. She had fought that tiny urge to root for him: that he might overpower the urge to be the man he had always been in the past and tell Tori that he was not interested in anything she had to offer him. Well, he had supposedly done that last night, and hearing that from Tori, Monica wanted that to have been enough for her to pull the plug on this entire affair. But if she were to trust him again, he needed to be tested. It would've been far too easy for Nate to have turned down Tori's first advance. But if she were to continue, to really pursue him, force herself on him over and over again, as Monica instructed, and Nate still resisted, then and only then would she have considered the possibility that he had changed, that their son would no longer be in danger by Nate's actions, and then, Monica could sincerely consider taking him back. But as she stared down at the pictures: Tori's arms thrown around his neck, her hand in his crotch, her leaning over kissing him—they proved, as they were meant, that Nate would never change.

Monica shut the camera off and set it aside. She started up the car, glanced at herself in the rearview mirror, wiping a finger under her eye before driving off.

47

For the second night in a row, Daphanie sat up in what used to be the guest bed—the bed Jennifer had slept in—but was now hers. As Trevor instructed yesterday, Daphanie came home and carried armloads of clothes from the drawers and closet from the room she had shared with Trevor, to the guest bedroom.

When Daphanie had gotten home yesterday evening, the guest room had already been cleared of Jennifer's belongings, as though the girl had started working the moment Trevor had broken the news of the move to Daphanie during lunch.

Daphanie's back against a pillow, she held her baby in her arms. The boy looked up at her lovingly with his big dark eyes, his face very close to her breasts; she wanted nothing more than to try feeding him again; her body yearned to give him the nutrients he needed to grow strong, but she never knew when the door would fly open, Jennifer or Trevor trying to catch her as though she were a teenager, blowing marijuana smoke out of a cracked bedroom window.

A knock came at the door.

Daphanie closed her eyes, exhaled: "Who is it?"

The door opened. Jennifer stood in the doorway a moment, then without permission, walked across the carpet, halted beside the bed, and held out her arms for the baby. "It's dinnertime. Trevor wants you to come down and cook."

Trevor sat at the head of the dining room table holding Nat while Jennifer hung over his shoulder, tickling the baby, laughing with Trevor each time the infant giggled. Daphanie, like a defiant house slave, brought food in from the kitchen in glass serving trays: baked chicken, green bean salad, baked sweet potatoes and gravy, and set them before the couple.

Daphanie had been cooking in the kitchen for an hour while Trevor and Jennifer worked on a large bottle of red wine. Daphanie could hear them talking and laughing on the other side of the kitchen door, and more than once she stopped, a wooden spoon or cutting knife in her hand, walked over and pressed an ear to the door.

On one occasion she heard Jennifer giggling then saying: "But really. Why keep her here? I can cook for you, clean, take care of the baby, and…" slyly, she said, "I've already proven I can give you whatever else you need."

"Stop that, woman," Daphanie heard Trevor playfully say, and she imagined the girl sitting on Trevor's lap, reaching down between his thighs to prove her point. "Daphanie is here for a reason."

"You still love her?"

Her ear still pressed to the door, Daphanie's breath hung in her throat, waiting for the answer. Not that she still loved Trevor—if she ever really had—but hearing that he still had feelings for her would, hopefully, allow him to only be so much more cruel to her. Listening intently, she prayed that would be the case, because she didn't know just how much more of this torture she could take before she just up and snapped.

His answer came after a thoughtful pause. "No. I don't still love her."

"You'd never put her before me, would you?" Jennifer asked.

"Of course not."

"Prove that to me. I'll make it worth your while."

"I don't know how," Trevor said.

"You sure?" Jennifer said.

Daphanie heard the tinkle of what she thought was most likely Trevor's belt buckle. A moment later, she heard him moaning, and remembering the baby was still in the room with them, Daphanie wondered how adept Jennifer was in her sex skills: jack a man's dick in one hand while holding a baby in the other?

Daphanie intentionally dropped the heavy knife she was holding, causing enough racket to stop what was going on in the dining room, then went back to her cooking.

After serving the meal, Daphanie stood to the side of the table, hands clasped in front of her, truly feeling like a servant; all she needed was a white apron and kitchen bonnet.

Trevor looked over the food, seemingly pleased. Jennifer sat in the chair adjacent to his, the baby had been put down not long before.

"Where's your plate?" Trevor asked of Daphanie. "I want you to eat with us."

All Daphanie wanted to do was go upstairs, kiss her baby goodnight, then burry her face in her pillow and cry herself to sleep. "I'd rather not. I'm not hungry."

"Get yourself a plate and eat with us," Trevor ordered.

Daphanie set her eyes on Jennifer. The girl smiled, seemingly doing everything possible not to bust out laughing.

After the meal was eaten, Trevor set his napkin on his empty plate. "Food was good, Daphanie."

"Thank you," she said, softly. She barely touched the food in front of her, only nibbling from it whenever Trevor suggested she eat.

"I don't think it was that good," Jennifer said. "Actually it was horrible. The potatoes were undercooked, the salad was dry…and the chicken taste like wood," Jennifer said in a sing-songy-Rapper's Delight voice.

Fed up with Jennifer, Daphanie looked past her to Trevor to see how much of this he would allow.

"Like I said," Trevor said. "The food was good. Why don't you clear the plates," he told Daphanie.

She came around the table, grabbed Trevor's plate and his utensils, then walked around Jennifer, set Trevor's plate down so that she could stack Jennifer's plate and utensils on top of his. While doing that, Daphanie felt the heat of Jennifer's stare on the side of her face.

"Next time I'll come in the kitchen and show you how to cook food properly," Jennifer said.

It wasn't a particularly scathing remark—didn't cut Daphanie very deep—it was just one more atop a million others: the last smart-ass comment Daphanie could take without firing something back at her. "You should do that, if you can find time to pull your face out of another nigga's lap."

The swipe from Jennifer came swiftly, her hand rising and flying across the table toward Daphanie's face. But Daphanie's response was quicker, catching the girl by the wrist and stopping her arm in place. She heard Jennifer's wince, while Daphanie stared hatefully in her eyes as the girl struggled to pull away.

"Daphanie, let go of her!" Trevor said. When she did not, Trevor made the request again, raising his voice.

Daphanie released Jennifer, the girl pulling back her arm, rubbing her wrist with the opposite hand.

"Now apologize for what you said to her," Trevor demanded.

"What? Hell no!" Daphanie said, looking to Trevor, which stopped her from seeing, this time, when Jennifer raised her hand to slap her. The assault came hard and loud across Daphanie's cheek.

"Apologize!" Jennifer said.

Daphanie stared defiantly at the girl, her face burning from the attack, but Daphanie said nothing.

Jennifer slapped Daphanie again, the sound echoing louder through the room, Daphanie's face burning hotter. "Apologize to me!"

Daphanie's eyes narrowed, her frown growing more hateful, but still she remained silent.

"No?" Jennifer said and slapped Daphanie again. The entire side of Daphanie's face felt as though it had been held against the burner of a red-hot stove. Then she was slapped yet again, harder: her bottom lip splitting, spilling blood down her chin.

"Bitch, you better—" Jennifer said, raising her hand to strike Daphanie for the fifth time when Trevor said, "Stop!"

Jennifer looked at Trevor as though she had just been violently snatched from a trance, and Daphanie cut her eyes at him: the left one starting to swell after being struck so many times. She ran her tongue over her cut lip; the blood tasted metallic and made her want to throw up.

"Jennifer, I need to talk to you in the kitchen," Trevor said, standing from the table. "Daphanie, I need to go the store. Grab my car keys and wait by the door."

48

His head snapped back, and he blinked his eyes quickly trying to keep them open; it was important Freddy not doze off where he was. He tried ignoring it, but his leg started hurting again, almost more than before. He figured it was because of the tight space he was in and the fact he hadn't moved it in what felt like almost an hour.

Lying on his side, he slid a hand into one of his coat pockets and pulled out the small bottle of generic aspirin. It took some doing, moving about back there, getting the cap off and dumping out a handful of them into his palm. He pushed the powdery pills into his mouth and crunched down, grimacing as he forced the crumbled aspirin down dry.

He shoved the bottle back into his pocket, and unable to wait any longer, Freddy did something stupid: lifted his head up from under the garments that were already lying in the back seat of the Nissan SUV, and peered out of one of the tinted back windows.

He quickly looked around the shopping mall parking lot. That's where he had been for the last hour: the south side Macy's corner lot, because that's where, after looking for twenty minutes, he finally spotted Kia's mother's truck.

After patching himself up the night he had gotten shot, Freddy slept on a half dozen broken down cardboard boxes. The stack was so thick that some of them were even dry. He pushed the sheets of board around, arranging them like a child making an imaginary fort, then Freddy shimmied in between them, his leg still feeling as though there was a rat trapped inside, trying to gnaw its way out. He lay there as the constant drops of rain continued to pelt the boards and drive him slowly insane.

There, fighting both sleep and pain, he thought about who might've had his child since he had killed Kia. At first he thought the police could've taken the baby—and that might've been true—but they would've only held him for a day, maybe, then returned him to the next of kin: Kia's mother.

The next night, after it had gotten dark, Freddy tried to go back to Kia's house to have a conversation with the mother, but there wasn't just one police car there then, but two. There was probably even an officer posted at the back door, and maybe even one inside. There was no way he'd be able to have a sit down with Kia's mother that way; he'd have to find another route.

Roaming the parking lot this evening, he hoped Kia's mother still drove the aging burgundy Nissan Pathfinder, and hoped she still worked at that Macy's, and hoped one of the doors of her truck was unlocked. Freddy was lucky and all of his prayers were answered.

Looking over his shoulders, holding open the back door, Freddy slipped in and under what might've been dry cleaning waiting to be dropped off. Under the mess, he hid himself on the back floor of the truck.

Now, after eating the aspirin and taking a peek out of the back window, Freddy was startled to see Kia's mother just a few feet from the car. She was with another older woman: white lady with red hair, dressed in similar K-mart bought business attire.

Freddy quickly ducked back down behind the seats.

"Thank you, Evelyn. Thank you so much," Freddy heard Kia's mother say. The car door opened, Kia's mother climbed in and shut the door behind her.

For the longest moment there was silence and Freddy only knew she was still in the car because he could feel her presence. Then he heard her crying.

He lay there, the crotch of a pair of polyester slacks over his face, his hand clutching the gun in his pocket, knowing this wasn't the time to make the move, but fearing he'd be found out if he waited any longer.

He heard Kia's mother sniffle and say, "Lord, I know Thy will must be done, but give me the strength to endure this. Jesus, please." More sniffling, then the sound of keys jittering against the plastic cased steering column and the car's engine came to life.

They were moving then stopping—probably at a stop sign before leaving the mall parking lot—then moving again. When Freddy felt they were a safe distance away—a minute's time of driving—he waited for the car to come to another stop. When it did, he quickly rose up from behind Kia's mother's seat and with one hand, grabbed the aging woman around her mouth and with the other, stuck the tip of the gun into the side of her neck.

Her scream was muffled, but still loud. Freddy's head whirled about glancing out both passenger and driver's side windows, making sure no one was stopped beside him witnessing what was happening.

"Ms. Banks," Freddy said. "Take me to my son right now, and I swear I won't kill your ass!"

49

Monica sat in the driver's seat of Nate's car, Nate sitting beside her. The car was parked in the lot of a small West-Loop, Italian restaurant, a big oak tree obscuring most of the car from the half dozen others parked there.

"I appreciate you meeting me here to have dinner, even though I get the feeling—with Ford still running around—you don't feel safe to be around me."

At dinner, Nate drank more than he should've. Monica sat there in front of him, taking the occasional tiny sip from her single glass of wine, not happy with herself for still being disappointed by the snapshot proof she had gotten earlier this afternoon. But Nate was right, Monica was looking over her shoulder even though she had moved in with Tabatha. Practically every moment of the day, she wondered if that crazy bastard, Ford, was plotting his moves, if he had shot somebody else, scratching off the names on his kill list, as he prepared to put another bullet in her head.

"Don't be ridiculous, Nate. I wanted to see you," Monica lied.

Nate smiled, scooted over in his seat so that he could be closer to her. "You were quiet at dinner. Everything all right?"

"Just...the business. You know how it is," Monica said, her left hand fiddling with the leather stitching on the steering wheel. "It's always on my mind."

He set his hand on her thigh, grabbing it lightly. "Well, I wanted to tell you I spoke with a financial consultant friend of mine today at work, and I think he'll really be able to help us."

"Oh, really. What else did you do today at work?" Monica said, recognizing the mistake she made in asking that question the minute it fell out of her mouth. It was drenched in resentment and suspicious accusation. She sounded like a jealous girlfriend who had busted her boyfriend cheating countless times, but promised she wouldn't have a problem forgiving. She hoped that mistake hadn't triggered Nate's antenna. That would ruin all the work she had invested thus far. "Because you seem kind of tired this evening," Monica said, working damage control.

She had felt Nate's grip tighten on her then relax.

"The routine work stuff," he said. "And yeah, it's been a long one, but I'm not too tired to have a little fun with my wife." Nate leaned in and kissed the side of Monica's neck. She felt his fingers of one of his hands fumble with the buttons on her shirt, the other hand sliding down between her thighs. Monica sat stiff, gripping the steering wheel with both hands, not certain of what to do: let him have his way with her, as any supposedly happily married woman should do when propositioned with spontaneous car sex, or reject him, because she still struggled with the thoughts that after his lunch with Tori, he could've taken her somewhere and had done to her, what he was attempting to do to Monica.

She brushed Nate off a little with her shoulder. "We shouldn't. Someone'll see."

Nate wrenched his head back to look out one of the car's windows. "No one can see us," he said, sliding a hand up the front of her shirt.

"Nate really, I should probably be going," she said in a lighthearted, giggly sort of voice, trying not to offend him or possibly cause more suspension.

"Then we can make it a quickie," Nate said, his voice low and guttural and wanting. His hand, feeling foreign and invasive now, was even busier, managed to unclip her bra and spring her breasts from their restraints.

"I said, no Nate!" Monica said, forcing his hand from under her shirt, spinning away from him, pressing her back against the driver's door, and crossing her arms over her chest.

"What's the problem?" Nate said leaning away. "Did I do something wrong?"

The picture of Tori's hand in Nate's lap at lunch would not fucking fade from her brain. "No!"

"Then what's wrong? If it's the business—I told you we'd—"

"It's not the business, Nate!" Monica said, again, speaking too quickly.

"Then what," Nate said, reaching a hand toward her face, wanting to caress her.

Monica tuned further away, shaking her head, the voice in her brain ordering her to do as he wanted or risk losing the chance at rescuing her son: something she continued to tell herself she still wanted.

"You don't want to do this with me?" she heard her husband ask.

Unable to look at him, Monica said, "I'm sorry, just not right now, okay."

It took him a moment to respond before saying: "I've hurt you in ways I can probably never make up for, but I'm trying. It's taken me this long to realize you are the only woman I love, the only woman I'll ever love. You're my soul mate, Monica."

Still looking away, she felt Nate grab her face, turn her to look him in the eyes.

"I'd die for you, you know that?" Nate said, his face as serious as she's ever seen it.

Monica nodded, and despite how much she might have wanted to, she could not believe a word of what he had just said. Nate leaned forward again, lightly kissed her lips, then without speaking another word, climbed out of the car.

50

Daphanie drove her Infiniti, crying, her seatbelt strapped across her torso, both her hands on the wheel, occasionally removing one to brush tears from her face.

"Stop that crying," Trevor said from the passenger seat, his arms crossed over his chest, not wearing his belt, as he never did when being shuttled about.

Moment's after Trevor ordered Daphanie to stand down, allowing her to catch a pretty serious beat down from Jennifer, he took the nanny in the kitchen to talk to her, leaving Daphanie to feel like a punished second grader, standing in the middle of the dining room. All she needed was a Dunce cap to wear. She tried not to cry, hearing the hushed whispers behind the kitchen door: female voice attempting to make a point: male voice interrupting. Daphanie didn't have to hear to know Jennifer was lobbying to have her thrown out. Sadly, Daphanie knew she was becoming all too much for Trevor to handle. Yes, he wanted to make her pay for deceiving him, wanted to make her suffer, but she knew his peace and calm was far more important to him than his quest for revenge.

Trevor would put an end to the chaos, possibly tonight, and as Daphanie smeared tears from her cheek, she thought that's what the drive was most likely about. He was taking her on the "the long ride". It was what Daphanie's mother did in the past—two times—when Daphanie brought home stray dogs: animals she begged her mother to keep, promised she would care for, but when she didn't, the dogs would come up missing. Daphanie would come home from school, no dog excitedly wagging its tail at the door. Daphanie's mother would tell her that while at school, the dog had jumped the fence and ran away, when she had really driven the dogs for miles, opened the back door of the car and released them back onto the street from which they were found. Trevor was about to do the same thing tonight, Daphanie feared.

She had been playing nanny to her own child, relegated to a house staff position, but at least she was in the house—in Nat's life. If Trevor did what Daphanie thought he would, she would never get her son back, or maybe even see him again.

On the drive for not even five minutes, Daphanie said: "I'm sorry for what I said to Jennifer. I'll apologize to her when we get back."

"I asked you to do that and you wouldn't."

"But the way she talks to me, looks at me, and you allow it. You let her hit me! I don't deserve that. I'm your son's mother. I'm a good mother!" Daphanie said, slowing the car to a red light.

"I know that. You would be if I allowed it," Trevor appeared pained to admit.

Daphanie looked at him shocked. "Then let me."

"You lied and tried to keep my boy from me. As long as I'm alive, that child has no mother. I am his only parent."

"But you have her there, caring for him as if she's his parent too," Daphanie said, becoming anxious, thinking what she feared might actually come true. "Just let me go home and be a part of our child's life. I don't care, keep the woman, sleep with her in your bed, just let me be with my son."

A car horn alerted Daphanie to the green light above her; she pushed the car through the intersection.

Trevor gravely shook his head. "I loved you once, Daphanie. And for no reason, you left me. It hurt, but relationships end. If I wasn't good enough and you wanted better or different, there was nothing I could do about that. You had that right. But to lie to me, take my child and attempt to give him away in order to snare another man." A look of disgust covered his face. "There's nothing you could ever do to make me forgive you. I brought Jennifer in to make things hard for you, to make you suffer, to try to make you feel what it is to be denied your own child."

214

"And you did that!" Daphanie said, tears growing faster in her eyes, her hands gripping the steering wheel tighter, her foot, unknowingly, pressing down harder on the gas. "I understand now!"

"No. You never can and you never will, because you're heartless. Only that kind of woman would do what you did."

Daphanie could feel it coming. He was about to tell her that he had already discussed it with Jennifer, then when they return, Daphanie was to go about gathering her things and not say a word to Jennifer as she packed, and not attempt to wake up Nate as Trevor escorted her down the hall, his fist clamped around her upper arm.

"Trevor please, whatever you're about to say, whatever you intend to do—don't!" Daphanie said, the needle on the speedometer creeping higher, the wind whirling louder through the partially rolled down windows, the trees, billboards and other stationary objects outside the car, starting to blur as they sped past them.

"Daphanie," Trevor's tone was apologetic but firm, like a judge about to render a life sentence to a fourteen year-old. "You didn't care about my feelings when you..."

And yes, he was starting on his explanation why it made sense to tear her from her child forever. How, at first it might sting for a little while, but that the pain would lessen over time, because time healed all wounds. And maybe she would find another man, fall in love and get pregnant with another child. But Trevor would warn her—one last dagger to totally finish her off—don't lie to the next man about being the father, because she had learned her lesson of how that could turn out.

Daphanie heard none of that speech, if that was indeed what Trevor was saying, because in Daphanie's head, she envisioned carrying her things down the hallway, then bursting into Nat's room, waking the baby, both of them screaming and crying and clawing for each other as Trevor grabbed her around the waist, lifted her off the floor and carried her, kicking and howling, out of the house. He would get a restraining order no doubt, and she would have no legal right to see her son. That would be it. She'd be done. And if Daphanie told Tori earlier that all the things Trevor had done to her was killing her, if what Daphanie just imagined came true, she knew that would definitely leave her dead.

"No. No. No!" Daphanie heard herself saying over the whipping wind noise, the rev of the car's engine and the occasional honk of a car as she flew through street lights, speeding out of a commercial district and onto a dark, two-lane street, lined with huge trees. But somewhere in the manic chaos exploding in her skull, she heard the advice Tori had given Daphanie: about doing whatever it took to get her baby back, whatever it took not to die. Tori hadn't been specific, but with Daphanie's arms outstretched, elbows locked, palms drenched with sweat and glued to the wheel, she could only see one option.

From Trevor's side of the car, she heard the phrases "…find a place to stay", Trevor telling her there was, "nothing you can do" and "call the police if necessary" and she knew it was going down: her worst fears realized. And that moment—no more thought required—Daphanie decided she would rather die than have done to her what Trevor was attempting.

Fifty feet ahead, just down the road, she set her eyes on a huge oak tree. She held firm to the wheel, pressed the gas pedal down till it would not go any further, and ignoring the high-pitch scream coming from Trevor and his attempts to grab the wheel, she yanked it hard, sending them racing toward the hulking oak. There was no squeal of steaming brakes or flash of bleeding taillights from the back end of the car as it rocketed forward, two inches before impact.

Daphanie's car struck the hundred year-old tree with a thunderous force, enough to snap branches thirty feet above them and rattle the ground beneath. The car's front end wrapped around the tree, crinkling like an aluminum can, the back end hiking up, then slamming hard to the ground. The front driver's and passenger's windows shattered completely, falling out the frames, sprinkling the ground like diamonds. Thousands of jagged white crack-lines ran down the back shield, as at the same time, a blood-rimmed hole opened up on the passenger's side of the front window, Trevor's body

216

shooting out of it, his head striking the tree, his body falling hard on the car's compacted hood.

Daphanie lay still in her seat, the belt pulling tight between her breasts; she quickly assessed her injuries: gingerly moved her feet: raised both her hands, slowly tightening them into fists to make sure she wasn't paralyzed. She was okay save for the pounding in her head, the dull pain in her neck at the base of her skull, and the weird feeling of something crawling down the side of her face and onto her lips. She lifted her fingers to whatever that was, brushed it away and saw that her hand was covered in blood.

She reached down weakly, fumbled with the seatbelt lock and managed to release the clip. She went for the door handle, but was startled when she heard her name called.

"Daph-nie."

She whirled around as fast as she could to see Trevor's body lying on the hood of the car like a struck deer on a dark road. One of his eyes was open, staring right at her through the hole in the window he had been ejected through. Again he called, softer than before. "Daph...nie."

Daphanie was able to shoulder the driver's side car door open, and with a trembling hand held against the length of the car's edge, she slowly made her way to the hood, where Trevor lay on his stomach, Slinky-like, his legs folded forward over his head. As Daphanie neared him, she saw that he was trying to say more, and wondered how that was possible when he was contorted in only a way a very limber, three year-old gymnast could've pulled off; his back was clearly broken.

"You...you..." Trevor gasped, still only one eye open, it following Daphanie's every move.

"What Trevor?" Daphanie said, feeling terrible now, despite what her intentions had been for him only moments ago. "What are you trying to say?"

"You..." he said softly, seeming nearly out of breath. "Stupid...bitch. You...got in an...ac...accident."

What sympathy Daphanie had drained from her as quickly as it had filled her. The man had not changed, even moments away from meeting the good man upstairs, he was still an arrogant, evil little, self-righteous prick.

"No," Daphanie said, laying her face down on the car's warm hood, just in front of Trevor's, so she could look in his eye. "I didn't get in an accident," she said in the tone of a third grade teacher, speaking to a petulant child she could not stand, but had to be kind to. "I saw that you weren't wearing your seatbelt and I ran into this fucking tree intentionally." She saw as Trevor's single working eye ballooned, heard one of his already shallow breaths catch in his throat. "And to think, if you just would've let me help you care for our son like I had asked, you wouldn't be smashed all over this windshield like a fucking bug."

The eyeball darted around in Trevor's head, no other part of his body moving. "Tell...our son I love..." he whispered.

"No," Daphanie said, knowing that Trevor would die in mere minutes, if he had that long. "I won't tell him that. I also won't tell him what a horrible, unloving man you were. You know what I'll tell him about you?"

Trevor's brow rose in a question over that one working eye.

"Absolutely, nothing at all," Daphanie said.

51

After putting the gun to Kia's mother's head, the older woman screamed into his palm, immediately went for the buckle on her seatbelt, fumbling desperately, trying to free herself. Freddy pressed his hand tighter against her face, pulling the back of her head into the car seat, and pushed the tip of the gun deeper into her temple.

"Calm the fuck down, or I'll do you right now!" Freddy whispered harshly.

Her chest heaving, still whining, she stopped struggling and set both her hands on the steering wheel as Freddy told her. He instructed her to drive, giving explicit directions that landed them—not ten minutes later—in an alley deep within a number of abandoned low-income housing buildings.

"Now I'm gonna come around in the front seat with you. Make a move, and I swear you're dead. You hear me?"

Kia's mother whined nonsensically, and eyes still teary, she nodded her head, her hands trembling on the wheel of the car.

Freddy pushed open the door, limped around the back and climbed into the front passenger seat. Resting the gun in his lap, pointed at the woman, Freddy said, "The two cop cars parked in front of your house, I want you to have them called off so we can go get my baby."

"Wha...what are you talking about?"

"Don't act like you don't know shit," Freddy said. "You Kia's mother. After I killed her, you the one they would've given my baby to."

Kia's mother's face crumbled into a mask of emotional agony. Her eyes shut and tears spilled from out of them. Suddenly, she lunged at Freddy, calling him a bastard and only freezing when the barrel of Freddy's gun was pressed to her forehead.

"You know I don't got no problem killing," Freddy said, holding the gun steady, staring sternly into the woman's eyes, and with his other hand, he was elbow deep into her purse. He wrapped his hand around her cell phone, pulled it out and held it before her. "Call the police and tell them cars to leave. Now!"

"No!" she sobbed.

He tried to force the phone into her hand. "I said call!"

She wouldn't take it and let it drop to the floor. "No!"

"Get out the fucking car," Freddy said, jabbing the gun in her face.

"No, no, no," she sobbed.

Freddy pushed open his door, climbed out, pointing the gun at the woman through the windshield as he hobbled around the front of the SUV. He yanked open her door, grabbed Kia's mother by her hair, then dragged her over to a metal dumpster and threw her against it. He pressed the gun against the back of her head. "Tell the cop cars to go so I can get my baby, or I swear I'll—"

"The baby's not there. I don't have him. I swear!"

Freddy grabbed the woman by the shoulder, spun her around to face him. Her face smeared with tears, mucus running from her nose over her lip into her mouth, she shot her trembling hands into the air.

"Bullshit! You the next of kin, so they would've—"

"They knew you'd come looking," Kia's mother sobbed. "That's the reason for the cars, the reason I let them keep the baby in custody."

"Custody?"

Sniveling, shaking her head, she said, "I agreed not to have the baby brought to me until you were arrested."

Freddy spun away from the woman, paced a couple of infuriated steps, then turned back, fished out his own phone—the most recent he had stolen from a high school kid—held it out for her to take. "Then tell them to give him to you."

"Please," the woman cried. "I'm telling you they won't. Not until they catch you. Let me go. There's nothing I can do."

Freddy shut his eyes for the briefest moment. In the darkness behind his lids, he saw Kia's pleading face, heard her beg him not to do what he was about to. Freddy opened his eyes, stared at the bawling older woman, and before pulling the trigger, he said, "Then why the fuck I need you?"

Catching a glimpse of only her legs stretched out from behind the dumpster as he drove away in the SUV, Freddy took solace in knowing now that Kia was not alone in heaven.

52

The accident had quickly attracted a crowd of onlookers and bystanders, and not much later, the cops and EMS had pulled up, lights flashing.

Not long before that, Trevor had breathed his last breath, closed his eye and died. Daphanie limped back to the driver's side of the car, found her cell phone on the floor, gingerly lowered herself to the curb and dialed the only person she felt she could've asked for help.

When the police arrived, they took Daphanie's statement, told her that investigators would be in touch, and left her for emergency medical services to treat. There on the back of their wagon, a big man with a wiry red beard, stitched up Daphanie's head while she sat, a white sheet draped over her shoulders, spatters of blood droplets staining the front of it.

The big man cut the thread after the last stitch, snapped off his latex gloves and told Daphanie: "Ma'am, I really think you should allow us to take you to the hospital." He glanced again over his shoulder at Daphanie's car; a towing company was hooking it up to drag away. "You were in a really bad accident."

"No," Daphanie said, standing, adamant, pulling the sheet from off her shoulders, holding it out to the big man. "I'm fine. I need to go home."

"Ok. Suit yourself," he said. "Do you need a ride anywhere?"

"No," Daphanie said, her arms crossed over the dried blood that had also stained her shirt. She looked up the street to see a car slowing as it neared her, then saw Tori in the back seat, the woman's eyes round as ping pong balls, her nose nearly pressed to the window, as she saw the cops cars, the emergency vehicles and all the wreckage Daphanie had made.

Moments later, in the back of the late-modeled Nissan Altima, after Daphanie had told Tori everything that happened up to that second, Tori said, "And so you got me in the car with some stranger coming to get you? Haven't you heard about the Uber driver killing those people?"

Daphanie caught the reflection of the Indian man's eyes in the rearview mirror. "Don't mind her. Just drive faster, please," Daphanie said to the driver then turned to Tori. "You're the only person I knew would come," Daphanie said near tears, still shaken up.

Tori lay an arm around her shoulder and pulled her close. "I'm sorry. Sorry about Trevor…about all of this."

"Me too."

"Don't you think you should go to the hospital?"

"No," Daphanie said, her eyes glazed over, her body rocking gently beside Tori's as the car rolled over the pot-holed Chicago streets. "I need to get home to my baby."

Walking into the house, Tori closed the door behind her and Daphanie.

"Trevor, that you?" Daphanie heard Jennifer call from the kitchen. "Where you been? I was worried sick. Nate woke up hungry and—"

Jennifer was unable to finish her sentence when she turned and saw Daphanie standing in the kitchen doorway, stitches in her head, hair flown all about, dried blood staining the front of her shirt, and one of her eyes already starting to blacken and swell from the impact of a lose article flying about the car, Daphanie hadn't even realized had struck her.

Jennifer gasped and appeared shocked standing there, holding Nat.

"So this is the skinny bitch, trying to take your kid?" Tori said, crossing her arms.

Daphanie nodded. "She's the one." Daphanie limped forward, her arms outstretched. "Give me my baby."

Jennifer took a step back, shifting Nat from one hip to the other. "Trevor said you were never to touch this baby without permission from he or I, and I'm not giving you—"

"Bitch, give me my baby right motherfucking now!" Daphanie screamed, her voice sounding so shrill and crazed she didn't recognize it as her own. What she had gone through had just been too much, and only then, that very moment—Daphanie staring at Jennifer as though she had snapped—did the weight of what just happened: Trevor dying—and all it took to push Daphanie into killing him—finally dawn on her. Yes, something that moment—as she carefully scooped her baby under the arms and out of the hands of Jennifer—came unhinged in Daphanie's head; she tried controlling it, but realized she might've been going a little crazy that moment.

"You ever hold a baby?" Daphanie asked, not looking at, but speaking to Tori, who stood behind Daphanie, for her eyes were glued on Jennifer.

After Tori realized the question was meant for her, she said, "Oh, me? Yeah. Give him to me."

Daphanie passed Tori Nat, keeping her eyes on Jennifer, who appeared frightened and had pushed up against the fridge, asking, "Where's Trevor?"

Taking Nat, Tori asked: "Why do you want me to hold the baby. What are you—"

"That was the last time you will ever touch my baby," Daphanie said to Jennifer, ignoring Tori, circling around the nanny, the look in her eyes that of a tigress sizing up an antelope for slaughter.

"Where is Trevor?" Jennifer asked again, not sounding nearly as in control as a moment ago.

"Go upstairs, grab your shit and—"

"I said where is Trevor?" Jennifer asked, more insistent.

Daphanie considered not telling the heffa anything, but calmly said, "That nigga dead."

Jennifer's mouth fell open as she started sucking huge gulps of air. "He's...he..."

"Died in a car crash. He's gone, and you're homeless. Now get out."

"No," Jennifer said, sounding uncertain, as though telling herself it was a bad idea to defy Daphanie, but deciding to do it anyway. "I'm not going anywhere, because I don't believe you."

"Whaah!" Tori droned, bouncing Nat in her arms. "I would get out of her if I were you."

Jennifer glanced past Daphanie at Tori, then at Daphanie to see the crazed look in her eyes. Seeming to obey Tori's warning, Jennifer pulled herself off the fridge, then quickly tried to pass, when Daphanie said: "Wait. You owe me an apology for how badly you've treated me."

Jennifer turned, dread on her face, seemingly recognizing what Daphanie was demanding. "Okay, I don't know what's going on, or what you did to Trevor, but I am so—"

Before Jennifer could say the next word, Daphanie reared back and slapped Jennifer across the face with an open hand, spinning her in a half circle.

"I said you owe me an apology."

"And I said..." Jennifer began, rubbing a hand across her face, a tear running quickly from an eye. "That I'm—"

Daphanie whirled around again, catching Jennifer with the back of her hand. Jennifer twirled, knocking dishes from the counter, where they shattered onto the floor. She latched onto the front of the kitchen sink, stopping herself from falling to her knees, pulling herself up, turning, breathing heavily, bleeding from her mouth and sounding as though she was gargling with cheeks full of mouthwash. She tried again: "Please...I...am—"

Daphanie swung a final time, catching Jennifer on the side of the head, a blow that hurt Daphanie's hand as much as she figured it pained the nanny. Jennifer fell on her hands and one knee, breathing exhaustively, then pulled herself up and started toward the kitchen door.

Daphanie looked around, quickly grabbed one of the cans of Similac from the counter the tramp was going to feed to her child, and slung it toward the fleeing woman, missing, but catching a corner of the wall and taking a chunk of plaster out of it.

Daphanie turned to Tori, her chest heaving, her arms extended, her hands reaching out for her child.

Tori pulled Nat close, kissed the baby on side of his head, and only have joking, asked, "Mommy, you sure you're calm enough to take him?"

Daphanie's brow furrowed, she looked at the counter behind her, then back to Tori. "Give me my baby, woman, or I swear I'll throw this other can of Similac at your ass."

53

Monica sat on Tabatha's sofa, her feet up, head thrown back, halfway watching Atlanta Plastic on Tab's flat screen. Tabatha sat on the edge of the big recliner, a half glass of wine in her hand.

"See girl, I could use just the tiniest bit of lipo right here," she said, trying to grab onto the little bit of fat on her flank, "And maybe stick it in my butt, like chick did right there, and I'd be able to snag any man on the street."

Monica hadn't paid a word of attention to what Tabatha had said. Monica's head was still back in the car with Nate, seeing that look of disappointment on his face after she rejected his invitation to steam up the windows like high school students. Why was he so disturbed? When she was last married to Nate, he went for weeks without sleeping with her, because he had Tori on the side to fulfill his needs. Why was this any different? Why did he pretend so to be faithfully doing this thing with Monica, when that was the furthest thing from the truth?

"Monica, are you listening to me?" Tabatha said, standing in the mirror across the room, wearing nothing but her bra now. "Seriously, you think I should get my arms done, too?"

"Girl, put your clothes back on your skinny ass and sit down," Monica said.

Tabatha waved Monica off with a hand, grabbed her shirt and pulled it down over her head. "So are you staying over another night, or you going back home to your loving husband?" Tabatha said, pushing her other arm through the shirtsleeve.

"I'm here until further notice: until I've accomplished the mission I've set out on," Monica said, not appreciating Tabatha's teasing. "How many times I gotta tell you that?"

"Say what you wanna say, girl," Tabatha said, plopping onto the chair adjacent to Monica, drinking again from her wine glass. "I like the whole story about you going after the boy: the heroic crusader and all that jazz, but you don't have to go through that to save face with me. Just say you wanna get back with the man. Yeah, I'm gonna talk shit for the rest of our lives, but you're my girl and I'll always love you," Tabatha laughed.

"Fuck you, Tab," Monica said, letting the girl get under her skin. The doorbell rang.

"Who the hell interrupting my show? Pause that till I get back," Tab said, pointing at the TV.

Monica grabbed the remote, punched the pause button and called out: "Who is it?"

Tabatha walked back into the room, a perturbed look on her face. "Your husband is here, but you have to step out if you wanna talk to him. I'm not letting that man in my place."

Monica pulled Tabatha's condo door closed and stepped into the hallway. Before saying a word, Nate took her in a hug. It was tighter than normal: his arms clutched around her waist as though he was going off to war, might die on the battlefield and not ever see her again. His face in the crook of her neck, she felt his breathing coming faster than normal.

When he released her, Monica asked: "Are you all right?"

Looking down the hall, he appeared to intentionally avoid her eyes. "Yeah."

"Why didn't you call? You can't just pop up on me here. This is not my place or the store, and you know how Tabatha feels—"

"I don't give a damn about how your friend feels about anything," Nate said, his eyes on Monica.

"O-kay," Monica said, surprised by the anger coming from him. "So—"

"I've been getting the feeling that something's not working," Nate said. "You know I love you. We're married. We have the family we've always wanted. I'm giving and talking and doing everything I can to prove to you I'm committed to this, but I keep feeling that something's just not right."

Let's start with you trying to fuck a bitch on the side, Monica wanted to say. "I don't understand."

"I feel…a distance. I know you, Monica. Tell me it isn't there. When we talk, make love…what happened in the car tonight. Hell, right now. Tell me there isn't something between us."

"Nate, I…" Monica said, not knowing how to respond, wondering how long he's sensed this.

"Just say it. I married you because I love you, and I thought you loved me."

"I do!" Monica said more quickly than she had planned.

"I don't think you're entirely certain of that."

"But I am," Monica said, unsure of what she was fighting more for: the chance to take this man's child, or for the man himself.

"Yet, you've left me and your son to live with your girlfriend."

"No, Nate. You know the reason I'm here. And it's not to live here. It's just until Ford is caught."

"Yeah," Nate said, sarcastically. "Let's continue to go with that." He turned, took two steps away, but spun right back around. "I know I've done horrible things to you, but I'm becoming—no," he said. "I am a better man. I think I'm proving that. And considering all we've been through, I don't see the point in doing this if we aren't honest with each other. So…" Nate paused as though standing on a cliff, uncertain as to whether he would leap.

"So what, Nate?" Monica asked, concerned.

He swallowed, hesitant. "So we can work out custody arrangements regarding Nathaniel and I can have my attorney's draw up the divorce papers. Just let me know," Nate said, again staring at Monica a beat longer, as if imprinting her image on his memory. He turned and before Monica knew it, he was walking down the hallway away from her.

Monica felt all of a sudden weak, leaned back against the wall, clamped a hand around her forehead and dizzily called out: "Nate."

He didn't listen, approached the elevator and pushed the DOWN button.

"Nate?"

A "ding" and the doors slid open.

Monica pulled herself off the wall. "Nate! I don't have to think about it."

He stuck out an arm, stopped the doors from closing before he got on, and looked back.

"Don't talk to your attorneys. I don't wanna lose you or our family. Okay?"

The corner of one side of Nate's mouth turned up slightly, he nodded, then disappeared into the carriage, the doors sliding closed before him.

Feeling exhausted, as though she had gone through some physically traumatic ordeal, Monica turned and pushed open Tabatha's condo door to find her friend right there, arms crossed, shaking her head.

"Way to stay strong, Monica. Mission accomplished."

"Whatever, Tabatha," Monica said, a hand up as she walked past her friend toward the guest bedroom.

Locked inside, sitting on her bed, Monica waited for the phone to be picked up.

"Monica," Tori said, answering. "Did someone take the pictures at lunch?"

"I got them. What happened afterward?"

Tori paused a moment. "What do you mean?"

"Exactly what I asked. What did the two of you do after lunch?"

"Oh. Nate took me back to the apartment."

"And?"

"We didn't have sex, but…do you really wanna hear this?"

"It's why the fuck I'm paying you a million dollars, now tell me, Tori," Monica said, her temper short.

"I…I gave him a blowjob."

"You did what?" Monica said, unprepared for the information.

"I sucked his dick, he came in my mouth. You know: a blowjob."

"I know what the fuck a blowjob is," Monica said. It was exactly what she supposedly had wanted, what she was paying Tori for, but Monica shut her eyes tight against the image.

"He seemed to enjoy it," Tori said, waiting for a response from Monica. "Are...are you there?"

"I'm here. This is not moving fast enough."

"What are you talking about? I just—"

"Tomorrow, you'll need to make sure he goes all the way. I'll be needing video of the act."

"But Monica—"

"I'm tired of waiting on you. I'm paying you to—"

"No, Monica," Tori said. "You keep saying that, but you haven't paid me shit, yet."

"Fine. Get me you and Nate on video having sex, I'll give you half of the million for it. Does that work?"

"Works just fine," Tori said.

"I'll send Lewis over tomorrow morning with the video equipment. Seeing how you've done this before, I'm sure you'll know how to work it."

54

Freddy cut the lights on Kia's mother's Nissan as he rolled slowly toward the small mansion in which Nate lived. The last time he was there, Freddy walked right up to the door, rang the bell, filled Nate full of lead and accidently popped his wife, Monica, in the head.

As Freddy slowed to a stop a half a block away, but within view of the home, he realized there were so many reasons to kill Nate, and he lusted for the moment when he did it, stood over the man's body, watching the desperate man's eyes whirl around in his head then settle on his killer, knowing he would die. Freddy would take his time with Nate, maybe shooting him in the groin first, then the gut, in the chest then finally finish him off with one tap to the dome.

Freddy grabbed the gun from the passenger seat, and after getting out of the car, shoved the weapon into his jeans. His original plan was to have rescued his boy, have him sitting safely in the front seat of the stolen car, kill Nate Kenny, then take off. Under the stars of a clear night sky, a warm breeze blowing through the open windows, he and his son would cruise south on the interstate, Freddy stealing proud looks over at him, as he planned the rest of their lives together. But that dream was dashed, just like the old lady's life, because she gave his baby away to the cops, and Freddy knew he'd never get his kid back now.

Hobbling along the fence line, Freddy was reminded that the few houses on the block were good distances apart. That worked in his favor, making it less likely the neighbors would hear the shots; with the injury to his leg, it would take a bit of time for him to limp his way back to the car after murdering Nate Kenny.

Fifty feet away, coming to the end of the neighboring house's fence, Freddy halted and threw himself up against a wooden divider, after believing he saw movement far off in the front yard of Nate

Kenny's house. His gun in his hands, his back pressed against the fence, Freddy peered out from around the corner, and yes, under the light of the moon, he saw the shape of a man walking across the lawn, the undeniable shape of an automatic rifle slung over his shoulder.

Freddy looked passed that man, toward the house and saw another man walking alongside the house, carrying a similar weapon. He threw himself out the way, back up against the fence, realizing the odds he was up against, but still entertaining the possibility of shambling quickly across that lawn, picking the guards of with well-aimed headshots, then busting down Nate's door with him under it, stepping on top of him and shooting him in between the eyes. But Freddy didn't know how many guards there were. He'd most likely die in the attempt, not having killed Nate Kenny, which has become his sole reason for living now.

Starting back toward the car, he knew this would not be the place where he'd take Nate Kenny's life. He didn't know how, but he'd have to find a way to catch the man out, away from his protective detail and kill him then.

55

After climbing out of bed, brushing her teeth and showering, Tori stood, her stomach growling in front of a kitchen cabinet. She held the doors open, staring at the empty space where food should've been. All the other cupboard doors were open, as well as the fridge's: cold air spilling out of it.

Her doorbell rang and she turned suspiciously toward the sound. Walking over and opening the front door, she tied her bathrobe closed and smiled at the sight of Lewis holding and arm full of green mesh Whole Foods shopping bags.

"I thought you told *me* to call *you* if I needed something. Not that you'd just drop by all unannounced."

"Why? What's up?" Lewis said, then whispered. "You got a married man in there?"

Tori pursed her lips with attitude. "No, but I could've had. Don't just be rolling up on a sista."

"Thought Monica told you I was coming, but got it," Lewis said, turning around, starting back down the walkway. "I'll call you later and see if I can drop these groceries off tomorrow."

"Boy, you better come back here with that food."

Inside, Tori stood leaning against the kitchen wall very close to Lewis, eating a bowl of cereal, while he filled the fridge and cabinets with the groceries he had bought.

"So she never told him that she hadn't really gotten the abortion?" Tori asked, holding her spoon midway between the bowl and her mouth, she was so shocked and transfixed by all Lewis told her about his friend, Freddy.

"Nah," Lewis said, putting away the last item of food then closing the cabinet. "We both thought it was best. But we also knew if he ever found out…" Lewis hunched his shoulders, a sad expression on his face. "I used to bring her bagels and coffee on some mornings. But now that she's gone…"

"I'm so sorry," Tori said, setting a sympathetic hand on his arm.

Lewis stared down at it then up at her, smiled and said, "Think that's why I just got up this morning and went shopping for you. After losing my girl and Kia now being gone, it just feels crazy not having somebody to take care of."

Tori thought it so sweet and amazing how this man felt guilt for wanting to do for someone else. She couldn't help but lay her hand against his smoothly shaven face.

"Like I said, I am really sorry about your friend, but…" she said, smiling just a little, giving his face a couple of light pats. "You can buy me groceries anytime, okay."

"Yeah, okay," Lewis said, grabbing his car keys from the counter. "Guess I'll be going."

"You forgetting something? Monica said something about video equipment."

"Damn. Right," Lewis said, tapping his forehead with the flat of his fist. "I'll grab it out the truck."

Lewis placed two tiny cameras, the size of ring boxes in the living room: one behind pictures on the mantle, another peeking out from around some books on a shelf.

In the bedroom, where they were now, Lewis finished placing the second of two cameras on the dresser behind some bottles of make-up and other casual looking clutter.

Stepping back, he looked at the bed: the direction the camera was supposed to be pointed and shook his head, trying badly to hide his disapproval. "So, that's for you when…you know…with Nate?"

Tori sat on the edge of the mattress, shaking her head. "I don't even know why I agreed to have her set those up. I guess because she's going to give me five hundred thousand if I give her video of me and her husband fucking. Trust me when I say I'm in desperate need of it, but that's never gonna happen."

"Why? You said you guys used to hit before."

238

"Don't tell her, but I've been lying to Monica up to this point, telling her we did some things, when Nate's not even interested. Dude really has changed. At least it seems that way to me."

Lewis walked over and sat beside Tori. "Then you just won't get your money."

"That's not an option. I'll drug his ass, make him look like a willing participant before I just walk away from a half mill."

"You watching too much Empire," Lewis chuckled.

Tori stood, paced the carpet of the small room in front of Lewis, obviously troubled. "I can't continue to live the way I've been living. I need this."

"Maybe if you tell Monica the truth, she'll still give you the money."

"No the hell she won't. But..." Tori said, her face lighting up with an idea. "Maybe Nate will."

"What?" Lewis said shocked, standing from the bed. "You're talking about telling him?"

"I won't say a thing, won't even tell him what it's about until he promises to give me the money back he took from me. Only then will I tell him everything Monica has planned."

"Are you crazy?"

"Crazy-ass broke," Tori said, her expression never more serious.

"Don't do it," Lewis said, looking genuinely concerned for Tori. "You don't know if he'll lose his mind, go the hell off, throw you down a flight of stairs or out of a window."

Glassy-eyed, seeing either of those potentialities play out in her mind, Tori focused Lewis into view and trying not to sound too frightened, said: "I guess I'll find out tonight."

56

Monica waited on Tim's doorstep for someone to answer the door. It was early, the morning air was chilly, but she knew he worked from home, and she needed to have the questions that were swirling in her head—had been all night—answered. She rubbed her arms, looked over her shoulder and fought the eerie feeling she was being watched.

In bed last night, staring into the dark, a pillow bunched under her head, she kept thinking about the conversation with Nate: choosing not to leave him because something told her he was being sincere. For the very first time, she believed every word he had said to her. But she needed confirmation. She called her brother-in-law twice this morning, and when he didn't pick, she drove right over.

"Monica," Tim said, startling her. She turned to see Tim holding the screen door open. "What are you doing here?"

"I'm sorry, but I tried calling and...I need to talk to you."

Tim pushed the door open wider. "C'mon in."

Shaking her head, she said, "I'm not going to stay. Just need to ask you a few things."

Concern came to Tim's face. He looked back into the house, then stepped out onto the porch and pushed the door closed behind him. "This has something to do with Nate?"

Monica nodded sadly, knowing Tim was the one person Nate told everything. Back when Tori was his secretary, Nate would often use his brother as an alibi while seeing her. When Nate struggled with issues regarding his affair, he would come to Tim for advice, and guiltily and begrudgingly, Tim would give it.

"Is he seeing someone?" Monica finally asked.

"What?" Tim appeared thrown by the question, as if Nate never committed adultery in his life. "No, Monica. I told you—"

"You have to tell me the truth. He's acting as though he's being faithful and sincere, but I know he's not capable of that," Monica said, staring in Tim's eyes, watching him shake his head, as though he was about to continue lying for his brother, which she could not tolerate. "Just tell me!"

"It's not like that. He loves you. This time he's really not doing anything."

"Then why is he seeing Tori Thomas again?"

Tim appeared stunned. "How do you know about her?"

"It doesn't matter. He keeps on about how he's this changed man, how much I matter to him, but I know he's seeing her again. Just confirm it for me Tim, please!"

"He's talking to Tori, but that's only because he feels guilty about everything he took from her. He bumped into her at the gym, saw it as an opportunity to fix things. And yes, he said she's repeatedly tried to start something again between the two of them, but he won't allow it. There's nothing's going on there, Monica. He loves you."

Monica stared at her brother-in-law, trying to read him, weighing his words, testing them for truth. In the years she's been married to Nate, she's learned to discern when her husband spoke the truth and when he lied: the fidgeting with his hands, his lack of eye contact, the funny fluctuations in his voice. This time, there's been none of that. Especially the conversation last night: it was just Nate baring his soul in a manner Monica could not help but believe, and cause her to question the information she was getting from Tori. Yes, Monica had a couple of snapshots of them at lunch, but it was nothing to prove Nate was having an affair. There was only Tori's word, and considering how desperate the girl was for money—considering Monica was threatening not to pay if Tori didn't deliver—it would come as no surprise if she'd been lying this entire time.

"Are you certain?" Monica said.

"He would've told me, Monica. He always has in the past. For the first time, I'm happy to say," Tim said, smiling. "You're wrong about my brother, because he really has changed."

Monica only returned a half smile, knowing she was able to trust Tim's word in the past, but she would wait to see if Tori could produce the video Monica had asked for. Nothing would tell Monica where she stood more than that.

57

"You can have a seat," the aging white man said to Daphanie, after escorting her into the dark walled office. "Would you care for something to drink? Water? Soft drink?"

"No, if we could just take care of the business, I'd appreciate it."

This morning Daphanie received a call from Mr. Longmire, the man that was gingerly lowering himself into the leather executive chair behind the huge desk in front of her. He informed Daphanie that he was the executor of Trevor's will and asked if she'd be so good to come in so that they could talk.

"I had no idea Trevor had a will," Daphanie said over the phone.

"He does."

"But what does that have to do with me?" Daphanie asked, knowing the agony Trevor displayed handing her a twenty dollar bill to run to the store with for ice cream.

"We can discuss that when I see you."

Now, sitting in front of him, she watched the brittle looking man open a leather bound folder and shuffle a few papers out of it. Daphanie shifted uncomfortably in the chair, nervous about what the man would say, believing there was the chance it would be along the lines of Trevor wanting Daphanie to have nothing else to do with her child, and enclosed, would be some sort of posthumously activated form stating exactly that.

"That it? His will?" Daphanie asked, imagining herself snatching it out of the old man's hand, setting fire to it, or shoving it in her mouth and gulping it down before Trevor could continue to ruin her life from his grave.

"Yes."

"I'm in it?"

"You are."

"And my...his son, Nate. There's something about him in there as well?"

"Yes," Mr. Longmire said. "Would you like for me to read it to you? That is why I called you here today."

No. She didn't want that, because as things stood right now, she was the only living parent Nat had, which, in her opinion, made her the boy's true legal guardian. But if there was something in the will: adoption papers naming Jennifer Nat's new mother, or anything to that affect, Daphanie was better off not knowing about it.

"Just get it over with," Daphanie finally said.

The older man took up the page off the folder and adjusted his glasses on his face.

Daphanie zoned out, turned off her hearing to what Mr. Longmire was reading, not wanting her few blissful days alone with her son to come to an end. But while watching the old man's lips, she heard him say something about "...leave all of my worldly possessions, to include monies associated with those holdings and all monies earned by sale of said possessions to my son, Nathaniel Charles."

No surprises yet, Daphanie thought. She hadn't expected the man to leave her a single cent. What she waited for now was to hear what financial planning institution he'd put in charge of his estate, and the date Trevor set for Daphanie to gather her things and get the hell out of his house, because she knew, somewhere scribbled on that page, that date was there.

"But till the day of Trevor's twenty first birthday," Mr. Longmire continued, "I leave Daphanie Coleman in control of all assets, holdings and monies, and being my son's birth mother, upon my death, I grant her all legal rights and custody of my son, Nathaniel Charles."

Daphanie sat in the chair, gripping the leather bound armrests so hard her fingers ached. Her entire body tense, Daphanie said, "Is...is that it?"

The man set the paper back down on the folder and gently closed the top half back over the forms. "For the most part. Yes, that's it," he smiled.

"That means Nat, I mean Nate...he's..."

"Yours to adopt if you wish. I can start the paperwork here, if you'd like."

She felt a smile, all teeth and squinty eyes want to show itself upon her face, but she suppressed it for fear it would reverse all that was happening that moment.

"And the house? When am I supposed to leave?"

"As the will declared, in 21 years, that is, only if your son no longer wishes you to live there."

Daphanie lowered her head, brought her hands to her face attempting to the catch the tears that were spilling from her eyes.

The older man stood, came around his desk and set a hand on Daphanie's shoulder. "Ms. Coleman...are you all right? Is there anything I can do?"

Daphanie looked up, shaking her head, her face shiny-wet with tears. She stood, attempting to pat her cheeks dry with her fingertips, then held out her arms and said: "I'm so happy, I need to give someone a hug. Do you mind?"

"Of course not," Mr. Longmire said, smiling, taking Daphanie in an embrace and politely patting her on the back.

58

Tori's cell phone rang. Nate's name appeared on the screen. She took a moment to compose herself, knowing that how she performed from that moment on would determine the complexion of the rest of her life. Exhaling, she swiped the green answer box on the phone's screen, placed her cell to her ear and said, very sweetly, "Hello Nate."

"Just calling to make sure we're still on. There something I need to give you."

Her doorbell rang at a little after 9 P.M. Tori hurried to it wearing a satin teddy with a shear, thigh high cover; the faint shadow of her darkened nipples could be seen through both. She had decided she'd make a final attempt to corrupt Nate; chances of success with Monica's plan were far greater, she believed, than with hers of drugging Nate, or even telling him the truth; she would save that as a last resort.

When Tori opened the door, Nate stared surprised at the very sexy lingerie she was waering, but in a way that suggested he was sorry for such a late-night intrusion, not in a way that said he wanted to grab her up and rush her off to the bedroom.

"Good to see you," Tori said smiling, holding open her arms and standing on her bare toes, waiting for a hug. Nate stepped in, took her in an embrace, held her only a moment, ending the hug with three polite pats on her back.

"Can I come in?" he said, afterward.

"Sure."

Nate stood in the middle of the living room, wearing khakis, a t-shirt and a blazer he wasn't pulling off to make himself comfortable; he just stood there as though waiting to take care of some business then promptly leave afterward. Tori could not afford to let that happen.

Walking toward him, Tori untied the belt of her robe. "Mind if I take this off. It's hot in here."

"Maybe you should leave it on."

"I think I prefer it off," Tori said, stripping it down from off her shoulders, setting it on the spine of the sofa, then held out a hand. "Now you have to take off your coat, or you'll make me feel like I'm walking around here half dressed.

Nate smiled, shouldered off his jacket and gave it to Tori to place on the sofa as well.

"How about something to drink?" Tori said walking into the kitchen, pulling glasses from the cabinet and starting to pour before Nate could tell her that he really hadn't planned to stay very long. She seductively walked the glasses out of the kitchen, holding them shoulder high, her hips dancing beneath the shiny satin, her nipples hardening and pressing against the gown.

"Here you are," Tori said with a smile, handing him a drink.

"I really didn't come here for that, Tori."

"Take one anyone."

Nate took the glass filled halfway with bourbon.

Tori lifted hers a little higher. "To bumping into each other at the gym—part two?"

"Sure," Nate said and took a sip from his glass.

After downing all of her drink, Tori lifted the bottom of Nate's toward his lips with two of her fingers. "C'mon Nate, I don't remember you being a light weight."

He smiled obligingly and kicked back what was left in the glass and held it out to her. "Okay, so like I said, I'm not going to stay long. I just wanted to come by—"

"Hold that thought, and let me take these glasses to the kitchen."

Walking them back, Tori stood, both hands pressed flat against the counter. She knew she was letting her opportunity to no longer live in abject poverty slip quickly away from her. She had to do something: make a move that Nate couldn't just shrug off: a move that would demand his attention and make him want to act. Fuck being a better man. Like Monica said, if the pussy was just too easy to take, no man, bad or good could turn it down.

Tori slipped the spaghetti straps from off her shoulders and let her gown fall to the kitchen floor. She turned toward the door, closed her eyes, breathed in and exhaled, knowing if this didn't work, she would have to resort to plan B: spilling all the marbles, coming totally clean to Nate, then risking being prey to whatever diabolical plan he would use to destroy her.

She stepped into the living room wearing nothing but the almond colored skin, dimpled, cratered, scarred and marred, her very shapely body was wrapped in. As she walked toward Nate, she forced herself to remember living in the squalor of the shit box she inhabited for the last year. And even though he was no longer a threat, she told herself to relive the torture Ja'Van inflicted on her, because if she didn't collect any of the money that was on the table before her, she might find herself relying on another knucklehead to support her.

Tori stopped her bare feet on the living room area rug and cleared her voice. "Nate?"

He turned around, and Tori only waited long enough to see the look of total shock on his face before she quickly moved on him, pressing her body to his, her lips to his lips, kissing him passionately, attempting desperately to slip her tongue into his mouth.

Nate turned his face left and right, her kisses wetting his cheeks, as he tried to grab Tori's busy hands, then finally took hold of her shoulders and was able to push her off.

"What are you doing?" He said, wiping his face as though he had been jumped by a slobbering St. Bernard.

"I…" Tori said, embarrassed, feeling like a fool, but worst, knowing she failed and would be sent home as broke as she was flown here. "I…just wanted to…I don't know. I'm still attracted to you, Nate. You've been so nice to me, and I guess I wanted to…" she shrugged her shoulders. "…repay you."

251

Shaking his head and sighing, Nate said, "That's ridiculous, and I'm the one who should be repaying you." Then, as if just realizing she was standing naked in front of him, Nate grabbed his jacket off the sofa and quickly threw it around her, pulling the lapels together.

"Sit down, please," he said, taking the seat right next to Tori on the sofa. Staring at her, he said: "You're beautiful, and any man would have to be blind not to be attracted to you, but I'm married, and I'm taking it seriously this time. I need for you to understand that, once and for all. Can you do that?"

Tori nodded sadly, feeling the heavy, stank wetness of failure start to weigh heavy upon her, forcing her to resort to the long shot of snitching on Monica. Still she believed it was a foolish idea, but it was all she had left, so she started begrudgingly: "Nate, I have something I really need to tell you."

"No," he said. "You've been cutting me off since I walked through the door and—"

"But it's something I really think you'd wanna know."

"And you can tell me, but after I take care of the business I came here to handle."

"Sure, okay." She lowered her head, shamefully.

Nate stood, took a step away from the sofa. "I need for you to stand, too."

Tori did as instructed.

"You know," Nate said. "I had a conversation last night with my wife, and it's been rough going, proofing to her that I'm different. So much that I was ready to give up: walk away. But I decided, regardless of how hard it gets, I'm going to keep on trying till she allows me to make things right."

"Why are you telling me this, Nate?" Tori asked, not very interested in hearing it.

"Because it dawned on me. I'm fighting tooth and nail to make things right in one place where I'd done some damage, when over here, it would be very easy to fix what I've screwed up."

Shaking her head, Tori said, "Still don't get you?"

"Do me a favor and go into that inside jacket pocket and take out what's in there."

"This one?" Tori said, patting her left breast.

Nate smiled. "Yes. That one."

Tori opened one of the lapels, sunk a hand into the silk lined pocket, felt the edge of a folded slip of paper and with two fingers, pulled it out. "What is this?" she asked, already identifying the pale blue paper as a bank check.

"Open it up and see."

Her heart racing, Tori very carefully opened the paper to examine it. It was, indeed, a bank check, and it read:

Pay to the Order of: Tori Thomas
The sum of: Two Million Dollars and zero cents

59

Nate watched as Tori stared unbelievably down at the check. She glanced up at him, back down at the creased slip of paper, then again at Nate, this time with watery eyes.

"This can't be real," she said then threw herself into him, wrapping her arms around his neck. "Thank you, thank you, thank you!" she cried into his shoulder.

"It's nothing considering what you went through because of me," Nate said, holding Tori around the waist. "Think you might be able to finally forgive me for that?"

Tori leaned out of the hug and smiled happily. "You're forgiven! Today. This minute."

Nate laughed. "Then I guess I should be going." He let Tori go.

"You can't, not yet. Not after one more drink to celebrate," Tori said, hurrying to the kitchen. "I promise nothing sexual, and I promise I won't come out naked," Nate heard her call from around the kitchen's corner.

"Okay. But only one then I'm out of here," Nate called back, feeling his cell phone vibrate in his pocket. He fished the phone out, saw Abbey Kurt's name on the screen then called out to Tori again. "Can I use your restroom?"

"Sure," she said, still in the kitchen. "Down the hall, first door on the left."

His voice lowered, Nate saying into the phone: "One moment." He found the bathroom, closed himself inside then flipped both switches on the wall: the light to see, the vent to cover his conversation. "Everything okay, Abbey?"

"Yes, Mr. Kenny. I found the information you were looking for. Would you like that now?"

Nate leaned a hip against the sink and stared up at the angst ridden, concern-filled expression on his face in the mirror. The information Abbey Kurt was talking about, Nate wasn't sure he really wanted to know because there was the possibility it might dispel the reality he had been living in for the last several days. But worse, that information might destroy a future he had been hoping for, a future he had been working harder than he ever had, to guarantee. It was information he had told Abbey Kurt to dig up because of something he had seen the day he had bumped into Tori for the first time at the gym.

After walking her down to her car, he was happy to discover that she hadn't seemed to hold a grudge against what he had done. Making plans to see her again, he said goodbye, and walked through the parking structure—several rows of cars lined up between painted white lines—feeling good about potentially making up for the money he had taken from her.

At his car, Nate pulled the keys from his pocket, but they slipped and fell from his hand. He grabbed them from the ground, then upon standing, he saw a car slowing to a stop at a sign and believed he recognized the driver. As the car rolled on and toward him, he quickly ducked out of sight, then slowly peered over the roof of his car at the aging Infiniti sedan.

The entire ride home, Nate forced himself to believe it was a coincidence: seeing two out of the three women he last had relationships with—two of the three woman, who's lives he ruined.

That night at dinner, he couldn't look at his wife without the wheels whirling in his head, trying to determine if she had anything to do with the chance occurrence.

"What?" Monica had said, catching him staring at her. "Everything okay with you?"

"Yeah, yeah," Nate said, hoping, praying that the thoughts in his head were false, because he had told Monica, this time he wasn't playing games, and this time he really did mean that.

That night he lay in bed on his side, streetlight stripes pushed through the blinds, painted the walls, the bed linen, and curved across Monica's sleeping face. Nate's pillow balled under his head, his eyes wide, he gazed at her. He mouthed the words, you promised me. Then softly, but aloud, he said them: "You promised me, and I'm going to believe you." He closed his eyes, attempted to force suspicion from his mind and allow trust in, but that was incredibly hard to do, for Nate was always a suspicious man.

Rolling onto his back, then away from his wife, he climbed out of bed, took the stairs down and got Abbey Kurt on the phone. "Sorry for the late call, Abbey."

"I was up, Mr. Kenny. What may I do for you?"

"You remember Tori Thomas, my secretary from several years ago?"

"Yes, sir."

"And Daphanie Coleman, a pharmaceutical rep I used to date?"

"Yes, Mr. Kenny."

"It's probably nothing, but I want you to dig around, find out what each of them are up to now, and if they might be up to it together."

"Yes, sir. Anything else?"

Standing in the center of the living room in the middle of the night, wearing his pajama bottoms, Nate paused, telling himself he needed to trust his wife and even if she was up to something, it might've been best he didn't know. And the best way to never know something is to never ask. But again, that wasn't Nate. "Do some light digging on my wife as well, and let me know what turns up."

Now standing in Tori's bathroom, the overhead air ventilation going, Nate's reflection staring uncertainly back him, this was his last opportunity to tell Abbey Kurt he wasn't interested in what she found out. It wasn't as though this was something that he had been urgently awaiting. And no, Nate had never told her to call off the inquiries, but on many occasions, he had wished he had never asked her to go digging. So this was his chance to tell her to just forget about it, and if there was something going on: if the three women were somehow conspiring against him, Nate could just do his best to weather

257

whatever offensive they put forth, forgive Monica for what she was attempting, then he and his wife could go on with their lives; he would have the wife he wanted, Nathaniel would have the mother Nate wanted the boy to have, and things, in Nate's opinion, would be what he had always intended them to be.

"Mr. Kenny," Abbey Kurt said. "Would you like that information now, sir?"

Nate dropped his eyes, ashamed that he could not fully be the trusting person he so whished to be—that he asked his wife to be, then looked himself again in the mirror and said, "Go ahead, Abbey."

He listened as Abbey told him of Daphanie's situation: Trevor had died in a recent motor vehicle accident and she received full custody of their infant child. Abbey could find no interaction between Daphanie Coleman and Mrs. Kenny. She went on to tell Nate that Tori Thomas was penniless and was brought to Chicago by Mrs. Kenny, confirming that Monica was up to something, most likely dangling money over Tori's head, hoping she'd seduce Nate, get them sleeping together again, but why? That answer came next.

"She's working with an attorney, Mr. Kenny," Abbey Kurt said.

"For what? To divorce me?"

"Yes, sir. But she first wants custody of your son."

"But I already allowed her to adopt him."

"She wants sole custody, sir. She wants the courts to take Nathaniel away from you."

"What did you say?" Nate said clenching the phone so tight he felt he could've crushed it in his grip.

"I have a connection in that firm. I have copies of the paperwork right here, Mr. Kenny."

Nate heard footsteps just outside the bathroom door then heard Tori calling for him. "Nate. You fall in, or what?"

In the mirror, Nate's face glistened with sweat; his chest swelled with each furious breath he took. "Abbey, have everything you found ready for me tomorrow morning." Nate ended the call, grabbed the bathroom doorknob and swung open the door to find Tori standing in front of it, still wearing Nate's jacket, smiling.

Lunging forward, Nate clutched her by the throat, bulldozed her backward. Stumbling and tripping over her bare feet, Tori's head and back banged loudly against the hallway wall, a gush of air rushed from her mouth and Nate felt her go almost completely limp in his grasp.

"What is she doing?" Nate yelled, spittle flying from lips as he tightened his grip around Tori's throat.

"Nate! Who? Wha...what..." Tori tried so speak, but Nate's tightening hold on her prevented it.

"Monica!" he yelled. "What is she doing?"

Tori whipped her head about, hair flying into Nate's face, as she beat at his arms, and kicked at his shins. "Can't...can't...breath!" Tori cried.

"She's trying to take my son. You knew about this? You knew and—" Nate yelled louder, holding a trembling fist by his head, fighting courageously not to let it fly, smash her face back through the plaster wall behind her.

"I...I...can't..." Tori coughed and gagged, her eyes shot with terror, her light skin becoming cyanotic—tinged with blue. And as her nails dug violently into his skin, drawing thin red lines down his wrist, he felt he could take her life for what she was aiding Monica in doing. What saved Tori's was that she was only an accomplice; he knew the idea wasn't hers. It was Monica who would have to pay the ultimate price.

Nate snatched his hand from out of Tori's throat. Tori sunk to her knees, and as if breaking the surface of water her head had been submerged in for hours, she took a great gasp of air.

Nate paced away from her, hearing Tori crying behind him, trying to speak. "I...I tried...to tell you. I was going...was going to tell you what she was doing."

Nate walked back to her, dropped to a knee, snatched Tori by the chin and forced her to look at him. "Before I gave you the check? That's what you were going to tell me?"

Sniveling, snot running from both nostrils, tears pouring from her eyes, Tori nodded and cried, "Yes!"

He held her face pinched in his grip a second longer. Believing her, Nate said: "However she got you to agree to this, I know it had to do with you being poor. That's my fault. I caused you to have to do it," Nate admitted, making her slight against him no less painful. "For that reason, you keep the fucking money. But don't you ever let me see your face again." He shook her away from him with enough force to send her face brushing against the wall, then stood and stormed away.

60

Lewis walked up to his truck after just visiting his daughter at Tim's house. She had asked him when she could come home, if he had heard from Eva and when she'd be able to play with her sister, Tammi, again.

Kneeling down, Lewis took her hands in his and whispered, "I've spoken to Eva, but I don't think Daddy and her are gonna be girlfriend and boyfriend anymore."

"Okay," Layla said, not seeming phased. "But will she still be my mommy?"

"Don't think that's gonna happen either, baby. I'm sorry."

Layla appeared sadder than the moment before, then moved closer, hugged Lewis and patted him between the shoulder blades. "Are you gonna be okay, Daddy?"

Smiling, he patted her back. "As long as I got you, Daddy's gonna be fine."

Layla leaned out of the hug, smiled and said, "Then I'm gonna be fine, too."

Clicking the remote to his truck, the locks disengaged on the Range Rover, and Lewis pulled open the door and climbed in as his cell started ringing.

He pulled the phone from his pocket, saw that it was Tori calling. He smiled, lightly pumped his fist, happy to know he wasn't the one always trying to make contact.

"Hello?" What Lewis heard was crying, sniffling and heavy gasping. "Hello? Tori! That you?" He said, frantic. "Are you okay? Are you hurt?" Leaving her house earlier today, he knew she wouldn't have been stupid enough to tell Nate about the scheme Monica was running, but by the sound of it, she had done just that. "I said are you hurt?"

"No," Tori sobbed. "Just…just…come over!"

61

Nate threw open the front door of his house. The guard posted in the living, watching TV, stood and reached for his rifle off the coffee table when Nate came rushing inside.

"My son..." Nate said, passing him. "Is he upstairs?"

"Yes sir," the guard said.

Nate was only mildly assured by what the man told him, as he continued tripping up the stairs. Monica wasn't the master manipulator he was, but considering she planned enough to get Tori here, possibly involve Daphanie, and have Nate thinking Monica was committed to the idea of being his faithful, dutiful wife and the mother to his child, she might've been conniving enough to have had Nathaniel swiped right out of his bed, right from under Nate's nose.

Nate pushed open his son's bedroom door. His eyes ballooned and his heart sank when he saw that his son's bed was empty and the window was open: a breeze pushing threw the sheer white curtains hanging over it.

Nate lunged for the blanket on the bed, whipped it off to make sure that, indeed, his son had been kidnapped again, only this time by his fucking wife. The blanket held up over his head, Nate saw nothing there but the fitted sheet and a pillow.

"Nathaniel!" he called out, yelling loudly, as though he was in the middle of a crowded football stadium. He went to the window, hoisted it further up, stuck his head out, scanning the dark yard frantically for his son. "Nathaniel!" he cried, desperately again. When he heard no reply, he shut the window, wanting to put his head through the glass for being so stupid to allow his child to be taken again.

"What's wrong, Daddy?"

Nate whirled around to see the little boy standing in the doorway, holding his favorite stuffed animal, his body silhouetted by the hallway light behind him. Nate leapt across the room, threw himself on the floor, scooped his son into his arms and pressed him firmly to his body.

"Nothing's wrong now, son. Nothing at all."

62

Lewis had managed to calm Tori down. She was no longer hysterical, most likely due to the empty bottle of Jack Daniels sitting on Tori's dining room table. Lewis had stopped to pick it up on the way over, thinking he might need it to calm her nerves; he had been right.

While drinking almost three quarters of it, Tori told Lewis all that had happened tonight. She sat in one of the kitchen chairs, her knees pulled into her chest, her arms locked around them, still appearing defensive. Staring up at Lewis, she saw the lost look on his face and said, "Sorry I brought you into this. I didn't feel safe here alone, and there was no one else to call."

"It's all right." Lewis walked over from where he stood in front of the fridge. He looked down on the table at the check Nate had given Tori. It sat in front of her, crinkled, dog-eared and ink smeared by dried tears.

"You're gonna have to do something with that. Take it to the bank or something. Get it cashed."

"Yeah, I guess," Tori said, trying to flatten it out using her palm against the surface of the table. Her eyes halfway lidded, she felt severely drugged by the huge quantity of alcohol she had downed.

"You think Nate's gonna go after Monica after what you told him?"

That moment, Tori's cell phone lit up, rumbling on the kitchen table. Tori fumbled for it, picked it up then said to Lewis: "It's Monica: her third time calling." Her words slurred and her eyes swam a bit when she asked: "What should I do?"

Lewis threw up his hands as if knowing less to do than she did. "You have to pick it up. Tell her something."

"Tell her what?"

Lewis stooped in front of her, whispering. "Whatever you have to."

The phone vibrated again, seemingly harder and louder. "I don't know what to say! You tell me."

"I'm not in this Tori!"

"Tell me what to do!"

"I don't know. Just talk to her!"

Tori shut her eyes, pressed the phone to her chest, as though saying a silent prayer, sighed then answered the call. "Hello, Monica."

"This is my third time calling you. What were you doing?"

"What you're paying me to do," Tori said, trying to sound as though she hadn't downed more than a half a bottle of whiskey by herself. "Nate...he just left."

There came a long pause. Finally: "Do you have the video? The two of you have sex?"

Tori's eyes rolled up, landing on Lewis. "Yeah...yeah, we had sex."

"You did? You just had sex with my husband?" Monica said, not sounding convinced.

"Yes! Why are you asking me this?" Tori said, her eyes still on Lewis. "I told you, we just fucked, okay."

"I'm not sure if I believe you, Tori."

"What do you mean, you don't believe me?"

"Sounds like you've been drinking."

"Of course I've been drinking. That's what people do when they fuck!" Tori said, shooting up from the chair. "You know what Monica, maybe we should talk tomorrow." All she wanted to do was get off that phone.

"No, no, no! All right, fine. But I need to ask you some questions, and I need for you to be totally honest."

"Questions about what?" Tori said worrying Monica might've known what she was up to. Tori pulled the phone from her ear, pressed her palm against it and mouthed to Lewis: "I think she knows."

Lewis stared back at her, still helpless. Tori placed the phone back to her ear and sat back down.

"Have you really been sleeping with my husband, Tori?"

Tori paused, feeling frightened of being found out, not knowing why, considering she had been busted already and was just paid twice the amount Monica had promised her. "I said yes."

"Tori, if you expect to still get paid, I need for you to tell me the truth. Now I know Nate's not sleeping with you."

"How you know that? Did he tell you?"

"His brother Tim did. I just need for you to confirm that."

Sobering from the moment Tori picked up the call, she said, "And you'll still give me the money?"

"Of course. That's what we agreed on."

Monica was lying, but that didn't matter now, Tori thought, realizing only then that she had been holding Nate's crumpled check in her hands, nervously dog-earing the corners and folding them open as she spoke. She was flush with cash and there would come a certain pleasure from telling Monica she had been played the fool.

"Tori, I'm going to ask you one more time. Have you slept—"

"No," Tori said. "We haven't had sex. I haven't given him oral. We haven't really even kissed. He wasn't going for it, Monica. Like I told you after the first night. But you didn't wanna believe me. Told me if I wanted to get paid, I needed to make something happen. So I did."

The other end of the phone was so quiet for so long, Tori said: "Hello?"

Monica's voice sounded small and hurt when she said, "You lied to me?"

"All Nate did was talk about how devoted he was to you. Guess the fuck what, Monica? He really was. If you would've sat down and just listened to him, instead of being so bent on taking the man's kid, maybe you would've seen it too." Tori could hear Monica breathing heavily and angrily on the line.

"I don't have to tell you that you'll never see that million we discussed."

"Yeah, I know," Tori said. "It was the reason she held back the bit of information about Nate knowing everything. While Monica was foolishly thinking she could possibly run to Nate, tell him she trusted him and call the whole thing off, knowing Nate, he was most likely strategizing how to tear Monica's life to shreds.

"Enjoy life on the streets, bitch!" Monica said. "That's where you'll be headed."

Tori ended the call without responding, then tossed the phone on the table, feeling upset and unnerved. "What is really happening?" she said, wrapping her arms around herself.

She heard Lewis say, "You did good."

"There's nothing good about any of this," Tori mumbled into her chest.

Lewis stepped closer to her. "It's what you had to do."

Looking down, she saw Lewis's shoes, the legs of his jeans, his t-shirt falling against his flat, muscled stomach. She could smell the faint scent of cologne he probably sprayed on twelve hours ago. She only knew this man through his association with the people she was now dealing with, only knew that he had gone through an almost identical situation and somehow came out better than he went in. Right now, she could've known a lot less and would've been okay with him being in her house. She was scared to death, believing that Nate came very close to killing her, and Lewis being there now, made her feel safe. But even after earning two million dollars, she didn't want to think about any of that. She wanted to let the intense buzz she tied on continue to heighten. She wanted to lay down somewhere, go to sleep, and wake up seeing that all her problems had disappeared.

Tori set her eyes on Lewis's hand hanging at his side. She reached out and slipped hers into it. "I wanna think nothing more about any of this right now." She stood, the room spinning, and took a step closer to Lewis: one of her shoulders bumping gently into his chest. She placed a hand on his shoulder, moving it up, slipping her fingers into the thick curls at the nape of his neck.

"What are you doing, Tori?"

She felt him try to step back, lean away from her, but he wasn't trying very hard and she wrapped the other arm around his neck, pulled tight to him. She stood on her toes, and with her open mouth, she pressed her lips to his, kissing him deeply. "I don't wanna think about this anymore," she said after the kiss. "Just do something to me so I don't have to for a while."

Lewis stepped back, held her by her shoulders, and through her fuzzy vision, saw him look square into her eyes and ask, "Are you sure?"

She smiled drunkenly, nodded her head and said, "Please, I'm sure."

She felt Lewis reach down, scoop her up, the world suddenly spinning horizontally, as he lifted her in his arms and carried her into the bedroom.

63

When the front door opened, Tim stood groggily in the doorway, looking to have been woken from dozing in front of the TV. With both hands, Nate grabbed his brother by the shirt, swung him out of the doorway, out onto the porch and slammed his body against the exterior house wall.

"Did you know about what she's doing?" Nate said, his teeth clenched, so filled with rage, his entire body rumbled.

"What?" Tim said, his voice high-pitched and surprised. "What who's doing?"

"Don't, Tim," Nate warned, shaking Tim by the front of his shirt. "She talks to you. She confides in you. She's trying to take me son. She's trying to take Nathaniel from me. Did she tell you?"

"No," Tim said, trying to push his brother's hands off of him, appearing as shocked as Nate. "I asked her. I asked her specifically if she was back for any reason other than she loved you. She said that was it! I'm telling you, Nate! That, and to be with her son."

Staring into Tim's eyes, Nate's breathing slowed. He unclenched his fists from around Tim's shirt then let his arms hang at his side.

"Nate, I'm sorry."

His head hung, turning his back to Tim, Nate said, "I was honest this time. All I wanted was to be a good man for her."

"And you were that. You are that."

"No," Nate said under his breath.

"You are!"

"But she didn't see it. She didn't care." Nate spun. "She's trying to take the one thing that matters to me."

"Nate…"

"Nathaniel's in the car sleeping," Nate said. He turned in a circle as if not knowing where to direct his vengeance. "I'm bringing him in. You keep him here and don't you tell her anything."

"What are you going to do?"

Nate stared at Tim, his lip quivering he was so angry. He thought to confide in him, thought better, then brushing a tear from the corner of his eye, said: "Keep Nathaniel here and don't tell Monica anything."

64

The next morning, Abbey Kurt hung the suit on the changing room wall hook, locked the fitting room door then dug the explosives out of the big leather tote she had gently set on the room bench. Also from the bag, she pulled a small power screwdriver and two thin metal braces she would need to affix the explosive devise, out of sight, onto the bottom of the bench.

She had already outfitted the first two AERO locations: the suburban and the west side stores. This one, Mr. Kenny instructed, was supposed to be done last.

Abbey lowered herself to the floor, turned on her back, triggered the flashlight on her cell phone, set it facing up and started the work Mr. Kenny had called her to take care of last night.

"Mr. Kenny," Abbey said, sitting up on an elbow in bed, her sleeping mask hiked up on forehead. "Your wife's stores, Sir?" she said after hearing his specific instructions.

"If you have a problem with this, just tell me and I'll find someone else."

"No, Sir. No problem at all."

After drilling the last screw into the underside of the bench, Abbey flicked a small switch on the device, activating a blinking red light that would correspond to the remote detonator used to set off the explosives. Abbey slid out from under the bench, gathered her tools and any other signs she had been there, dropping them all back in the bag then stood. Turning, she caught her reflection in the changing room mirror. She was held by the almost undetectable amount of guilt that no one else would've been attuned to, but she could clearly see in the emotionless façade that was her face. She had been with Mr. Kenny for ten years. He's done many things that she didn't agree with, but what she was doing now: what he had her do earlier this morning; had her seriously consider leaving him. But Abbey was taught long ago, never to question the actions or the reasoning of her employers, so she did not.

In the mirror, she smoothed the front of her skirt, snapped the bottom of her jacket to free it of wrinkles, then shouldered the bag, grabbed the suit from the hook and stepped out the dressing room.

"How did that fit?" The thin man in the purple, ruffle-collared, shirt asked.

"I'm not interested," Abbey Kurt said, handing the man the garment, stepping past him.

As she walked through the nearly empty store, she saw Mr. Kenny's wife coming toward her. The woman appeared harried and uncertain, paying little attention to everything around her, except for whom she appeared to be searching.

Abbey continued on, the remnants of the bomb she had just placed in the bag over her shoulder, as Mrs. Kenny hurried by, oblivious of the woman that would be responsible for the destruction of all her stores.

65

Monica walked into the downtown store surprised to see that it was busier than usual. There were easily a half dozen men browsing the suit collection, another couple checking in on the spa side, and a smartly dressed woman that walked past her on her way out. She might have had to stop being so hard on Tabatha about drumming up business and congratulate her when she saw her, that was, if Tabatha was in the office, where she was supposed to have been.

Walking deeper into the store, Monica saw Roland. He waved to her from deep in the racks of suits. "Hey, Ms. Monica."

"You being good?" Monica asked.

"On my best behavior, as always," Roland smiled.

"Good," Monica said, walking in the direction of the hallway that led to her office. "Tabatha back there?"

"She hasn't come in yet."

Monica stopped, turned back. "You sure?"

Roland set down the suits he had in his arms then walked over to Monica, not wanting to put store business out amongst the customers. Lowering his voice, he said, "When I got to the store it was locked. I opened today."

The look on Monica's face had Roland set a hand on Monica's shoulder. "Everything cool?"

"Yeah, yeah," Monica said, trying not to show the angst that was starting to fall over her: the exact same feeling she had experienced earlier.

This morning she woke with a slight pain in her temple, feeling unrested and troubled. She patted the blankets around her for her phone. It was in bed, because she had fallen asleep waiting for Nate to return at least one of the dozen calls and texts she had sent to him last night. After what she had found out from Tori, she had to speak

275

to him, apologize for the distance he had felt between them, without coming right and saying it was because she hadn't trusted him.

Feeling the device, she brought it out from under the sheets to see she hadn't had a single missed call from her husband; there were no text messages waiting. She pressed the redial button, waited and cursed when the call was diverted to voicemail and she was notified the mailbox was full.

"C'mon, Nate," Monica said, ending the call, pushing back the blankets and throwing her legs over the side of the bed. Sitting there, she took a moment to really think about the news she had gotten last night from both Tim and Tori. Could it be that Nate had finally changed? What did that mean for Monica, for little Nathaniel, for the three of them as a family? Could she now forget about continuing with her plot to take the boy from Nate, because…he was now a decent, maybe even a good husband?

Monica stepped out of bed into her slippers and couldn't help but smile as she pulled on her robe.

She walked down the hall and into the kitchen, expecting to see Tabatha sipping coffee, eating yogurt and watching the last bit of the morning newscast, before going to work, but there was no sign of her.

Monica walked back down the hallway to Tabatha's bedroom; the door was open. She stuck her head in, knocked softly on the frame of the door. "Tab, you in there?" Monica called toward the bathroom door on the other side of the bedroom. "You're gonna be late for work, and you know the owner might fire you," Monica joked. When no response came, she walked through the room, nudged open the bathroom door and found that it was empty as well.

Tabatha might've actually left early to work for once in her life, Monica thought, chuckling to herself, heading back toward the kitchen. She'd have a little breakfast, get dressed and decide just how to inform her best friend that she had never been more wrong about Nate, and maybe, just maybe—Monica thought holding out her left hand to stare proudly down at the wedding ring—she might've done a good thing by remarrying the man.

But now, in the store, Roldand standing in front of Monica telling her he hadn't seen nor heard from Tab, left Monica worrying, having no idea of where her friend could've been.

"Yeah, well, she's probably out at IHOP or something treating herself to pancakes," Monica said, faking a smile, trying not to let on just how concerned she was. "I'll get her on her cell phone and tell her to get her ass in here before she really gets fired."

66

After her eyes opened, it took a moment for who was in front of Tori to come into focus: Lewis wearing old jeans and a t-shirt with the sleeves hacked off, exposing shoulders and biceps that any Men's Health model would've been jealous of. He smiled and held a tray of food—what smelled to Tori like scrambled eggs, sausage and skillet-fried potatoes.

She wiped her eyes, blinked and slowly pushed herself up in bed. As she did, the comforter slid from off one of her shoulders, exposing her bare breasts. Embarrassed, she quickly pulled the blanket back over herself. "I'm sorry."

"It's okay. I've seen those on a woman before." Lewis smiled, placing the tray over Tori's lap. There was a small glass of orange juice on it beside a steaming cup of coffee that smelled like the best she's ever gotten a whiff of. There was even a narrow vase with a single yellow tulip in it.

Tori shook her head, trying to remember if any man has ever done this for her before. She smiled. "You didn't have to cook me breakfast."

"Then what would we have done with the food I bought you yesterday?"

"I know, right," Tori said, nodding, picking up one of the diagonally sliced halves of toast. "I don't have any clothes on," Tori said, before Lewis got out the door. "Did we...you know?"

"We didn't. You were drunk and shaken up after that stuff with Nate, and I'm not the kind of guy to take advantage."

Even more embarrassed, Tori said, "Sorry about that. It's just..."

"Really, it's okay. And just to be clear, it's not because I didn't want to." He smiled. "Eat your breakfast before it gets cold."

Lewis shut the engine off in the Bank of America parking lot five minutes after the bank opened. "This is where you said the check is from, right?"

"Yeah," Tori said, staring out the window like a child being dropped off on her first day of kindergarten; she was frightened.

"So you okay to do this?" Tori heard Lewis say.

"Yeah," she said, not feeling okay at all.

"Well, I'll be here when you're done."

Tori whirled around. "No! You're coming with me."

"Why?"

Tori didn't know why, exactly. This felt so much like a trap. She felt guilty for having the money, as though she had stolen it. She worried Nate might realize he'd made a grave mistake and send the police after her. "Because I'd feel safer if you just came. Will you?"

"Of course," Lewis said, pulling the key from ignition and unbuckling his seatbelt.

Opening the account went much more smoothly than Tori had anticipated, even though she could not help looking over her shoulders, expecting S.W.A.T. to burst through the windows, guns drawn. A little more than half an hour after she and Lewis sat down with a bank account manager, they were on their way: Tori with a new bank account, in which fifty thousand of her soon to be two million, was available immediately.

In the truck, before starting it, Lewis asked Tori, "How do you feel?"

There was a huge smile on Tori's face and a sense of relief she hadn't felt in years, knowing she actually had money of her own and would not have to rely on anyone else, but she still felt a feeling a dread, as though there was more of a price to pay before she was truly free.

"I feel good," Tori said, nodding.

67

Freddy stood just outside the back of his Uncle Henry's house. Unlike last time, where the window to his mother's room sat slightly ajar, allowing Freddy to hoist it open and climb through it—now it was locked, the curtains separated just enough for Freddy to see his mother laying in bed, huddled under the blankets.

He stood there, flames of pain roaring up his injured leg, his narrowing body drenched by cold sweat under the heavy winter coat. He watched her lovingly, as he had done when he was nine years old, on the occasions just after his father had beaten her, then pulled on his trousers and boots and went off to work. After that, Freddy would sneak into his mother's bedroom, crawl on his hands and knees so as not to wake her, then sit at the corner of the mattress that lay on the floor and watch her as she slept, her face puffy with black and purple patches, her eyes and cheek swollen twice their normal size. Freddy knew—climbing in bed behind her, spooning her, wanting to get as close to her as possible, wanting to climb inside her so that he could give her his strength to defend against his father— that would be the last time the man would touch her like that. Freddy kept his promise.

The next day, after waiting three hours on the living room sofa for his mother to walk in from work, his father's blood clinging to his face, arms and hands, absorbed into the front of his tee shirt and caked onto the baseball bat he had set on the coffee table, his mother didn't scream when she pushed open the front door and saw him. She didn't cry or fall to her knees and sob, asking God why she was cursed with such an evil son. She looked at Freddy then toward his father's bedroom door, and with knowing eyes, she held out her hand, and when Freddy got up and took it, she walked him to just outside the bedroom, told him to wait a second, then she stepped in to witness what her son had done. Only a moment later, she was out again, had lowered herself to her knees, and had wrapped her arms around Freddy. The words she said were soft and comforting and he still heard them, now as a grown man, sitting outside her bedroom window. "It'll be all right, Fred. Everything will be all right," she said more than two decades ago.

That was because she knew Freddy killed his father because he would not let the man abuse her. Just like he would not let Nate Kenny live after doing the same. Since childhood, he was his mother's protector, as he was Joni's and Kia's, and his baby's. No, he hadn't been able to shield them from harm as he had wanted, but killing the bastard who had caused them pain would make up for his failure, at least in his mind.

Freddy knocked softly on the pane as quietly as he possibly could. Uncle's Henry's pickup was in the driveway, and if the old man knew Freddy was lurking outside the house, there would've been a confrontation, and afterward, Uncle Henry would've lay dead on his sister's bedroom floor.

"Ma," Freddy said, tapping again, ever so lightly on the glass. "I need for you to wake up and let me in. I need to talk to you," Freddy said, his face pushed very close to the window. He pushed back the hood, wiped a hand across his brow, wiping it of the cold sweat that beaded up there. "I think I'm gonna die soon, but I don't want you to feel any kind of way. Don't feel bad for the people I killed. Don't feel bad for how I fucked everything up. You loved me, gave your life to me and you was the best mother I could ever want. I just wanted a chance to hug you one more time and tell you I love you," Freddy said, pulling the few wadded up bills he had left in his pocket—eighty six dollars—smoothed them out with trembling hands, stacking and folding them and sliding them into a grove under the window where they would be later found. "It ain't a lot, but I hope it'll help, that you can do something with that."

Knowing she would not wake, that this goodbye would have to be enough, Freddy pressed his hand against the window, his body aching with the pain of knowing he'd never see his mother again.

"Goodbye, Ma." He pulled his hand down, moved to turn away, but not before seeing his mother stir in bed, open an eye, look to see if Freddy was still there, then quickly closing it again, seeing that he was. He paused, thought of being angry, thought to feel ashamed, thought to put his fist through that window, dig, armpit deep through the shattered glass, around in the room until he caught her by the throat, and sobbing, ask his mother why she would ignore him when he told her he thought he was so close to death. But he stopped those thoughts, stared his gaunt-faced reflection in the eyes, then turned away and shuffled off instead.

68

It was late, and after not having heard from Nate the entire day, worrying that something truly had been wrong, Tabatha's doorbell rang. When Monica opened the door, Nate magically stood before her, looking lost and exhausted. Happy and relieved, Monica threw herself into him, wrapping her husband in a hug, and telling him how much she missed him. She took him by the hand, dragged him through the condo, saying—her voice suggestive and sultry: "Tabatha's not here so we can be as loud as we want."

But entering the bedroom, Nate seemed neither happy nor overly excited to see her. Throwing him up against the closed door, kissing him, grinding her body against his, she got the sense he was more melancholy than anything, as though he was suffering a loss.

Pulling him over and sitting herself down on the edge of the bed, she stood him up in front of her. She wanted to ask him if he was okay, but was more concerned with pleasing him physically, showing him how much she missed him, valued him...loved him. She wanted to thank him for being the man he's been saying he was: the man she didn't believe he was capable of being.

All during today, dialing and redialing his number, hoping that he'd pick up, an anticipatory smile on her face thinking of what she'd tell him, she fantasized of what their lives would be now that she knew he was truly onboard with what she wanted when they were first married.

"Baby, you okay?" Monica finally asked, staring up at him as she unbuttoned his shirt and pulled his belt from the loop.

He said nothing, just nodded, glancing down at her momentarily, then away, as if not to disturb her from what she intended.

She opened his trousers, pulled him out, stroked him ready then took him in her mouth. She heard Nate moan. He pressed a gentle hand to the back of her head and pulled her into him as he thrust gently deeper into her mouth.

Earlier, while scrambling to make contact, wondering why Nate had not returned any of her phone calls, a sense of dread fell heavy over her: the thought that Nate had somehow found out what Monica was up to. That would've ruined everything. Nate would've been outraged, would've sought revenge, and of course, he would've left her, which she thought—as she wrapped her moist lips around his throbbing penis, stroked him along his shaft—would've been the worst of it, because she did love him. Tab and everyone who had negatively commented had gotten it right. She was a fool for Nate: stupidly in love with him. But that was only a bad thing when the man acted a fool. Nate no longer was doing that.

Monica felt tiny convulsions emanating from Nate's center, felt him pulling her hair tighter and eased away from him, holding him in her fist, lovingly kissing the tip of his dick, looking up at him and saying, "I want you in me."

The room was dark, but nighttime street light coming through the windows allowed her to see him nod his compliance. Monica stood, shed her clothes as he was doing, pushed out of her panties, unclasped her bra and freed breasts with nipples so engorged they pulsated almost painfully.

He stood before her, now naked. She took his hand, and lying down he climbed on top of her. His body weight felt so comforting, so right and was so missed that she wondered how she could've ever lived without him. She took his face in her hands, smiled, squirming under him, her thighs open, her clit popping with dizzying sensations every time the dome of his dick grazed it.

"I love you so much," Monica said, staring into his eyes.

She had called Tori Thomas today, wanting to know if she had any information that could help her find out what her husband was thinking, give her a clue as to why he had not contacted her. Monica sat in traffic nervously drumming her fingers on the steering wheel, waiting for the girl to answer. "C'mon, c'mon, c'mon, pick up!" Monica wasn't surprised when she didn't. "I need to speak to you," Monica said, leaving a recording. "It's really important. If you can, just call me." She was about to hang up then said, "And Tori, I'm sorry about...just call me back. Maybe we can still get you some of that money I promised."

Monica hung the phone up, no less worried that Nate had discovered Monica's plan. She then called her attorney, but when Joyla answered and asked Monica what she needed, Monica froze a second.

"Monica, everything okay?" Joyla asked.

Suddenly sure of the decision, Monica said, "Cancel the custody suit, Joyla."

"Monica...what? Why don't you come in so that we can discuss this before you just cancel everything?"

"I'll come in, but just to pay you for your time. I'm no longer filing."

Now, Monica's head swimming as Nate entered her, she pressed her lips to his, swallowed his tongue, pulling on it as she did his dick, pressing her hands against his ass, opening her thighs wider, wanting him to go deeper, intensify the tingling of the first impending orgasm she was already starting to feel.

"So much, baby. So much! I love you," Monica said again. And still Nate didn't respond, didn't even look her in the face, just turned his head, grunting, fighting the urge not to come.

He slid stiff and dripping from out of her, pulled back on his knees, then grabbed her by the hips, flipping her onto her stomach, where she rolled up on her knees and elbows.

His face was in her ass, his wet, hot tongue snaking around inside of her, sending shivers across her entire body, triggering an explosion and releasing an orgasm that collapsed her onto her belly. But Nate was grabbing her again by the hips, pulling her, then pushing back into her, pounding her from behind.

Her face buried in the pillow, her muffled screams coming out of it, she grabbed hold of it for dear life, feeling herself come again and again, hearing Nate behind her, telling her that he had loved her so much, that all he wanted was for them to be a family. Then she felt his muscles stiffen, felt him grab tighter to her fleshy ass, and he was erupting, hot and thick, inside of her, as she pressed back against him, coming again on his dick, beating a fist into the mattress, wondering again, how she had almost fucked this up.

Moments later, she lay peacefully on her stomach, trying to keep her lids from falling, which was almost impossible. Nate lay on top of her, his body warm, his breathing slowing, becoming normal, and she felt, for the first time since they've been remarried, things were as they should've been: were right, and that from then on, would remain that way.

Drifting off, she heard his voice, heard him talking about what they've been through, how hard he had tried to prove himself, and how incredibly important his son was to him. Monica continued to battle sleep, but was losing, falling off, but nodding her head as though awake, making agreeable noises, as though listening to and understanding what Nate was saying, when really she was about dead to the world. She stared up at him through the dark room, unable to stop her eyelids from lowering, the last thing registering in her memory was Nate saying how hurt he was to find out that Monica had been trying to take what was most dear to him, that she would pay horrifically for what she had done and would learn firsthand what it felt like to experience that kind of pain. Drunk with sleep, and not comprehending any of it, Monica smiled, said, "I love you, too," then watched Nate's face fall out of focus as her eyes closed completely.

69

Pushing up on her hands, Monica jerked herself out of sleep, whipping her head about the room, sensing something horrible had happened last night, but not remembering what.

"Nate?" Monica called, seeing that her husband was not still in bed with her, but remembering how wonderful it was to have had him there. He was exquisite—they were together, and Monica lowered herself back down on to her stomach to think about their lovemaking for just ten more seconds before getting up and readying herself for work.

A smile on her face, a pillow pressed tight to her chest, her arms wrapped around it as though it was her husband, she thought how catastrophic things could've been if Nate had found out what she had been up to before she called Joyla yesterday and cancelled her petition for custody. She smiled, also thinking about how lucky she was that her husband would never get wind of that.

"Nate," Monica called, walking barefoot down the hallway, wearing a robe and trying to fix her hair into something presentable. Stopping at Tabatha's closed bedroom door, she pressed an ear to it, giggling, hoping her friend didn't come in last night at the peak of hers and Nate's lovemaking. She would've heard way more than she should've, and Monica figured after that, Tab would've really had no love for Nate.

Knocking twice lightly, Monica pushed open Tabatha's door to find her not in bed and that the bed appeared not to have been slept in. Monica pushed all the way into the room, searched the bathroom to find that everything looked exactly as it had yesterday; she had gotten the frightening feeling that Tabatha still had not come back.

Monica hurried to the guest bedroom, grabbed her cell phone, checked it for messages, and saw that nothing had come from Tabatha.

The phone to her ear, walking toward the kitchen, Monica got Roland, who she was sure had not left for work yet, on the phone.

"Has she tried to call you? You spoken to her yet?" Monica asked.

"I been trying to call her, but it goes straight to voicemail," Roland said, sounding as concerned as Monica felt. "But no, I haven't heard anything from her."

Monica told Roland again that everything would be just fine, something she was increasingly having a hard time believing herself. She thanked him, and told him she would find Tabatha one way or another. Hanging up, she realized that Nate was not there in the condo with her either. She thought to call and ask him why, but knew he had to get home, prepare Nathaniel for daycare and get to work himself, but was comforted by the thought they would definitely catch up later.

She went to the fridge, took out the orange juice and poured herself some, saying softly to herself, "Tab, Tab, where are you, girl?"

Drinking, wracking her brain, hoping something would come to her that would help locate Tabatha, Monica slammed the glass to the counter, choking on some of the juice, disturbed by a thought she prayed was not real: the image of Nate's face hovering over her last night as she drifted off to sleep, speaking words she could not remember, but that moment, felt were ominous and frightening.

She shook off the bothersome thought, knowing it had been a dream, because Nate finding out had been something that had been troubling her, so it appeared while she was sleeping last night— nothing more.

Needing to think of anything else, Monica spotted the TV remote on the coffee table, walked around the kitchen counter into the living room and clicked on the flat screen to Eyewitness News. A newscaster's voice reported again on the shooting of a rookie female cop that was slain, sitting guard outside of a south side home. "If

anyone has information that may help police, please call the Chicago Tip Hotline." A number was flashed across the screen. Monica shook her head, walking back into the kitchen, thinking sarcastically that it probably was Freddy Ford who had killed the poor woman, and wondered if police had caught him yet.

She opened one of the overhead cabinets, and holding onto the door, she heard Nate's voice in her head, saw that memory of his face again, and she questioned had it really been a dream—for that moment—it felt so real to her. He had said something about finding out Monica was trying to take Nathaniel, but she knew that the memory could not have been real, for if it had been, she probably wouldn't have standing there in her bathrobe, in relative comfort, but possibly in a trunk somewhere, being driven off to the woods to be taken care of.

Monica grabbed the can of coffee, knowing she needed a really strong pot to wake her up, shake that craziness out of her head and prepare for what she might have to do to find her friend. She pulled open a drawer looking for the filters. Finding them, she went for the coffee pot, prepared to lift the lid when she noticed an envelope sitting under the corner of the machine. It wasn't there last night. She would've seen it if it was.

With a slight tug, she pulled the corner of the envelope from under the coffee maker examining its outside, feeling the weight and rigidity of something inside: something that felt like a card.

Monica lifted the flap, saw the colorful, glossy top of what looked like a photograph then slipped the item out. She gasped, her breath snagging in her throat, the picture dropping from her hand and floating end over end to the floor. She stood gawking down at the white backside of it, wishing that if she didn't pick it up, what she saw on the other side would cease to be true. She bent down, lifted the photo from the floor and stared at the close-up of Tabatha's face. Her poor best friend's eyes were bulging with fear, her hair was plastered to her forehead, her face covered with sweat, her mouth wrenched open by a gag stuffed tight into her mouth.

Feeling tears well up and spill out of her eyes, Monica thought back, allowed the images of Nate staring down at her, the words he spoke last night to enter freely into her memory; he said something about making Monica pay horrifically for what she had done, learning firsthand what it felt like to experience the pain he suffered, and Monica knew without a doubt that Nate was behind Tabatha's disappearance.

70

Tabatha struggled again with the ties that bound her wrists behind her back and tethered her ankles. She screamed for the thousandth time, but figured no one would hear her because of the bandana jammed in her mouth she was forced to bite down on. She had no idea of where she was. A blindfold covered her eyes, allowing no light whatsoever to be seen by her; she was in total darkness. She only had a bad estimation of how long she had spent there: twenty four to thirty six hours, she guessed.

What she remembered from early yesterday morning was getting out bed, getting ready for work and going into the kitchen to make coffee, when a soft knock came at her condo door. Because of the early hour, Tabatha figured it to have been one of two neighbors down the hall, needing to borrow Splenda or a jump because their car battery had gone dead.

She opened the door to see a small, muscular woman, standing in the doorway, wearing a pants suit, holding one arm behind her back. Tabatha looked at her oddly, then asked: "Can I help you?"

"Tabatha Anderson?" the woman asked.

"Yes, why—"

Before Tabatha could say another word, the woman jabbed her in the belly with a Taser, causing her so much pain, she could only describe it as having her insides incinerated.

That was a while back. Since then, she nearly wanted to pass out from hunger. She could no longer feel her arms: just an occasional tingling where she believed they were, and she smelled of urine, for an hour ago, the pain of trying not to release what had her bladder distended to the size of a basketball finally became too much. Warm piss from in between her thighs, covered the seat and ran down her legs. She wept as she did this: less from humiliation than from the belief that who ever had taken her and tied her up and let her pee on herself, had no intentions of letting her live.

She needed to escape.

She knew the first step in accomplishing that was to get out of that chair. She pumped her hands into fists, coaxing blood into them, hoping to regain some feeling. When she could sense the tips of her fingers, she wiggled them, made contact with the chair and felt the thing was constructed of wood; it could be broken. In movies she'd seen it done: captive rocked the chair till it toppled over, and when it hit the ground, the thing fell apart. It sounded ridiculous, but that was all she had left.

Blindfolded, her face titled upward, and in total darkness, she tipped the chair back and fourth and back, until the piece of furniture was teetering, then fell completely over, hitting the floor. But the frame of the chair never made contact with the ground, because it was buffered by one of Tabatha's arms, which immediately broke. She sustained what doctors referred to as a high humeral open fraction. The arm snapped somewhere between her shoulder and elbow, the bone splintering and tearing through the skin, blood spilling from the wound. Tabatha screamed out in agony, feeling so much pain she blacked out there on the floor, jagged bone shooting out of her skin, cold urine drying between her thighs.

71

After depositing Tori's check yesterday, she and Lewis went back to the apartment just long enough for her to get the few articles of clothing she wore from California. Inside the bedroom, as she peeled off one of the expensive outfits that was bought with Monica's money, Lewis sat on the bed, his back turned until Tori finished dressing in her old clothes. She wanted nothing else to do with Monica, or anything Monica had purchased for her.

"I think you look better like that anyway," Lewis said, turning back around.

"Then let's go shopping so I can buy what I want," Tori said.

They spent the day together, Lewis in no rush to leave her side, and Tori seeming content enough to continue to hang out with Lewis.

When night came, Tori had Lewis take her to the Mandarin hotel downtown. In the SUV, sitting in the drive in front of the lobby doors, Lewis turned to Tori: "Well, guess this is it, huh," he said, trying to mask the bit of sadness he knew he'd feel watching her go.

Her bag slung across her shoulder, one hand on the door handle, appearing hesitant to climb out, Tori said, "Where you gonna go?"

"Home, I guess."

"No," she said, adamant. "That crazy dude is still out there, right?"

"You mean Freddy?"

"Yeah. I mean he could be laying for you."

"I don't know," Lewis said. "But where else am I gonna go?"

Tori glanced out her window as if looking for a solution, turned back to Lewis and said, "Just stay with me tonight, okay."

Lewis happily agreed and carried all the bags of Tori's new clothes up to the elegant and beautiful fifth floor suite, but when it was time for bed, he picked up the phone and called down to the concierge. When Tori asked what he was doing, he told her with a smile: "Having them bring up some blankets for the sofa. Don't know if I can be trusted to do the right thing two nights in a row."

This morning, squinting against the sunlight that pressed through the hotel room windows, Lewis set up on the sofa to see Tori wearing a big white, hotel bathrobe, standing beside a large room service table, two silver domed platter covers on top of it, along with glasses of juice, water and mugs of coffee.

"What's this?" Lewis said, trying not to look so happy by the surprise.

"You made me breakfast in bed," Tori said, crossing her arms, looking proud of herself. "Just thought I should return the favor."

After checkout, Tori and Lewis ended up in Hyde Park, on the big rocks bordering the lake: one of Lewis's favorite spots in all of Chicago. To the north of them was the skyline: among all the other buildings lining the waterfront like huge chess pieces, the Sears Tower and the John Hancock building stood, reminding Lewis of the days when he would ride his bike on the Westside of Chi, poor as dirt, but happy as hell.

The two walked across the grassy park and found a place where there were no other people around. "I used to love this spot," Tori said. "Thought I'd never see it again when I moved to California. Folks out there think the ocean is a big deal, but give me Lake Michigan any day. I love Chicago."

"Then you shouldn't leave again," Lewis said, looking over his shoulder at her as he plucked a rock from the ground.

Tori showed a sly smile. "You're saying I should stay here? Why?"

"Dunno," Lewis said, standing and tossing the rock, not looking back at her. "You just should." Finally he gave her a glance, saw that she was blushing a little. He couldn't help but smile back. "Well?"

"Well, I'll have to determine if there's enough reason to stick around."

"Yeah, okay," Lewis nodded, confidently. "I hear you," he said, feeling his cell vibrate in his pocket. He pulled it out, saw Nate's name on the screen and held it up so that Tori could see.

"Why is he calling you?" Tori asked.

"Only one way to find out. Hello," Lewis said into the phone.

"Hello Lewis," Nate said, his tone businesslike. "I'm going to ask you once and I need for you to tell me the truth. Did you know that Monica was trying to take my son and didn't tell me?"

It sounded like a trick question, and knowing Nate like he had, Lewis figured it most likely was. But no longer being under the man's control, no longer having to answer to him, Lewis said: "I only found out a couple of days ago. And yeah, I figured it was something you might've wanted to know. But I don't deal with either of you two like that anymore, so that business is between ya'll, and none of mine."

There was a brief pause. "Then you should probably pick your daughter up from my brother's house, since you don't deal with me like that anymore."

Lewis nodded his head in acceptance. "Fair enough."

"Goodbye, Lewis."

"Goodbye, Nate."

72

All day, Monica had been searching for Nate and trying to make some form of contact with him. She had gone to Kenny Corporation, Nate's downtown offices, and had been promptly turned away by the two thin, supermodel-like receptionists, wearing headsets behind the counter.

"I'm sorry, Mrs. Kenny," but Mr. Kenny is not available, the brunette said with the smile and tone of a seasoned airline flight attendant.

"I don't care if he's available. I need to speak to him. Do you know who I am?"

"His wife, yes," the redhead said, "But—"

Knowing they'd never allow her through, Monica took off, hurrying by the reception counter, around the maze of cubicles, along the wall of ceiling high windows over looking Lake Michigan, toward Nate's office, where ten feet shy, she was stopped by two tall men, wearing security uniforms. Monica was promptly wrangled and escorted—the men carrying her by her arms—to the elevators and told not to come back till given authorization by Mr. Kenny.

She went back to the store, grabbed Roland off the floor and told the new girl she had hired two weeks ago to cover. Closed in her office, after sitting Roland down, Monica said: "I don't want you to be alarmed, but there's a chance that Tabatha's missing."

Wringing his hands, worry deepening the lines in his face, he stood quickly from the sofa. "Missing! I know she's fucking missing. What exactly does that mean, Monica?"

"Roland," Monica said, gently pushing him down, her hands on his shoulders. "I don't need you blowing this out of proportion or getting dramatic. I said there's a chance, but I'm not certain," Monica said, deciding that moment it was best not to speak another word until she was sure about what happened to Tabatha. "What I need you to do is keep the store running, and the moment Tab comes in or calls—which I really believe she will do—I need you let me know, okay?"

"I can do that, Monica," Roland said, standing, rubbing his arms, looking like the worried mother of a lost child. "The moment she calls or comes in."

Standing in the parking garage, her phone to her ear, listening as Nate's voicemail picked up, Monica stopped before climbing into her Jaguar.

"Nate, I've been calling you and you're not calling me back. I've been by your office, and couldn't even get in to see you. Is everything all right?" Monica asked, her tone calm, holding the picture of Tabatha in her hand, but still not entirely certain it was Nate that left it for her. Yes, she remembered the words she thought he said to her last night. But she also could not forget how he held tightly to her, his back arched, his face buried in her breasts, his fingers interlaced with hers. With each involuntary thrust of his body, with each surge of warmth he deposited within her, she had felt his love. Had that been an illusion? It was hard to imagine those actions, and the ones of someone who could kidnap Monica's best friend as being those of the same person. She would not be totally convinced Nate had spoken those words to her last night, that he had found out what Monica was planning until the man told her for himself.

"I need for you to contact me, Nate, because I went to the coffee maker this morning and found—" Monica was saying, when she was interrupted by Nate's voicemail cutting her off with a beep.

73

The sky was dark when Monica stopped her car in the circular drive of Nate's house, behind two unmarked police cars.

She had tried Tabatha's phone again on the way over, the call being directed straight to voicemail, not even ringing once, making Monica believe that wherever Tab was, her cell battery had already died.

Monica was on her way back from the police station, had spoken to an officer at the front counter, holding up Tabatha's picture, telling him she wanted someone to find her, that she wanted to file a missing persons report. The officer told Monica what she knew he would: her friend needed to be gone so many hours in order for a report to be filed and an investigation started.

Now she climbed out of her car and hurried up to the front door, prepared to enter her house, when the door was opened by a woman in a business suit. Appearing angular, her hair pulled slick back into bun, glasses on her face, Monica thought the woman looked familiar.

"How may I help you?" Abbey Kurt asked.

"I need to see my husband," Monica said, excused herself then attempted to push her way inside. Abbey Kurt stepped in her way, blocking her path.

"I'm sorry, ma'am, but my orders are not to let anyone in."

"Did you hear what I said? I'm Mrs. Kenny. I need to see my husband this minute," Monica said more assertively, trying to enter again. This time, not only did Abbey Kurt step into Monica's way, she shoved a hand into her shoulder, forcing her backward. Staring shocked at the woman, Monica saw a look that suggested the guard was given the authority to do much more if called for.

"Then let me see my son," Monica said.

"I'm sorry, Ma'am. That won't be happening."

She was so infuriated and frustrated, Monica felt she would break down and cry, but she had the sneaking sensation Nate was standing behind a window, staring out at her. She stepped back, glanced toward the windows on the front of the house then back at Abbey Kurt.

"You tell him I came by," Monica demanded. "You tell him to call me, and if I don't hear from him, I'll be going to the police," she said, that effort already failing, but having nothing else to threaten Nate with. Taking backward steps down the walk, away from the house, she shouted at the windows. "You hear me Nate? I'll call the police, tell them what you did, if you don't call me!"

Monica drove back to Tabatha's house, hoping that when she opened the door, her friend would be there, kicked back on the sofa, watching Lifetime TV. Turning onto the block on which Tabatha lived, Monica said softly to herself: "Be home, Tab. Just be home so I can have one less thing to worry about."

But pulling up in front of Tabatha's building, Monica couldn't believe what she saw.

Yanking the keys from the ignition, Monica climbed out the car, hurried around it, and was stopped cold, slapped in the face by what stretched out on the front lawn: every piece of Monica's furniture, to include the king mattress and box springs Nate had in storage and the two flat screens that they weren't even using. Also there was every article of her clothing to include bras and panties, and every dish, saucer, fork and spoon Monica owned. It was all dumped and scattered across the lawn, looking like the accident site of a plane that had exploded in the sky.

So shocked and distraught by the sight of her lingerie strewn over the ground, a bra hanging from a bush branch, the cracked screen on one of her TVs, and one of the wedding photos of her and Nate, shattered and slipping out the frame, she did not see the teenaged boys with sagging jeans, picking through her belongings as though at a garage sale.

Startled, Monica said, "Get away from here! This is not your stuff. Go!"

They dropped the 32" TV then hurried off.

Inside the condo, Monica threw her purse on the sofa, calling out Tabatha's name, as she searched again through the rooms. Back in the living room, Monica was fed up and exhausted. She grabbed her cell phone prepared to call the police again, beg them into action, when her phone lit in her hand with an incoming call, Nate's name blinking on the screen.

"What have you done with Tabatha? Do you have her?"

"I asked you if being with me, if being a family again was what you wanted. If not, I said you could leave. You chose to lie instead."

"Did you take Tabatha, Nate? Did you hurt her?"

"You tried to take my son when all I wanted was for us to be together. You needed to know how I felt. You tried to take who is most dear to me, so I'm doing the same to you."

"Do you have my friend?" Monica yelled into the phone. "Is she hurt?"

Silence on the line, then: "The wedding ring," Nate said. "I need that back from you. You no longer deserve to wear it. And yes, I have your friend," he said, Monica believing she detected what could've been shame in his admission, but she could not have been sure. "She had an accident, but she should be fine," Nate said.

"An accident! What have you done?"

"I said she'll be fine. But I've done more. Right now I'm holding a detonator. I had someone hack into your credit card account and your stores are rigged with explosives bought in your name. I could press a button now and they'd all go up."

Shocked, Monica gasped breathlessly. "No!"

"And with your stores being in the red, I wonder who the feds would come after for insurance fraud?"

"Nate!"

"You thought you could fuck with me and not pay for it."

"Please. Please don't do that."

The line went quiet, Monica believing Nate was calming some.

"Meet me and I'll think about not destroying your stores and having you thrown in prison. Give me the ring and you can take your friend then."

"Where?"

Nate gave her an address and a time with the warning that if Monica were to call the police, something terrible would happen to Tabatha. Monica didn't believe Nate had it in him to harm Tabatha, but the horrified look in her friend's eyes on that photo insinuated that he could've gotten someone else for that job. She took the instructions, Nate hanging up the phone before Monica could ask another question.

She grabbed her purse from the sofa, shouldered it, hurried across the room and pulled open the front door to find a gun stuck in her face, an emaciated and sickly looking, shaved-headed, Freddy Ford standing behind it.

74

The pavement, the traffic signs and lights before Freddy became fuzzy, blurry and split into three. On coming traffic on the other side of the street appeared to have been heading right toward him. He swerved twice almost hitting cars to his left, nearly ricocheting off a street light on his right. After the near misses, he saw an open parking spot, cut the car hard right and pulled in.

Breathing exhaustively, shutting off the engine and shifting the car into park, Freddy knew his senses going haywire was due to complications from the gunshot wound. He looked himself in the rearview mirror: his eyes had sunken back deep into his skull, the whites fading to a dull shade of yellow. He clamped his hands around his thigh, squeezed, wishing he could stop the pain, the flow of toxins traveling throughout his body like snake venom. All he could do was lay back against the headrest, the cold sweat on his neck, smearing across the leather; he needed aspirin.

He lifted his left leg out the door, setting his foot on the ground then carried his other leg out. When he looked up, preparing to hoist himself out of the car, he was startled by the sight of a small police precinct building, cop cars parked out in front, all slanted at an angle, sitting in front of him. Shocked, he started to climb back in, but stopped, his mind holding a moment to wonder if this had been a sign from something or someone telling him he could end it all—everything—that moment. That if he wanted, he could drag himself into that building, hands raised, and tell the cops who he was, all that he had done, and they would take him, pull the bullet out of him, give him meds, and he would live. They would throw his ass in jail, put him on trial, try to sentence him to death, but Freddy played crazy real good—enough to be given life instead, and that's what he'd be rewarded. But so would Nate Kenny, and Freddy would spend the remainder of his days, sitting in a drug induced stupor knowing the man who had taken all that Freddy loved, would've gotten away with it.

"Fuck that," Freddy said, starting the car, watching as cops walked in and out of the precinct doors, climbed in and out of their cruisers with their guns and batons and radios—a couple of them even glancing right at Freddy, then away. Freddy thought what fools they were for not being able to identify a killer of one of their own sitting right there in front of them.

He'd taken off driving, knowing how heavily guarded Nate Kenny's house was, but having no where else to go, he landed there, telling himself he might catch the man coming or going, inside of his car alone. So he would wait, follow him down a vacant side street, ram his car, hobble up to him when he got out and kill him in the middle of the street.

Freddy had been parked down the street from Nate's house only fifteen minutes, when instead of seeing Nate, he saw Monica leaving the house, driving past him. Freddy quickly hiked himself up in the seat, fumbled to stick the key the in ignition, then sped up to follow her. After twenty minutes of driving, he parked a half a block away from the building he saw her enter, all sorts of furniture and household shit strewn across the lawn.

Walking inside the apartment building, stopping at the elevator, he had no idea where Monica had gone, but he guessed the top floor and punched 3.

Staggering down the third floor hallway, he slowed before each door, leaning close, hoping to hear some indication Monica was in one of them.

The unit at the very end of the hall, behind the last door, he stopped in front of and heard Monica's voice: the conversation he knew was with her husband. Freddy grabbed his gun, thought to knock, but the door opened in front of him, Monica staggering back in shock. He raised the gun, pushing her back into the condo, slamming the two inside.

She stared frightened at him with terrified eyes, but they were also thinking eyes; Freddy saw the way they looked at him, at his leg: how he was injured, appearing weak. He saw she was figuring a way she could get past him: get away from him.

Freddy shoved the gun in her face. "Don't. I'll fucking kill you," he said, swiping at the sweat running cold down his brow.

He walked, grimacing, through the apartment, slowly dragging his leg behind him. Seeing they were alone, he told Monica to sit on one of the bar stools. He eyed a block of knives on the counter to Monica's left and slid out one of the larger ones, holding it out before her.

"I'm gonna kill your husband," Freddy said. "I know you just got off the phone with him. Now," Freddy said, his eyes glancing at the knife he held, then back to Monica. "Imma' ask once. Where the fuck is he?"

Desperation on her face, Monica said, "I can't—" then she screamed, grabbing agonizingly at her leg, for Freddy had lifted the knife and plunged it deep into her thigh, just above her knees. Monica howled in horrific agony. Freddy clamped his hand over her mouth, yanked the cleaver from out of Monica's leg. Blood smeared on its metal skin, he brought the knife beside her face and said: "I'm gonna ask one more motherfucking time."

75

Lewis did as Nate suggested and picked up his daughter from Tim's house. Tim's brother was reluctant to let Layla go. "But Ford is still out there, right? They haven't caught him yet?"

"Not yet," Lewis said. He and Tori stood on Tim's front porch watching Layla play with Tim's kids on the front lawn.

"So what are you going to do?" Tim asked concerned. "Why take her now?"

"We'll work it out," Lewis said, truly unable to answer the question "And you'll have to ask Nate why. It was him who said I had to get her."

After leaving Tim's, Layla said she was hungry, so the three of them ended up sitting at an outdoor, McDonald's table. Layla stared at Tori in between dipping French fries into her strawberry sundae and popping them into her mouth.

"It's not polite to stare," Lewis said, taking one of Layla's fries and chomping down on it.

"Just checking her out, Dad," Layla said, squinting an eye at Tori, as if observing her under a microscope. "She going to be my new mom since you broke up with Eva?"

"Wow!" Tori said. "And I thought I was direct."

"Layla—" Lewis said.

"Sorry," Layla said. On the way from Tim's house, Layla had already grilled Tori, asking how old she was, where she lived, if she had any kids and did she have a boyfriend. Lewis paid close attention to the answer of the last question and was pleased to hear that Tori wasn't attached.

Lewis's cell rang on the table beside his crumpled burger wrapper. Hello?" He said, answering.

Although the man sounded like he just crawled across miles of desert sand without water, Lewis recognized Freddy's voice immediately.

"Freddy…" Lewis said, looking over at Tori. He immediately saw the concern she felt for him. Lewis stood and walked his conversation toward the parking lot, out of his daughter's earshot. "You don't sound good," Lewis said.

"Got shot. Pretty sure I'm not gonna make it. But I ain't going before killing Nate Kenny's ass."

"You'll never get to him, Freddy. Just turn yourself—"

"Wrong. On my way to him now; his wife taking me."

"Monica?" Lewis said, alarmed. He heard her call his name, then heard Freddy yell: "Shut the fuck up!"

"If you hurt her, I swear I'll—"

"Too late. She's bleeding pretty good, but she'll be okay, she do what she told," Freddy said, sounding as though he was out of breath and in pain.

Pacing furiously across the parking lot, Lewis said: "Let her go, Freddy. What do you want?"

"Exactly what I told you: Nate Kenny ass dead, and I want you to be there, just like you was when I beat my old man to death. But I swear fa' God, you call the police or you call that nigga Nate, I'll put a second bullet in this bitch's head. You feeling me?"

From across the parking lot, Lewis looked at his little girl, then stared at Tori, watching her look worriedly back at him. He nodded, turning away. "Yeah, I feel you, Freddy."

76

Freddy pushed Monica into the storefront of the soon to be high-end strip mall: a cinderblock skeleton of stores that stretched east and west for blocks in the up and coming shopping district. In the front of the building there were gaping, empty squares, covered with heavy plastic where the windows would go. Inside was a maze of walls and corners with wooden frames, drywall nailed to some of them, creating partitions Monica could not see around. The gun to her back, she was pushed over the threshold and stumbled across a dust-covered wooden floor, beneath beamed ceilings, exposed electrical wiring hanging from them.

Freddy hobbled behind her, forcing her to stay hidden, pressing the tip of the gun deeper into her ribs, whispering to "Keep the fuck quiet!"

Inside was close to pitch-black, save for the streetlamp light that snuck in through openings in the building's unfinished façade.

Monica realized she had seen this place before. Nate had taken her here a week ago. It was one of the many remedies he had suggested to bring her business back to profitability, informing her that developers had huge plans for the area and a lot of money could be made if she were to open a fourth AERO store here. But she did not trust him, holding her hand as they strolled through almost the exact area she was in now, Nate waving an arm about, asking her to envision what the space might look like after she added her touches. He had stopped in the middle of the store then, turned to her, telling Monica she had nothing to worry about, that they were together now, that he had her back, and there would be nothing but good ahead of them.

Monica was snatched out of her thoughts by another shove in her back, Freddy whispering from behind her, the stench of his warm breath in her ear: "Where is he?"

Nate was in there somewhere; she saw his Bentley parked far off in the lot, the shadow of a figure sitting in the backseat: possibly Tabatha, possibly the person who had snatched her from her condo two days ago.

Monica listened and heard movement deep in the store—to the left—behind one of the walls. Having must have heard it too, Freddy halted, grabbing tight to Monica's arm.

"Call him!" Freddy whispered.

She didn't, not wanting to expose her husband, make him vulnerable, fearing Freddy might just aim his gun in that direction and start firing.

"Do it!" Freddy demanded, shaking her.

"Nate," she said. Silence. "Nate, are you here?" Monica called again, cautiously.

"I'm here," he called back from the darkness.

Still holding onto her arm, Freddy's body leaned against Monica's as though for support. Like if she stepped away, the man would simply topple over. He was weak, panting and smelled of near-death. He released her, ordering: "Go out there, but do or say anything crazy, I'll kill you both."

Monica limped in the direction of Nate's voice, grabbing hold to her left leg. The dishtowel Freddy cinched tight around the wound did nothing to stop the pain and little to stop the bleeding; she felt warm blood oozing down her thigh as she walked.

"That's far enough," Monica heard Nate say, still not able to lay eyes on him in the dark room. She stopped in the middle of the huge space: long and wide, the size of a typical department store without the clothing racks and shelves. Glancing over her shoulder, she caught Freddy ducking out of sight behind a corner, twenty feet away.

"Why are you limping like that?" Nate asked from the shadows.

"It doesn't matter," Monica said, anxious and starting to anger because she could not see him, because she did not know what

Freddy would do, and wasn't sure if she or her husband would live through this or die bleeding on the dusty wooden floor. "Where's Tabatha?" She asked, worried for her friend.

"You call the police?" Nate said. "Anybody with you?"

"I didn't fucking call the police, Nate. And no, there's nobody else here. Where's Tabatha?" Monica asked again, searching the darkness, wishing there was a way to get a message to Nate, to signal him that he was in danger, but she could not even see him.

"Where's the ring?"

Monica looked down, felt saddened as she reached to pull it off her finger. She staggered a step forward, holding the ring with two fingers out in front of her, still guessing where Nate could've been.

There was silence and no movement.

"Do you want the ring or not?"

"I...you're friend is in the car." Nate's said, his voice echoing off the cement walls. "I didn't hurt her. She broke her arm, but it was an accident."

Monica saw her husband step out from behind a wall into a slash of yellow streetlamp light that cut through an opening in the ceiling, giving her a look at his face: he looked saddened and hurt.

"Here, take your ring," Monica said.

"I don't want it, Monica. I want you."

"Nate—" Monica started, wanting to tell him this was the wrong place to have this conversation, but he stopped her.

"No. I was serious when I said I changed. Couldn't you have seen that? Weren't you able to tell?"

Yes, she could tell, but she had been too foolish to trust him, and it was too late for that now anyway, she thought, glancing over her shoulder again, unable to see Ford in the dark, wondering what he was waiting for, and why he hadn't jumped out at them yet.

"I was able to tell Nate," Monica said. "I could see, but I just chose not to believe it. And I'm sorry for trying to take Nathaniel from you. I didn't—"

"Don't be," Nate said, taking two more steps closer, shaking his head, forgiveness on his face. "I deserved that for all I've done. But

313

look at us. It's not normal or romantic or sane, but we're here: together. And I love you."

"Nate," Monica said, more anxious now, sensing that Ford was stepping out of the shadows.

"Tell me that you don't still love me," Nate said. "Tell me that you don't believe I still love you. Say you don't believe I'm capable of loving you right, and I'll leave this minute and never bother you again."

A tear spilled from Monica's eye because she did still love him, and believed that all he said was true, that he was committed to every word as he had been to his actions since they've been married again. She knew that if she had just trusted him, they would not be there that moment, Monica's head turning to see Ford dragging himself around a corner, the gun dangling from his hand.

"I know you can love me, Nate. I know it, but I'm so sorry," Monica whined. "If only I had believed you. If only—"

"It's okay," Nate said, and there was what Monica thought sounded like joy, relief and dare her think, happiness in his voice. "We haven't done so much harm that we can't fix things. It's okay," Nate said, walking toward her, his arm outstretched, his hand open. But he stopped ten feet short. Nate looked past Monica, his eyes narrowing, and she knew Freddy was somewhere behind her; she could smell him reeking there, his shoulders slumped, taking exhaustive breaths as though they caused him pain.

"Yeah, it's too late, motherfucker," Freddy said, hoisting the gun up, pointing it at Nate.

"Freddy Ford," Nate said, as though not surprised to see him. He raised his hands, shoulder high.

"I'm so sorry, Nate," Monica apologized, feeling helpless.

"Shhh," Nate said. "It's going to be all right."

"Think so, bitch?" Freddy said, dragging himself another step closer: the three of them, standing in a straight line at ten feet intervals. Freddy's face and neck was drenched with sweat, his tee shirt was dark with it under his coat. He held the gun on Nate, his arm trembling as though the weapon was too heavy for him. "Today is the day you pay for all the shit you've done."

"You've come here for me?" Nate said. "Not my wife?"

"Goddamn right."

After Nate heard that, Monica noticed a change in his expression, as though from hopeful to acceptance, as he'd have no problem giving his life as long as she'd be safe.

"I've done a lot of bad things," Nate said, closing his eyes momentarily as if trying to recount them all.

"Sure as fuck did," Freddy said.

Nate looked up at Monica. "And I'm sorry, baby. I'm sorry it has to end like this."

To her it sounded as though he was indeed accepting what Freddy wanted, that he was ready to die without any fight whatsoever.

"No!" Monica cried.

"Tell our son when he asks about me, that I've gone someplace from where I will always love him."

"No," Monica said, starting toward Nate, but was stopped by the sound of Freddy cocking the pistol. "Hold it right there, bitch!"

Monica froze, stared at Nate and watched him lower his hands, grasp them in front of him, close his eyes, lower his head, then: "If you're gonna do it, fucking get it over with, Ford!"

Freddy raised the gun as Monica watched his finger tighten on the trigger. When he started to pull, she screamed for him to stop.

Amazingly, he did.

Monica exhaled. Nate opened his eyes, as if wondering why he was not dead.

Freddy stood shaking his head, staring at Nate.

"Something's wrong. Your ass is too peaceful," Freddy said, gesturing at Nate, using the gun. "You reconciled with all the shit you did to me and my family. You accepted it and you good with the fact yo' ass should die and burn in hell. But," Freddy said, wiping sweat from his chin with the back of a hand. "You ain't feeling the pain I felt when my Mom's house was taken, when I lost Joni, when I killed Kia.

315

You don't know what it's like to feel you supposed to protect the woman you love, but ain't able to do it—let her get killed then have to suffer living without her, knowing your failure is the reason why. Well I'm gonna show you how that feels," Freddy said, pulling the gun from Nate, turning and pointing it at Monica.

"Ford!" Nate yelled. "She's got nothing to do with this."

"She's the one you love," Freddy said, glaring at Nate. "So she can die first—you can suffer—then I'll kill your bitch-ass."

His hands back in the air, looking as though he was doing everything to hold himself back from lunging for Freddy, Nate yelled: "I'm the one that stole your mother's house from her. Kill me! I'm the one that had you chased to Atlanta, that had your girlfriend killed, not Monica. I'm the one that put you in prison, allowed your girl to lie to you. I'm the reason your crazy ass had to kill her, leaving your son a bastard. Let my wife live, and kill me, Ford!"

Freddy turned the gun back at Nate, looking crazed in the eyes, his back hunching with each breath he took, his entire body seeming to rattle with rage. To Monica it appeared he would give Nate his wish. Then Freddy said: "Yeah, I'ma get to killing you, but the bitch goes first."

Freddy turned the gun back toward Monica. At the same time, Nate left his feet, started running toward Freddy. The gun already set on her, Freddy tightened his finger on the trigger, but when he saw Monica's staring over his shoulder, saw her eyes balloon and realized Nate was attempting to save his wife, Freddy spun back around just as Nate was closing on him. Nate's hand was outstretched, the tip of his finger grazing the shell of Freddy's coat when Freddy's gun went off.

77

Lewis was already in the building when he heard the gun shot: a noise that pushed him more desperately through the dark labyrinth of walls, his gun clutched tight in his hand.

After getting Freddy's phone call, Lewis rushed home to get the weapon, racing the car like a maniac, Tori's arms extended, palms smashed against the dash as through bracing for impact, Layla, screaming from the back seat for her father to slow down.

Inside his house, he told Tori to keep Layla there.

"No," she said, standing in the living room in front of him, shaking her head. "We're going with you."

"Look," Lewis said, "I won't let anything happen to you or my little girl. That can't happen again."

"And what if Freddy isn't really going where he told you, but coming here?"

It wasn't likely, but Lewis couldn't take a chance on leaving Layla and Tori unprotected.

Pulling up to the darkened cinderblock structure of buildings, Lewis told Tori not to move and lock the doors.

Now, a second after hearing a gun go off, Lewis hurried out from behind a wall, into a dark, wide-open space. There he slowed, seeing his friend standing over a fallen body, Lewis could only guess in the near pitch-black space, was Nate. Off to his side, Monica was pulling herself up from the floor.

Lewis raised the gun. "Freddy, stop! Don't move!"

"Sup, Lewis," Freddy said over his shoulder, sounding as though he barely had the strength to stand. He dragged his injured leg one more pace, putting him directly over Nate, pointing the gun down at the injured man. Freddy turned, looked back at Lewis smiling. "Damn, look at you…gun and everything. You a killer now?"

317

"Put it down," Lewis said, holding the gun on Freddy. "You okay, Nate?"

"I'm...I'm okay," Lewis heard Nate call from the floor, his voice weak. Lewis could see that he was bleeding pretty bad from the shoulder: the upper left half of his shirt had gone almost completely red with blood, but he appeared he'd live if Freddy didn't pull the trigger on him again. "Monica, you good?"

"I'm good, Lewis," Monica said, her voice shaking.

"Freddy, you need to put down the fucking gun," Lewis said.

"You know I ain't gonna do that," Freddy said, his eyes focused on Nate, one of Nate's arms up, shielding his face. "This nigga took all that I loved. Gonna shoot him in the heart and watch him die."

"You don't have to do this. We can get you some help."

"I killed, Lewis!" Freddy yelled, remorseful. From over the sight of the gun, in the dim light, Lewis thought he saw tears in Freddy's eyes.

"I killed so many motherfuckers—innocent people—to get to this guilty bitch right here!"

"Freddy..." Nate started.

"Shut the fuck up! My own fucking mama don't even want shit to do with me cause of who I am now: who this nigga made me, and what I've done!" Freddy yelled, jabbing the gun down at Nate, glancing quickly back at Lewis. "Worse, this shit got me so crazy, I killed my own baby's mama and walked away from the child like he was a piece of trash: my own seed..." Freddy said, patting himself in the chest with the fist that held the gun, then pointing it back down at Nate. "...like he was a piece of shit."

Sweat grew heavy in Lewis's grip, dripped from the handle of the gun he was so scared. "Put it down, Freddy. Just put it down," Lewis begged, glancing over, seeing Monica, on her knees weeping.

Freddy smiled at Lewis, and in that smile he saw the kid he rode bikes with, no-handed down the middle of the street: the kid he'd cut class to go with to the dollar movie: the kid he promised he'd be friends with for the rest of their lives.

"You gonna shoot me?" Freddy said, wrapping his other hand around the gun as though to steady his aim.

"Freddy, please!"

"I said," Freddy yelled at the top of his lungs. "Are you gonna shoot me!"

Knowing he'd have no other choice, Lewis cried. "I will!"

Freddy's eyes narrowed, something slipping into them, something that darkened his entire face, then he said: "Good, cause I'm ready to die."

Lewis had seen that look in Freddy's eyes before: it was the look Lewis saw when at eight years old, Freddy walked out of his father's room after killing him, the look that, over the years, when Freddy was determined to do wrong, do something illegal, something lethal, despite how Lewis would try to talk him out of it, Freddy would do anyway, to hell with the consequences.

It was why after Freddy admitted he had no fear of dying, Lewis knew Freddy would kill Nate, and Lewis knew he had no choice but pull the trigger of his gun. It went off in his hand, the sound deafening, the flash blinding him for a split second. The bullet struck Freddy in the temple, tearing into his brain, dropping his body to the floor, his gun falling from Freddy's hand and clacking harmlessly beside him.

Breathing heavy, only able to hear a steady ringing in his ears, Lewis stood frozen, staring at his dead friend, his arm still extended, his fist locked around the gun. "Monica, Nate…you all okay?" Lewis asked trembling, watching Monica as she limped hurriedly over to Nate, lowered herself to her knees, checking on him.

She looked up tearful, crying and gratefully said, "He's okay, Lewis. I think he's going to be okay."

78

It was a beautiful sunny Sunday afternoon and Monica paced outside the small, new single-family home, wearing a lovely pink spring dress and white heels. She watched as Nathaniel ran around, playing on the front lawn, wearing slacks, a short-sleeved, collared shirt and a clip-on tie, looking like a miniature version of his father.

"Boy, if you get grass stains in those pants!"

"Take it easy on the kid," Nate said, walking up beside Monica, his left arm still in a sling. Freddy's bullet had torn some ligaments, but exited cleanly, missing his bone. He had gotten a good prognosis and was expected, after physical therapy, to regain full strength and mobility. His treatment and recovery was far better than Tabatha's, who needed surgery, an iron rod inserted into her bone and was expected to be in a cast for two months. Nate paid all of her medical expenses and stood by her bedside to tell her he'd be paying her twice her salary while she recuperated.

Her hair a mess, lying in a white hospital gown, Tabatha looked sideways at Monica, as if for guidance in what to say.

Monica hunched her shoulders. "He's my husband, but that's between ya'll two."

"Well," Tabatha said to Nate. "I still don't trust or like you very much, but like she said, you're my best friend's husband, so I have to respect her decision, deal with you, and who knows, maybe one day you'll trick me into seeing what Monica sees in your ass."

Standing outside on the sidewalk in the upper middle class neighborhood, beside his wife, Nate said: "He's just doing what little boys do," in reference to his son's play.

"And I'm just doing what mother's do," Monica smiled. "Nathaniel, you hear what I said?"

The boy halted, his arms extended out by his side like airplane wings, and when he saw, standing behind his mother, his father wave for him to continue what he was doing and not worry about his mother, Nathaniel started running and making again with the jet engine noises.

Monica turned, catching Nate, and swatted him on his unhurt shoulder.

Nate all of sudden looked worried. "She's not going to show, is she? Why did I even think after all I've done, that she would?" He wore a lightweight, tan tailored suit. He looked healthy and as handsome as Monica had ever seen him, but she hated when he questioned himself like he did.

"All we can do is try, baby," Monica said, pulling him into her, giving him a hug and a quick kiss on the lips. "And you know the promise you made me—that you made to yourself."

"I know: to be a better man."

"This is part of that, so lets have a little faith, okay."

Looking down at her, he smiled. "I know, but I really want to do this for her. I really need for this to happen."

Just then Lewis's Range Rover pulled up to the curb. With the windows darkened, they were unable to see inside, unable to see if Lewis was successful in what he said he should have no problem pulling off.

The passenger side back door flew open, Layla bounding out of it, wearing a lavender and white dress with patent leather Mary Jane shoes. "Hey Nathaniel!" She yelled, running across the lawn to chase her friend, waving at Nate and Monica as she pursued him.

"Well," Monica said, walking with him toward the truck. "What do you think?"

"Guess we'll find out in a sec," Nate said.

The passenger door opened, Tori stepping out of it, her hair pulled up in a bun on top of her head. She wore a white spring dress, and her make up was impeccable. She walked up to Nate, looked him compassionately in the eyes then gave him a hug. "Hey Nate, how you doing? Feeling okay?"

"Stronger every day," he said, hugging her with his good arm.

"Monica," Tori said, as though she barely knew her.

"Tori," Monica said, back just as coldly, watching the younger woman as she walked around the back of the truck to the other side.

Nate whispered, "You guys gotta get over your little differences."

"Takes time, Nate. We're both committed," Monica said out the corner of her mouth. "But it takes time."

"What's up, Nate?" Lewis said from the street side of the truck, Nate unable to see him.

Nate raised a hand as though it would be seen over the roof of the Range Rover.

"Lewis, is it a go?" He asked, never really having a doubt as to whether Lewis would deliver. Dumb luck, fate or divine intervention— Nate wasn't sure what brought them together on that day years ago a younger, less responsible and desperate Lewis Waters crashed into Nate's car. But in the time Nate knew him, he's proven himself to be a good man that loved his child, his woman and kept his word. Lewis had a rough upbringing, spent time on the streets and was fearless enough to have saved Nate's life. It was for that reason when Abbey Kurt tendered her resignation, telling Nate she was unable to do anymore what was required for the job, Nate had called Lewis, told him to put on his best dark suit and meet him at Kenny Corporation.

Lewis standing in front of his desk that day, Nate said, "I heard you're not working."

Shamefully, Lewis said, "Not this moment. No."

"Well you are now. There'll be an internship period you'll have to go through with my outgoing person, but I need someone brave, resourceful and devoted to be my personal investigator. You'd be perfect. How does $150,000 a year sound?" Nate said, standing from his desk, holding out the hand on his uninjured arm.

Elated, Lewis quickly took Nate's hand, pumped it vigorously. Graciously, he said, "You mind if I give you a hug?"

Nate smiled. "Only if you don't hurt the shoulder, man."

Now, out in front of the house, Nate heard the back door on the other side of Lewis's truck, opening. He heard Tori and Lewis speaking patient instructions to someone, then the two of them came around the truck, standing on either side of Mrs. Ford. She wore a flower print dress, a white bonnet and gloves. She halted immediately when she saw Nate standing in front of her.

"I'm sorry about your son, Mrs. Ford," Nate said.

Appearing saddened, she lowered her head, nodded, then looked up and said, "And I'm sorry for what he put you and your family through." She looked around as though disoriented. "But can you tell me why I'm here."

Nate glanced up at Lewis to see him shaking his head, mouthing, "I didn't tell her."

Nate exhaled, looked at Monica for instruction.

"Just tell her," Monica said.

"I don't feel your son was always a bad man. I cheated and corrupted him and put him in a position where he felt he had to do some bad things in order to get back what he had lost...things he had lost because of me. He took my son, but I have him back," Nate said, turning to see his boy, laughing, rolling around in the grass with Layla. "And in a way, I took yours from you. I can't return him, and I can't ease the pain of you never being able to see him again, but I can fulfill one of his wishes: for you to have a home of your own again." Nate dug in his pocket pulling out a key. "It's paid for by me: maintenance, taxes, everything. You'll never spend a dime to live here. I know it's nothing you have to take, and knowing that it's coming from me, it's probably something you don't even want. But I'm asking, take this key, go inside, look around, give it a moment, then come back out and tell me what you think. Will you do that?"

Mrs. Ford glanced into the face of Tori, Monica, Nate then Lewis, and nodded her head.

Nate held out the key to Mrs. Ford.

"You want me to come with you?" Lewis asked.

"No. I think I can do this on my own," Mrs. Ford said, causing Tori to give Lewis a "well, excuse me" look.

The four of them stood on the walkway in front of the house and watched as Mrs. Ford took her time, climbing the stairs.

His arm around Tori's waist, a smile on his face, Lewis said, "It's a good thing you're doing, Nate."

He nodded, glad that the woman agreed to show. "Think she'll take it?" Nate asked.

"If she doesn't, I will. I'm thinking about opening a spa," Tori said, glancing at Monica.

"Oh, really," Monica said, cutting her eyes at Tori.

"Nah, just joking," Tori smiled.

They watched as Mrs. Ford unlocked the door and pushed it open.

The kids spotted her and called out. "Ooh, can we see the new house, too?" They ran over and up the stairs, only to be stopped by the aging woman, blocking their path inside.

"You can come in, but first you gotta take off your shoes. Don't be tracking mud into my new house."

Nate's arm around Monica, he laughed as he looked down and saw her smiling up at him. "Yeah, something tells me she's going to take it."

END 6.1.16

So...what'd you think of the novel. Please let RM know.

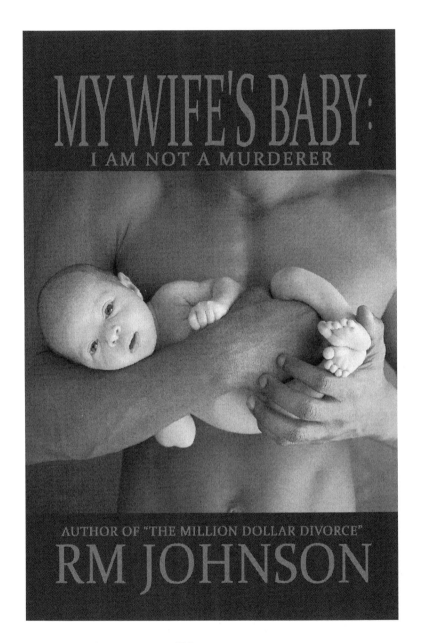

MY WIFE'S BABY:
I AM NOT A MURDERER

AUTHOR OF "THE MILLION DOLLAR DIVORCE"
RM JOHNSON

1

Twenty stories up, the harsh, cold wind swept across my face, tested my grip, tried to rip them from my hands. Sweat spilled from my brow in large round beads, plopped into the eyes of my wife who dangled from one of my arms. From the other, my thirteen year old daughter clung, crying, begging, "Daddy, daddy! Please don't let go!"

I can't remember how we found ourselves here—me hanging, waist deep out the window of our high-rise condo, the two people I loved most in the world, swinging from my ever loosening grasp. My palms were coated with hot sweat. The tendons in my shoulders felt as though they were on fire, would be ripped from their sockets if I didn't free myself of the weight pulling on them.

Squinting against the pain, so far below us, like tiny diligent ants, I saw the men file from the fire engine—red lights flashing on its roof, attempting to extend some giant ladder, rig a safety net, proposing to catch my wife and child as they plummeted toward the hard concrete. The thought comforted me only momentarily, because I knew those men could not make it happen: that ladder would never reach, the net would never open, at least not in time; a decision had to be made now.

I loved my daughter from the day she was born, from the moment her mother smiled in my face, pressed her warm cheek to mine, whispered in my ear that we were pregnant. I never thought I was the father she deserved, that she was worthy of, but she triumphed in spite of me, always telling me I was her hero, snuggling up to me nights when we watched TV, as though I were her favorite blanket. She made me the best man I could be, forced me to never stop trying to be better. Now hanging from my arm, my little girl glanced down, screamed then turned back to me, wind whipping her hair into her face. I saw the certainty in her eyes; she knew she'd die. I cursed God for putting me here, for making me choose.

"Stan…" my wife moaned, her hands wrapped tight around my wrist, her nails drawing blood from my skin; I saw the red lines crawling down, spiraling around her forearms, but her eyes were calm, she was content, ready to face what she knew was inevitable. "…I'll be fine. Just let me go."

My daughter heard her mother, cried out, begged her mom to stop talking like that.

"Dad, you can't! You have to pull us back up!" My child said. But there was no way that was going to happen, and her mother had to have known the decision I was going to make.

It had taken me a lifetime to find my wife, and when I did, I felt as though I was freed from a search filled with frustration and disappointment, loneliness and uncertainty. After meeting her, I no longer looked back at my mistakes, but looked forward to the good I could do, the wonderful life we would have, the beautiful child we would make. We did that.

I kept telling myself we could do it again. The love my wife and I shared could produce another example of our undying devotion to one another, and in that child, we'd see glimpses of the one I had to sacrifice in order to hold onto to my soul mate, to that one in a million I could never recreate or replace. This line of reasoning occurred in a fraction of second, my wife staring up—and knowing me better than anyone alive—she surmised the decision I had reached. Her eyes flashed wide with horror and in her attempt to save our child, she released her hold on me. But I caught her wrist before she fell, held her tighter than I had before.

"No, Stan! No!" My wife cried, begged. "Let me go! Just let me go!"

I turned to my daughter blinking against the tears that practically blinded me. "I love you so much," I told her.

"Dad?" My little girl said.

"I love you, baby," I bawled, staring into her eyes, trying to imprint her face forever onto my brain. "I love you so much! God, please forgive me," I said, shaking my daughter lose. And as punishment for not being strong enough to save them both, I forced myself to watch her sink to her death, her eyes filled with terror, one hand stretched out to me as though I wasn't the coward that released her, but the hero she had always mistaken me for, that would save her.

Up!

I gulped air, sitting in a puddle of sweat, sheets tangled about my legs and waist, shocked that I had not woken up Erica. She slept soundly on her shoulder, a pillow bunched under her head, beside me.

I freed myself from the sheets, trying not to wake my wife, surprised she hadn't gotten up, then figured she probably had been up at least once already, standing in the kitchen, staring sleepily as the seconds ticked off the microwave timer, a baby bottle warming inside the lighted box.

I climbed out of bed naked, wearing only boxer shorts—the way I always slept.

"Can you check on the baby?" The request came from somewhere under a jumble of comforters. "I'll be up in a minute. Thank you," she said sweetly, before I could answer.

I walked down the hallway, the wood floors cold under my bare feet. I stopped at the nursery door. It had been two weeks since I was finally able to convince my wife against letting the baby sleep in bed between us. I made countless arguments: "He'll get accustomed to it, and before you know it, we'll be sharing the bed with a 10 year-old." When that didn't work, I tried, "One of us will roll over in our sleep..." I said, allowing her imagination to do the rest, thinking she'd rush him out of our bed as quickly as possible. Instead, she confidently told me that would never happen. Mothers are unable to do harm to their infants, consciously or subconsciously. "Then how about sex?" I asked. "We haven't made love in...I had to seriously think about it, do the math in my head it had been so long. "Since sometime soon after you had gotten pregnant."

"It wasn't soon after. It was two months after," she said, sounding offended that I had kept track.

"Two months or not, what does it matter? We haven't had sex in forever."

"Fine," Erica said, and from that day onward, she would lay the baby in his crib at night instead of bringing him, sleepy-eyed and restless, to lie between us. But still, there was no sex.

Standing in the hallway now, needing to take a serious morning piss, I pushed open the door of the room Erica insisted I paint over when the first shade of baby blue didn't look exactly as it had in Home Depot.

I stuck my head in, heard movement in the crib: whining, plastic sounds of his diaper rubbing against the vinyl pad under his blanket as he shifted about, and I knew any minute he would start crying. I pulled the door closed, stood in the hallway and told myself my wife would happily deal with the hungry, crying baby. I took a step toward the bathroom, stopped, my head hanging shamefully low.

I pushed back through the nursery room door and walked to the crib.

The baby lay on his back, his face crumpled into a chubby, wet mask of pink irritation. He had already started crying, but stopped when he saw my face appear over the railing. He reached up to me, inflated little fingers grasping at air, smiling, anticipating me reaching in for him. There was nothing else I could do but smile back and lift him from the prison I had banished him to.

"Shhh, shhh, shhh," I whispered, bouncing him on one forearm, the hand of my other arm pressed gently to his back. "It's not that bad in there, Lil man. We could get you a Triple fat goose down mattress pad, maybe some pictures of some hot little girl babies to hang from your mobile. You'll be all set."

He smiled wide and toothless at me, playfully slapping my cheek and pulling at my earlobe as I walked him in his diaper and tiny t-shirt around the room.

Full disclosure: I didn't want the little guy, made serious moves to guard against him, even limped about, wide-legged, in a fair amount of pain for a good many days after getting snipped to make sure I would not father another child. He showed up anyway, and I had to admit, 99.9% of me was glad he had.

"Are you wet?" I asked him, sliding a thumb within the hole in the diaper his chubby thigh protruded out off, finding out that he was. I lay him down on the changing table on the other side of the room, cleaned him, applied talc and put him into a dry diaper. I hoisted him back up, held him over my head. He giggled down at me, appeared relieved, happy and appreciative.

"You're welcome," I said. "You just have to learn not to go potty in your pants."

I lowered him, thought to kiss his cheek, but held him elevated just over my face, staring into his dark, round eyes, feeling guilty for that .01% that didn't want him here and the selfish reason behind it.

I heard the door open behind me then felt Erica at my shoulder. I turned to her, the baby in my arms; he reached for her more earnestly than he had for me. She took him, scooping him under the arms, pressing her lips to his cheek, then laying him against her breast and feeling his diaper.

"He was wet, but I changed him," I told her.

She walked around me, her lavender satin robe open, and put him back on the changing table, undid the tapes on either side of his waist and examined the pad in between his legs.

"I told you I changed him. The diaper is right there," I said, nodding to the used one, folded up on the end of the table.

"Okay," she smiled at me, fastening his diaper back and scooping him back onto her shoulder. She started toward the door, leaving me standing in the middle of the room, feeling incompetent and kind of useless.

"Hold it."

Erica stopped in the doorway, turned back to face me, a question mark in her smile.

"I told you I changed him, but you checked him again. Why?"

"Just making sure, Stan, okay?" She walked to me, kissed me on the cheek; the baby swatted me jealously across the chest. "Okay, Stan?"

"Yeah," I mumbled. "Okay."

NOW AVAILABLE!!!

Made in the USA
Lexington, KY
07 August 2016